"You came."

The low voice slipped through him like a shot of Virginia moonshine, straight up. His body fired to immediate life. He spun around and found her not three feet away, standing in the shadow of a sycamore. She stood her ground when he crossed to her. "Who are you?"

"I think you know."

"Ah, that's right. My guardian angel."

She glanced around. "I wasn't sure you'd come."

"Sure you were. You know how the game is played."

"The game?"

And for a moment, all Ethan could do was stare. The pale blond hair and creamy skin, the collarbone revealed by a scoop-necked black T-shirt, the tight-fitting leather jacket and black jeans. But now? Now he couldn't look away from her eyes. They weren't just blue. That was too calm a color. Too common. They were pale, distant, an eerie shade of violet, translucent almost, like whitewashed sapphire rimmed by cobalt.

And in them, a man could drown.

Dear Reader,

Welcome to another month of excitement and romance. Start your reading by letting Ruth Langan be your guide to DEVIL'S COVE in *Cover-Up*, the first title in her new miniseries set in a small town where secrets, scandal and seduction go hand in hand. The next three books will be coming out back to back, so be sure to catch every one of them.

Virginia Kantra tells a tale of *Guilty Secrets* as opposites Joe Reilly, a cynical reporter, and Nell Dolan, a softhearted do-gooder, can't help but attract each other—with wonderfully romantic results. Jenna Mills will send *Shock Waves* through you as psychic Brenna Scott tries to convince federal prosecutor Ethan Carrington that he's in danger. If she can't get him to listen to her, his life—and her heart—will be lost.

Finish the month with a trip to the lands down under, Australia and New Zealand, as three of your favorite writers mix romance and suspense in equal—and irresistible—portions. Melissa James features another of her tough (and wonderful!) Nighthawk heroes in *Dangerous Illusion*, while Frances Housden's heroine has to face down the *Shadows of the Past* in order to find her happily-ever-after. Finally, get set for high-seas adventure as Sienna Rivers meets *Her Passionate Protector* in Laurey Bright's latest.

Don't miss a single one—and be sure to come back next month for more of the best and most exciting romantic reading around, right here in Silhouette Intimate Moments.

Yours,

Leslie J. Wainger
Executive Editor

Please address questions and book requests to:
Silhouette Reader Service
U.S.: 3010 Walden Ave., P.O. Box 1325, Buffalo, NY 14269
Canadian: P.O. Box 609, Fort Erie, Ont. L2A 5X3

Shock Waves
JENNA MILLS

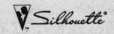

INTIMATE MOMENTS™

Published by Silhouette Books

America's Publisher of Contemporary Romance

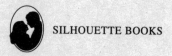 **SILHOUETTE BOOKS**

ISBN 0-373-27357-6

SHOCK WAVES

Copyright © 2004 by Jennifer Miller

All rights reserved. Except for use in any review, the reproduction
or utilization of this work in whole or in part in any form by any
electronic, mechanical or other means, now known or hereafter
invented, including xerography, photocopying and recording, or in
any information storage or retrieval system, is forbidden without
the written permission of the editorial office, Silhouette Books,
233 Broadway, New York, NY 10279 U.S.A.

All characters in this book have no existence outside the imagination of
the author and have no relation whatsoever to anyone bearing the same
name or names. They are not even distantly inspired by any individual
known or unknown to the author, and all incidents are pure invention.

This edition published by arrangement with Harlequin Books S.A.

® and TM are trademarks of Harlequin Books S.A., used under license.
Trademarks indicated with ® are registered in the United States Patent
and Trademark Office, the Canadian Trade Marks Office and in other
countries.

Visit Silhouette at www.eHarlequin.com

Printed in U.S.A.

Books by Jenna Mills

JENNA MILLS

grew up in south Louisiana, amidst romantic plantation ruins, haunting swamps and timeless legends. It's not surprising, then, that she wrote her first romance at the ripe old age of six! Three years later, this librarian's daughter turned to romantic suspense with *Jacquie and the Swamp,* a harrowing tale of a young woman on the run in the swamp and the dashing hero who helps her find her way home. Since then her stories have grown in complexity, but her affinity for adventurous women and dangerous men has remained constant. She loves writing about strong characters torn between duty and desire, conscious choice and destiny.

When not writing award-winning stories brimming with deep emotion, steamy passion and page-turning suspense, Jenna spends her time with her husband, two cats, two dogs and a menagerie of plants in their Dallas, Texas, home. Jenna loves to hear from her readers. She can be reached via e-mail at writejennamills@aol.com, or via snail mail at P.O. Box 768, Coppell, Texas 75019.

For my Tuesday-night girls—
Rebecca, Elizabeth, Seema, Margarita, Ann, Traci
and Liesl. Thanks for helping me keep the faith,
and for reminding me to believe in miracles,
even when they can't be seen or felt.
May all of you soon know the same pure joy!

And, as always, for Chuck. What a year it's been!
There's no one I'd rather share the adventure with.

Prologue

"The best and most beautiful things in the world cannot be seen or even touched. They must be felt within the heart."

—Helen Keller

"Touch her, and it will be the last mistake you make."

Late-morning sun cut through an expansive wall of windows, falling like a spotlight on the man with the gun. In his element, the fool laughed. "Look at you." He swept an arm toward the far side of the spacious room. "You're hardly in a position to be making threats."

The ornate mirror revealed the apparent truth of his words, a tall raven-haired man with his hands bound behind his back, his ankles secured together. Armed guards surrounded him in a circle of semiautomatics he recognized as MP-5Ns. Thick rope cut roughly into his wrists, but he welcomed the bite of pain.

It meant he was alive.

And so long as he was alive, the man with the suit of white, but a smile of pure darkness, would not be allowed to win.

"I have what you want. Killing me leaves you with nothing."

Contempt flashed in eyes that once shone with the lie of friendship. "Death doesn't always involve the body, my friend. Only if you're lucky."

The threat echoed silkily through the sunbathed room. White walls, white furniture, white carpet. But not white lies. The lies were black, and they had destroyed.

But not again.

So long as he had a breath in his body, not ever, ever again. This time it was personal, and this time it was going to end.

"The choice is yours," the man in the white suit announced. "The power has always been in your hands."

True enough. But he hadn't planned on the woman. She hadn't factored into his agenda. She was a complication, a risk he could neither afford nor risk.

Refusing to take the bait, he hardened his eyes and lifted his chin, stared beyond the weapons trained on him and through the window to the beach beyond, where the turquoise surf crashed against a carpet of sand so white, so sugary, it defied logic and possibility.

The flash of red hit without warning. A wave of it, surging up from the pale-blue horizon and sloshing over the beach, washing away the serenity. Seagulls squeaked. Gunfire exploded.

A woman screamed.

Deliberation shattered. He was running then, shouting, swearing, through the sudden blanket of darkness. He had to find her, find her fast. Before the man with whom he'd once broken bread broke something that could never be replaced.

"Stand down!" he roared. "It's over."

The flash of sunlight blinded him, but he saw her anyway, a slim silhouette against the impossibly blue horizon. She wasn't moving. Wasn't running, wasn't taking cover. She just stood there, her flimsy dress flapping wildly, the surf crashing against her calves.

Pain exploded against the base of his skull. He staggered, went down hard, refused to stop. He pushed to his hands and knees and lunged forward.

He saw the gun too late. The explosion of white blinded him, blanketed him, snuffed out his voice and his breath…

"No!"

In a small bed, she jerked herself awake. Her heart thundered in her chest with painful precision, hard, urgent, violent like the breaking surf. Sweat bathed her body, gluing her nightshirt to clammy flesh. Automatically she lifted a hand to her burning throat, fully expecting to find a rope constricting her breath.

Of course she didn't.

So real. So horribly, vividly real.

Coldness then, moisture pressing against her free hand. "Gryphon."

The Great Dane whimpered his concern, nuzzling closer. He knew. He always, always knew when the images struck. She'd once wondered how but had long since given up trying to understand. Gifts didn't have to be understood. Just accepted. Respected.

"It's okay, boy," she reasoned, but the words rang hollow even to her own ears. The taste of fear lingered like a vile poison at the back of her throat. The smell of blood sickened.

But there was no blood. Not yet. She knew that as surely as she knew the ugliness had found her again, dug its claws deep. A cold resolve sank through her as she fumbled for the bedside lamp and let light spill into the small room. From the drawer of her nightstand, she retrieved her grandmother's silver Celtic cross and curled her fingers around the talisman.

The infusion of heat fortified her.

For more than two years she'd kept the images at bay. She'd slept peacefully. She hadn't quite dreamed of white bunnies frolicking in a waving field of brightly colored poppies, but there'd been no darkness. No terror. No blood. No death.

Until now. Through the flood of light, she opened her fingers and stared at her palm, saw the deep crescent gouges her fingernails had cut, saw the ancient cross, the truth. And deep inside, she shivered. The tall man with the closely cropped raven hair stood in grave, imminent danger.

Her dreams were back, and they were never wrong.

Someone was going to die.

Chapter 1

She recognized him.

The tall man with the thick raven hair and piercing green eyes emerged from the federal courthouse and cut through the crowd of gathered reporters. He didn't spare those flanking him a glance. He just kept walking, his stride determined and powerful.

From her vantage point only a few feet away, beside a prolific crepe myrtle drenched in showy white blooms, Brenna Scott watched. The October sun beat against the leather of her jacket, making the crisp fall afternoon feel more like an inferno. Or maybe that was just the burn of inevitability.

"Is it true Jorak Zhukov has been found?" a striking young woman in a tailored jade pantsuit shouted at the man. She trotted after him, her photographer rapidly angling for the perfect image of one of Richmond's favorite sons.

Finally. At last.

Time drained quickly, Brenna knew, relentlessly, blood-drenched sand through a broken hourglass. Waiting for nothing. No one. Not her. Not the man she'd come to find.

"Reuters is reporting a raid on his compound," another reporter put in, this one a well-known personality with one of the major networks. "I'm told there were no survivors."

"If Zhukov is dead," the attractive woman persisted, "does that mean the threat to your family is over?"

Federal prosecutor Ethan Carrington never broke stride. He slid on a pair of sunglasses and descended the wide, concrete steps, leaving the squawking reporters in his wake. They didn't give chase. They obviously knew it would be pointless. It was a well-known fact the Virginia Military Institute graduate had a will of steel. He played by his own rules. He would talk to the media when he was ready and not one second before. That's what made him such a formidable opponent in the courtroom.

That's what made him as feared as he was revered.

That was also what made the action she was about to take as uncertain as a shot in the dark.

She'd tried to deny, stay away, avoid what needed to be done, but the tentacles of inevitability dug deep, through flesh and bone, deeper, to that dark place far inside. She'd fought hard, resisted, clawed her way back to the land of the living, but in the end the truth could not be denied. Once lives tangled, there could be no escape. No running. No hiding.

Not from Jorak Zhukov.

A chill whispered through her, much like the thin clouds skittering toward the sun. Slipping on a pair of dark sunglasses, she watched her target head down the busy Main Street sidewalk, a briefcase in one hand, a mobile phone in the other. His dark-gray suit could only be Armani. He walked with purpose, and she couldn't help but wonder if he anticipated the coming evening as much as she did. If he felt the same excitement.

The same chest-tightening dread.

Of course not. Men like Ethan Carrington didn't feel dread. They walked unblinking into the fire, dead sure the flame would not burn. Not them.

The quick twist of sorrow made no sense. She fought the unwanted sensation, slipped from her spot by the showy crepe myrtle toward her car. Ethan Carrington never looked back. He just kept walking, his brisk stride carrying him among pedestrians and tourists, businessmen and women. And yet, with disturbing insight, she knew the man walked alone.

Soon he might never walk again.

"It stops now." The light turned green and Ethan forced himself to slowly accelerate, resisting the urge to floor the Jeep. He could do nothing about the rush of adrenaline, however, the sweet taste of anticipation.

Indulging, savoring, he clenched his mobile phone tighter. Only a few more minutes. "It stops with me."

"Maybe it's already over," security specialist Hawk Monroe pointed out. "CNN reporters on location say there's no way anyone could have survived the fire."

"He survived." Of that, Ethan had no doubt. Jorak Zhukov had more lives than the proverbial alley cat. Until Ethan had irrefutable confirmation of Z's death or captivity, he wouldn't stop looking, wouldn't rest. And he knew his future brothers-in-law, Hawk and Sandro, wouldn't, either. They'd continue to stand guard around Ethan's sisters.

"You really think he's behind the meeting?" Hawk asked.

There was no one there to see him, but Ethan didn't care. He smiled. He'd been in D.C. when the first call came in, a scratchy message left on his work voice mail in Richmond. He hadn't thought much of the message, not at first, other than that the woman had one hell of a voice. Federal prosecutors got calls all the time. Everyone had *vital* information to share.

Then she'd called again. And again. At the office. At his home. Finally at the hotel in D.C.

And then she'd uttered the magic name.

"I don't believe in coincidence," Ethan said. Not when it came to Jorak Zhukov. The man was too cunning, too determined.

Hawk bit out a vicious curse. "Tell me where you're headed, bro. I'll be there, back you up."

Ethan swung the Jeep around another corner, leaving downtown's eclectic combination of graceful streets and intrusive high-rises in his rearview mirror. "No." He knew Monroe too well, knew his penchant for being in the heart of the action. But this didn't concern his twin sister's fiancé. It didn't concern anyone but two men, and until they again stood face-to-face, until all cards lay faceup on the table, especially the one Ethan had been protecting for years, the danger to his family would drag on.

And that, he could not allow. "He won't kill me," Ethan said. Not so long as he had what the other man coveted.

"You can't be sure of that."

But he could. He knew Jorak Zhukov in ways his future brother-in-law didn't. Couldn't. The bastard had been threatening Ethan's family for weeks now, prompting the Carringtons to live in the circle of a tight security net. And Ethan was tired of it. Tired of seeing his sisters struggle to be brave, tired of living in the dark and playing cat and mouse, tired of wondering when and where Jorak Zhukov would strike next.

Turning onto a narrow, bumpy road, he indulged another rush of anticipation. Six short weeks ago, Jorak had been behind bars; his father, the ruthless general responsible for kidnapping Ethan's sister Miranda, dead and buried. Ethan, a federal prosecutor and member of an antiterrorism task force, had built an iron-clad case against the man. With the court date drawing near, justice, a mistress too long denied, had been seductively close.

In the blink of an eye, everything had changed.

Z had escaped, and the game had begun anew.

"This has gone on long enough," he barked out. Not just weeks or months, but years. Years only he and his father knew about.

Years that had haunted him, driven him.

"I still don't like it," his friend muttered.

Old-growth forest rose up around Ethan and blotted out the sky, sycamore and oak, an occasional elm. It was damn hard to believe mere minutes separated this primitive world from the man-made jungle of concrete and steel downtown.

"That's because you don't get to have all the fun." He

glanced around the shaded, gravel parking lot, saw no one. "Trust me. There's no other way."

"This woman, you really think she's connected?"

He exhaled roughly, and even though alternative rock blasted from his radio, he could still hear her voice, low, throaty. His finger had been poised on the delete key when she'd whispered the name. He'd gone very still, all but his heart rate. "I'm about to find out."

But in his gut, he already knew. Instinct hummed through him. This was it. He felt it in his bones.

That's why he'd called her back, suggested an out-of-the way meeting place, dropped his security detail. He didn't want an audience. He didn't want interference.

Not even from Hawk.

"Maybe she just wants a date," Hawk mused.

Ethan shoved the gear into park, let the Jeep idle. "She mentioned Z by name."

"You could be walking into a trap."

"That's the plan." Again, he glanced around the clearing. He was early. "Not a word to Elizabeth."

A hard sound broke from Hawk's throat, equal parts amusement and frustration. "I won't have to say anything, bro. Your sister has radar when it comes to you."

As he had for her. He'd never forget the afternoon a few weeks before, when they'd come dangerously close to losing her. The spider tingle had crawled down the back of his neck seconds before the phone had rung. He'd known before Hawk had said a word.

Calling his sister, trying to assure her everything was under control while pretending to say goodbye, was the hardest phone call he'd ever made. He'd heard the fear in her normally confident voice. The sorrow. The belief that she would never talk to her twin, her family, again.

"I trust you can distract her." Elizabeth was a strong, capable woman, but Hawk had barely let her out of his sight since Jorak had escaped prison. The same was true for Ethan's younger sister, Miranda, and her fiancé, special forces operative, Sandro Vellenti. They were visiting Sandro's parents in California now, but with their wedding approaching, they would be returning soon. Apprehending Jorak before the Carringtons gathered in one place for the celebration was critical. "Maybe you can take her skydiving again."

Who would have guessed that beneath his sister's sharply tailored suits and neatly combed hair beat the heart of an adrenaline junkie?

Ethan grinned. They *were* twins, after all.

"She worries about you," Hawk said, ignoring the off-the-cuff suggestion. "She thinks you're obsessed with Jorak, taking this vendetta too personally."

The word *obsessed* hit like a swift shot below the belt. "I know what I'm doing."

"That's what worries her."

"It shouldn't." He was a lawyer by trade, but like every other Carrington male before him, he'd learned how to survive. His father and grandfather had seen to that.

"I'll update Sandro," Hawk said. "I'm sure he'll want to come on back."

Ethan flicked off the engine. At first he hadn't known what to make of the dark and dangerous-looking agent with the International Security Alliance, but as he learned of the time Sandro and his baby sister spent together in Portugal, the way Sandro had risked his life to save hers, misgivings had been replaced by gratitude, then camaraderie. The man had quickly become part of the family, even though he and Miranda wouldn't exchange marriage vows for another three months.

"With any luck, you won't hear from me again until it's time," Ethan told Hawk. The two reviewed the plan they'd constructed with the help of a few trusted FBI and ISA agents, then Ethan disconnected the line.

The aroma of burning leaves hit him the second he stepped from the Jeep. Cool air whipped against flesh exposed by the shorts and T-shirt he'd changed into before driving to the river. Every evening he ran along the tree-enshrouded shore of the James. To the world, tonight would appear no different.

Slowly he looked around, noted the canopies of the oaks and sycamores rustling against an increasingly gray sky, heard the river, running low, rushing nearby. A prickly sensation crawled over him, but he saw no one.

Disappointment pushed closer, but he held the useless emotion at bay. Either the woman would show, or she wouldn't.

Narrowing his eyes, he glanced toward the stoic old trees crowding out the light. "Come and get me, you coward," he snarled, but only a lone warbler answered. Restless, he wandered to the riverbank where, just beyond, Virginia's prized river, the James, ambled over the extensive scattering of slabs of granite. As kids, he and his sisters had leaped from flat rock to flat rock, playing chase and scaring their parents half to death. Once, Miranda had slipped, bounced into the water with an unceremonious splash.

Ethan had retrieved her before their mother could scream.

Now he stood on a carpet of damp, decaying leaves and watched the water trickle over and around the gradual falls. He let his arms drop to his side, held his body still, making himself the perfect target, just like Miranda had been a few short months before. He was a patient man. He'd waited this long. He could wait a little longer.

"You came."

The low voice slipped through him like a shot of Virginia moonshine, straight up. His body fired to life. With a kick to his heart rate, he spun around and found her not ten feet away, standing in the shadow of a massive sycamore. Pale hair blew softly against her face, a stark contrast to the black outfit encasing her willowy body.

The feeling hit immediately, a niggle low in his gut, a breath of familiarity.

"How could I resist?" he asked quietly. Anticipation quickened through him. She was different than he'd imagined when he'd first heard her throaty voice, softer, more slight in appearance. But she stood her ground as he crossed to her, never so much as flinching, never taking a step back, despite the purposeful steps he took. She reminded him of a defendant stoically waiting for the jury to pronounce her fate.

His blood ran hot. This moment. He'd been waiting so long. "Who are you?" he asked when he stood close enough to touch.

She angled her chin. "I think you know."

His fingers itched to see if her skin could be as soft as it looked, but he didn't trust himself to touch. Didn't trust her. "Ah, that's right," he said, and let his voice pitch low. "My guardian angel."

She glanced around, scanning the parking area as though looking for something. Someone. "I wasn't sure you would come."

"Sure you were." Certainty pulsed through him, giving birth to a slow, predatory smile. "You know how the game is played."

Her eyes, remote until now, flared. "The game?"

And for a moment all Ethan could do was stare. He'd been studying her in totality. The woman. The pale blond hair and creamy skin, the collarbone revealed by a scoop-necked black T-shirt, the tight-fitting leather jacket and black jeans. But now, God, now he couldn't look away from her eyes. They weren't just blue. That was too calm a color. Too common. They were pale, distant, translucent almost, like whitewashed sapphire rimmed by cobalt.

And in them, a man could drown.

For a moment he was a ten-year-old boy again, on vacation with his family in Ireland, staring at a mural of fairies hiding in a dark forest. His sisters had adored the mystical creatures and legends, but they'd haunted Ethan. He'd woken up in his bed at night, drenched in sweat, breathing hard, pinned to his mattress by the memory of pale blue eyes fading into nothingness, a single arm reaching to him, reaching...

He never made contact in time.

Because the memory jarred, he shoved it aside. "Who are you?" he asked again. His voice was rougher this time, harder.

Cool air whipped blond hair against the sides of her face. "My name doesn't matter."

The hell it didn't, but he let that slide for now. "Then what does matter?" He glanced around, half expecting to see the man he'd once called friend step from behind one of the oaks or sycamores. They'd met here before. Drunk here. Laughed here. "What's so important that you tracked me down all the way in Washington, D.C.?"

"I've seen you on the news," she said. "I know you're a good man."

Maybe she just wants a date. "And?"

The breeze picked up, swaying the canopies and allowing trickles of the fading sun to slip through. Against her face, shadow and light played a seductive game. "I couldn't live with myself if I didn't warn you."

Frustration bumped against anticipation. "Look, angel." The endearment slipped out by itself, but he went with it. "It's not that I don't appreciate foreplay, because I do, trust me, I do." He let his eyes heat, linger on her face, dip lower. Within the scoop neck of her black T-shirt, a weathered Celtic cross dangled from a tarnished silver chain. "But we both know where this dance is going. So unless there's a really good reason to drag it out, let's just get on with it, okay?"

Her eyes went dark. "I don't know what you're talking about."

"Sure you do." He stepped closer. She stepped back. "Tell me what you know about Jorak Zhukov," he said very softly, very quietly. It was a tactic that rarely failed him in the courtroom. "Tell me why you keep calling me."

Tell me why your voice has invaded my sleep, luring me awake during the dredges of the night.

She looked beyond him to the river trickling over the slabs of granite. "He's a dangerous man."

Ethan couldn't bite back the laugh. "Is that a fact?"

Her gaze met his. "He won't go down without a fight." The words came out on a rush, hard, desperate. "Men like him never do. You've got to be careful."

The thrill of the hunt whispered louder. Suspects and witnesses who talked in circles were nothing new to him. Sooner or later they always tripped up and tightened the circle into a noose. "How do you know that? Personal experience?"

She shook her head, sending a strand of blond hair against her mouth, not painted pink or red or coral, but moist and natural. "No."

The desire to lift a hand and brush back her hair had him curling his fingers into a fist. "Then how do you know what kind of man he is?"

She slid a finger along her jaw, pulling the hair from her mouth. "You don't have to know someone personally to recognize evil. I watch the news."

That stopped him cold. He'd tried and convicted her before ever stepping foot from his Jeep, certain she was involved with Jorak. But now he had to wonder.

Maybe she just wants a date.

Stories about Jorak Zhukov had dominated the media. Everyone knew the ruthless criminal had sworn to punish the Carringtons. A little over a month before, attacks against Ethan's sister Elizabeth had made headlines. More recently, the coverage had been of the hunt for Z's hideaway.

"He wants to hurt you," she added, and the breeze whipped harder, lifting the carpet of decaying leaves into a swirl.

Ethan didn't know how it was possible, but in the space of a heartbeat the temperature dropped ten degrees. "That's hardly a secret." The secret was why. "But trust me, I'd like to see him try."

It would be the last mistake the coward made.

The woman frowned. "I can see I'm wasting my time." Frustration and scorn riddled her normally throaty voice. She turned to leave, twisted back at the last minute. "Just be careful," she said very slowly. Very pointedly. "Personal vendettas are the most dangerous kind."

Everything inside Ethan went very still. Very hard. His blood, running hot moments before, turned icier than the James River in February. For a second there, a ridiculous second, he'd almost believed her. He'd entertained the possibility that she was no different from the others that had called him, wanting a moment of his time, a moment of notoriety, claiming knowledge of a crime about which they knew nothing.

Personal. Vendetta.

Christ, she knew. One mistake, damn it. One stupid, careless, naive mistake, a quick lethal slice of betrayal, and children were growing up without fathers. One child would never grow up at all.

He charged after her, caught her at the edge of the clearing. "Not so fast," he said, reaching for her. She pivoted toward him, scalding him with those unusual eyes of hers. He took her arm anyway, closed his fingers around her wrist. "Just what the hell is that supposed to mean?"

Dusk fell softly around them, the hazy shades of twilight, lengthening shadows blurring into the first hints of darkness. She held his gaze a punishing heartbeat, the blue of her eyes glowing against the disturbing paleness of her face, then she looked down at the contact between their bodies, his darkly tanned hand curled around her pale wrist. "Let go of me."

There was a hardness to her voice, a raw demand Ethan refused to heed. "Answer my question."

She tried to twist from him, but he held her tighter. "I'm not going to hurt you," he growled. Adrenaline blasted him. Blood roared in his ears. He was tired of waiting, of being patient, of playing Mr. Nice Guy. He wanted—

"I had a dream," she said softly, slowly, and then her eyes were on his again, and Ethan couldn't breathe. Couldn't think.

The evening went unnaturally still. The rustle of the breeze seemed to stop. Even the constant drone of the crickets and cicadas fell silent. "A dream?"

From the moment he'd spun around to find her watching him, he'd sensed a guard about her. A reserve. It was as though she had an invisible barrier tacked up around her, and behind it she could be as tough as she needed to be. All that was stripped away now, making her appear oddly vulnerable.

"About you," she said in that faraway voice. "I dreamed of you."

The simple statement flamed through him like a blowtorch. His body reacted, hardened, braced for the onslaught. The flash of heat came first, swirled cruelly. The shot of lust came next, drove deep.

"Did you, now," he drawled, hearing the soft Virginia blur of consonants. He let his mouth curve into a slow, heated smile, letting this woman who dressed in black and spoke in riddles know that he was imagining her there in the darkness of her own bed, eyes closed, body arching in her dreams, reaching for him, touching. Wanting.

In the deepening shadows, he looked at her standing there, soft pale hair tangled around her face, eyes wide and stunned. Her mouth was slightly parted, and Ethan couldn't help but wonder what those unadorned lips would taste like, what promises she would make. What truths she would reveal.

What lies she would conceal.

The thought drenched him like a bucket of cold water. He released her arm and staggered back, stared at her as if he'd never seen a woman before. He enjoyed sex. That was true. Enjoyed it a lot. Enjoyed boldness and creativity, frequency. It was also true he hadn't been with a woman in months. But he wasn't a lech or a pervert. He didn't go around mentally stripping off the clothes of the female attorneys he faced in a courtroom or the judges who presided over his cases, fantasizing about getting it on with every female witness he put on the stand or having a free-for-all with an all-female jury.

Wanting a woman who was in league with Jorak was as smart as playing Russian roulette with a fully loaded gun. Hoping to trade sex for information made it no better.

Angry now, more at himself than her, he grabbed the frayed ends of his control and knotted them together. He ignored the way she watched him, the sharp look in her eyes, the flickers of an emotion he refused to label as fear.

"Tell me, angel," he drawled. "Tell me about this dream of yours."

"It wasn't a good dream."

"No?" He treated her to a slow smile. "That's hard to imagine. Just what were we doing that wasn't good?"

She wrapped her arms around her middle, drawing her leather jacket more tightly around her waist. "I wasn't in it."

Frustration pushed against patience. They'd been at this longer than thirty minutes, and the circles kept getting bigger, not tighter. "Too bad." Very deliberately he looked from her face to her chest, the swell of breasts hidden by the jacket. He saw the mosquito slip in against her neck, brushed it away before he'd realized his intent.

She jerked, as though he'd skimmed his fingers along her inner thigh, not her neck.

"A mosquito," he tried to explain, but she skewered him with her gaze.

"I don't like to be touched."

"And I don't like to be played with." At least, not like this. There were definitely games he enjoyed, methods of playing he relished. "If you've got something to tell me, tell me. Otherwise, this conversation is over."

Somewhere not far away, he would have sworn he heard the crunch of tires on gravel. He studied the parking area, saw nothing.

"The point is my dreams come true," she surprised him by saying, and when he turned to look at her, he found the oddest expression on her face. With any other person, in any other situation, he would have called it sorrow.

"That's why I had to come to you." Her voice was flatter now, resolved. "Even though I knew you wouldn't believe me. To live with myself, I had to warn you."

He'd been so sure, damn it. He'd been so sure tonight was the night. That she was the one. Now his miscalculation burned. This woman didn't work for Jorak. She had no vital information. She just had dreams.

Hawk was going to have a field day with this one.

"I can see I've wasted both our time," he said, stooping to retie his running shoe. Night had fallen, but even with the dense cloud cover drowning out the faded moon, he could still get in his run. He knew the path by heart.

"It's been real," he said, straightening. Real what, he wasn't sure, didn't want to consider. He looked at her one last time, this blond woman all in black who'd been stalking him for days. She stood stiller than the night, watching him through those eerie, fairy eyes of hers, never blinking, never looking away.

Abruptly he turned and headed down the well-worn path.

"Contact Detective Brinker with the Richmond police," she called after him. "He'll tell you everything you need to know."

Ethan stopped, sucked in a sharp breath, slowly turned to face her. "And just what will he tell me, angel?"

"I used to work with him on cases," she said. "Mostly missing children. He'll tell you about my dreams."

A long moment passed before Ethan said anything. He didn't know what to say, just knew he needed to get away from this woman with eyes straight from his darkest fantasies.

"I'm a lawyer," he said, refusing to feel the sting of disappointment. In the darkness he smiled. "I need more than dreams."

The breeze, cooler by the second, blew the hair back into her face. "Then you're selling yourself short."

Frowning, she watched him vanish into the darkness. The towering sycamores and oaks swallowed him, carried him into the night. But still she stood, and still she watched.

He wouldn't call Detective Brinker, and he wouldn't heed her warning. He wouldn't be careful. It wasn't in his blood. She'd learned that about men like him long ago. Learned hard. There was a storm brewing, and Ethan Carrington was going to meet it head-on.

And when the clouds cleared, someone would be dead.

Dreams. Ethan knew all about those fleeting images that seduced from the fringes of sleep. He knew the temptation to believe, the price of succumbing. He knew reality had nothing to do with what occurred when a man was in bed with his eyes closed. Reality came only through the light of the day, when a man had his eyes open. Wide open.

There was very little of that light now. The sun had set, but the clouds prevented the moon from taking over. The water running to his right swirled darkly, invitingly. It had been the ultimate high of his teenage years, nabbing a six-pack with his buddies and swimming across the James.

Until the night Pete Kirkpatrick never made it to the other side.

He ran faster, harder, enjoying the feel of sweat bathing his body. He lengthened his stride and pumped his arms, not giving a damn about the occasional branch littering the path, the knobby knee of an oak. His sisters thought he punished himself, but to him, exertion was the ultimate reward.

Somewhere in the distance, back toward the parking lot, a scream ripped into the steady hum of crickets. He swung around, his heart still racing forward, realized it had only been an owl. Scowling, he continued down the path, needing to work off the sense of being stuck with his hands tied behind his back. He'd become an endorphin junkie during his years at the Virginia Military Institute. The natural high rivaled that of any illegal substance, with the added benefit of no hangover. Often, in the heat of a case, he crafted the majority of his closing argument while pounding the shady streets of Richmond's Fan District.

Frustration kept time with adrenaline. He'd been so sure, damn it. So sure. The woman's vague phone call had carried all the hallmarks of one of Z's ploys. Finally he'd believed he'd found a real and tangible link to the man who'd destroyed everything Ethan had once believed in.

Christ, he realized, testing himself with a wind sprint. He'd never even gotten her name.

He broke through the invisible finish line of the dying sycamore and stopped, leaning forward and bracing his hands on his damp thighs. He sucked in a breath, but the thick, humid air brought little relief. His body screamed for oxygen.

Refusing to indulge, he turned around and headed back. To-night was not a night for cutting slack. He'd already wasted too much time chasing shadows. He, better than most, knew the price of letting his imagination run away with him. He knew the danger of following paths that led nowhere. But the second she'd said Z's name in that mind-blowing throaty voice of hers, something inside him had surged to life. He'd been blind with the need to find her, get on with the game.

The path ahead of him brightened, prompting him to glance upward. The clouds had thinned, allowing the light from the moon to leak through.

I had a dream.

In his years as a prosecutor, he'd heard a lot of cockamamie stories and lame excuses. Claims of visions were nothing new. But, Christ, never once had he found himself tempted to be-lieve.

Wanting to believe.

She'd sounded so sure, damn it. So…unsettled. When she'd looked into his eyes and warned him to be careful, that men like Jorak don't go down without a fight, she'd sounded as if she knew what she was talking about. And God, yes, some stupid part of him had wanted to believe her.

It wasn't a good dream.

Frowning, Ethan pushed himself harder, enjoying the way the night closed in on him like a tomb with a heartbeat.

My dreams come true.

What did the woman with the eerie fairy eyes think she saw in the darkness of her sleep? What had she dreamed that dis-turbed her so, that made the color drain from her face and the light in her gaze go dark, that she refused even to speak of?

Nothing. The answer slapped Ethan harder than a low hang-ing branch from a pawpaw. She'd seen nothing.

He'd be a fool to think differently. He needed to finish his run, go home, shower. Call Hawk. Regroup. And above all else, he needed to forget that ridiculous moment she'd revealed that she'd dreamed of him, the images that had come to him immediately, an unstoppable current breaking through a dam, a man and woman intertwined, heat, intensity, a sense of urgency, a desperation he'd never felt before.

Darkness again, the clouds stealing the moon. Ethan ignored the sensation tightening through him and focused on the night, the land, the sense of release he always found alongside the James.

His family had been in Richmond for over 150 years. His great-great-great-grandfather had fought with Lee himself. Young Max Carrington had been full of bluster and righteousness until the moment he was felled by a Yankee musket and wound up in a field hospital across enemy lines. He'd drifted in and out of consciousness for days, comforted by the sweetest, softest voice he'd ever heard, and images of the most fascinating, green eyes he'd ever seen. He'd always fancied himself marrying sweet Olivia from Jamestown, not falling in love with a daughter of Boston, but from the moment he'd regained his strength, he'd vowed to move heaven and earth to keep Flora Marie Brown in his life.

And keep her he had.

Over the ensuing century and a half, the Carringtons had thrived. There'd been many children, but only one son per generation. And it was up to that son to preserve the family legacy.

It was a duty Ethan took seriously.

His former lover, Carly, had never understood that about him. She'd never understood the drive, the passion, the unquenchable thirst for life. It still stunned him to realize how close he'd come to marrying her, that once he'd thought she might be the one. Illusion, he knew. Fantasy. Dreams. They were dangerous commodities he had no time for, couldn't trust, not when he had a cold-blooded killer to land behind bars.

Not ever.

The clearing opened twenty yards ahead of him. He kicked it in, giving the last of his run all that he had. When his feet crunched down on gravel, he allowed himself to stop. Again he leaned forward and braced his hands against his thighs, found his skin hot and damp, just the way he liked it.

Then he noticed the insects caught in a stream of headlights.

He looked up abruptly, saw the black stretch limousine, felt a fresh flood of adrenaline.

Slowly he stood to his full height and smiled. One darkly tinted window rolled down, revealing the pale glow of an overhead light inside. He saw her then, sitting perfectly still, watching him through those disturbing blue eyes.

His heart kicked hard. He started toward her, heard the crunch behind him too late. Something hard slammed down against the back of his head, and the world went dark.

Chapter 2

"No!" Brenna lunged across the leather seat and grabbed the recessed handle, but the door didn't budge. "Ethan!"

He went down hard, his big body collapsing like a felled sycamore to the gravel of the parking lot. Horror jammed through her, broke from her throat. She climbed through the open window, heard the low hum too late. The sheet of glass pushed against her neck.

"I wouldn't if I were you," came the accented voice from behind her. Then the feel of cool steel against her neck. "You were warned what would happen if you fight us."

She had been. She just didn't care. Not when Ethan Carrington lay sprawled on the ground. Not moving. She'd tried, damn it. Tried to warn him. Tried to prevent this from happening.

But like so many other times, warnings changed nothing.

Because like so many others, Ethan had not believed.

A wiry man in black stared down at him in triumph, as though he'd felled him after a long hard battle, rather than with a cheap shot from behind. Leering, he kicked Ethan in the gut.

"He's of no good to you dead," she gritted out, but the man with the gun on her laughed.

"He's not dead."

She knew that. He would live to reach the beach compound. He would live to see the woman he loved in jeopardy. After that, everything became shrouded in darkness.

The thin man dragged Ethan's body toward the limo like nothing more than a sack of sweet potatoes. She cringed at the sight, gasped when she was yanked back from the window. The door came open, and he was shoved inside. He landed against her, forced her back against the seat.

"There's champagne chilling," the man who'd held the gun to her head said. Like an obscenely civil host, he gestured toward a bucket against the far seat, where a green bottle with foil across the top winked from inside an ice bucket. Two crystal goblets waited nearby. "The boss says you can pass the time any way you like."

Before she could respond, he stepped from the limo and closed the door. The window zoomed the rest of the way up, and the two front doors slammed shut. Brenna reached for the door handle, not at all surprised to find it wouldn't budge. For the window button, not at all surprised to find it did nothing.

"He's hurt!" She pounded fists against the dark glass, much as she had when they'd first locked her inside. Her bone and cartilage ached from the abuse, but she didn't care. "He needs a doctor."

The limo's engine purred to life, and the sleek car slipped into the night, gained speed. Trees rushed past them, slowly at first, quickly faster, and even though she could see beyond, she knew no one could see within.

"Ethan." His name came out on a hoarse whisper. Her heart beat harder, scraping the inside of her chest. "Why?" she murmured, easing him into her lap. The sight jarred her, seeing such a big man so still. "Why didn't you put up a fight?"

The warmth of his breath feathered across her cool flesh. With her fingertips she found his throat, the knobby protrusion of his jugular. The flutter pulsed, strong, true, bringing with it a ridiculous surge of relief. She slid her palm to his jaw, the newly formed stubble of whiskers, the moist warmth of his slightly parted mouth. Then his strong nose. Cheekbones. Eyes, closed. Then his forehead. His closely cut hair.

The jolt struck like lightning. She braced herself against the current, but didn't block. She allowed the images to surge, needing to know as much about this man as she could. She felt no fear in him, no doubt, no mercy, only a cold hard certainty, a determination made of unbendable steel. Then a flash of blinding pain. A blow to the head. A kick to the gut.

Instinctively she cradled his head close and started to rock. He was bigger than she'd realized watching him downtown. Taller, more broad in the shoulder. The beautifully tailored business suit had contained him somehow. But here, now, like this, in loose-fitting gray workout shorts and a torn old VMI T-shirt, there was nothing contained or restrained about the man. His skin was hot, damp, the muscle beneath hard.

Muttering something unintelligible, he turned toward her and buried his head against her abdomen. The urge to hold him closer, to kiss away his pain, staggered her. This man was not her friend, not her ally. He'd made that clear. And because of that, he was going to pay the ultimate price.

Still, she kept one hand on him, lifted the other to the chain around her neck and closed her fingers around her grandmother's cross.

Slowly, gradually, a sense of calm whispered through her. She breathed in deeply, pulling oxygen to the floor of her diaphragm and held the breath, let it out slowly. Over and over. All the while she eased a hand along Ethan's roughened cheek and murmured nonsensical words her grandmother had often used to comfort.

The future isn't etched in stone, her grandmother had always promised. Once, the chanted lullaby had soothed. Now, it scraped. *It's fluid, ever changing. Something to be cherished, not feared.*

Once, Brenna had believed. Because she'd wanted to believe. Desperately she'd wanted to believe. But then she'd learned the truth, that wanting only led to devastation. The future *was* etched in stone, couldn't be changed.

At least not by Brenna.

Swallowing hard, she looked down at the chiseled planes of Ethan Carrington's impossibly handsome face, and some place deep inside slowly, steadily started to bleed.

Time turned backward, returning her to an eerily quiet spring morning, when she and her cousin had stood side by side, with a warm breeze feathering between them. Leanne's hands had been as cold as ice, her eyes rimmed with red.

For Brenna, there'd been only numbness.

Saying goodbye to her grandmother had been the hardest moment of her life.

Knowing it was her fault had destroyed her.

She'd tried. She'd tried so hard. She'd only wanted to help, to stop the darkness. Instead, she'd invited it into her home. For as long as she lived, she'd never forget the flash of horror, the chilling instant of awareness. The blind run through the darkness. The broken window.

The smear of blood on the doorstep—

No. She wouldn't go back there. Not ever, ever again. Refusing to dwell, she focused on the man in her lap. He'd looked invincible standing against the night, with the James River ambling along behind him. She'd seen him on television before, countless times, and he'd always been imposing. But nothing had prepared her for the intensity of his presence, even something as simple as his walk. The take-no-prisoners voice. The way those penetrating green eyes had locked on to her and never let go.

"Why didn't you listen to me?" she whispered. He'd fought her, Brenna, the woman who'd come to help, but not the men who'd knocked him unconscious. He'd just stood there with a faint, knowing smile curving his lips, as though the limousine was the most cherished sight in the world.

Another moan, this one deeper, stronger. He shifted in her lap, and through the darkness, one of his hands settled against her inner thigh. The tingle of awareness was immediate.

Warmth penetrated denim and sank beneath her flesh, trickled deep. Instinct demanded that she pull away from him, his touch, but her body refused to obey.

So long. It had been so long since she'd allowed herself physical human contact, other than her cousin Leanne and a few co-workers. To have a man touch her, even though he didn't know what he was doing or who she was, to feel his fingers inch along her thigh, jammed the breath in her throat.

"Ethan." She tried for nonchalance, but his name rasped against the emotion in her throat.

"Mmm." His big hand kept moving. Each finger seared into her, left a lasting imprint. His thumb rubbed along her hip bone, another finger stretched along her stomach, his pinkie skimmed along her pubic bone.

And this time the heat tickled lower.

The limousine stopped abruptly. Brenna jerked her gaze from the sight of Ethan's hand exploring her body, toward the window, where a pickup truck with the windows rolled down idled beside them. The driver had his arm draped over the frame, a cigarette dangling from his lips. "Help!" She slammed a palm against the window, felt the sting deep, but the light turned green, and they resumed their forward motion.

"S-soft." The word was faint, reverent, and it brought her attention back to the man whose falsely intimate touch was slowly, surely, skillfully, unraveling her. His hand cruised higher, along the leather of her jacket and over her rib cage to her breasts, and everywhere he touched, skimmed, she died a little death.

The voice of reason screamed for her to jerk away, but another voice, this one softer, less used, pointed out there was nothing sexual to the slide of his fingers along her chest. He wasn't trying to make her breasts ache. He wasn't trying to make a low moan throb in her throat. He wasn't trying to unfurl a ribbon of sensation from her chest down between her legs. He was just using his hands to orient himself.

"Ethan." She felt the vibration of her voice against his palm as he slid it along her throat. "Can you hear me?"

"H-hear you." His hand slipped over her jaw, cradled. His index finger skimmed her lower lip. "F-Flora."

Brenna went very still. The name echoed between them, curled around her heart. He spoke it with an aching tenderness she hadn't thought possible from him. The quick slice of longing stunned her. She sucked in a sharp breath, felt his finger dip inside. Instinctively she closed her mouth, but his finger remained between her lips, against her teeth, bringing with it the coppery taste of blood.

"Ethan," she whispered again. "It's me. The woman from the river. Brenna Scott." Not Flora. "Are you—"

He moved so fast the rest of the question jammed in her throat. He jerked out of her lap and into an upright position on the plush leather seat. Through the dim, foolishly romantic lighting, she saw the lines of his face go hard. The hand that had been on her face dropped to snag her wrist. And when he spoke, his voice was that of the cutthroat prosecutor, not the raw whisper of the man whose touch brought her body humming to life.

"What," he demanded very slowly, very succinctly, "do you think you're doing?"

The question stung. Not so much the words, but the ragged edge to his voice, the harsh, mistrusting tone.

"You're hurt." She opted for the obvious, knowing he would believe nothing else. "I was trying to help."

"Help?" He made the word sound like an accusation. "Is that what you call it?"

She'd been born with sharp instincts, had trained them to be even sharper. They hummed now, hard, deep, in a primal rhythm she hadn't felt since the night she'd run into her darkened house, five minutes too late.

"You were unconscious." For a few fleeting moments the invincible lawyer's guard had been down, his defenses lowered. He'd reached for her, touched her tenderly. Called her Flora.

It was a side she innately sensed this man denied.

"You're bleeding," she added, and though she rubbed her

fingers together, his blood remained on her hand, in more ways than one. "I think it's from the back of your head."

A hard sound broke from low in his throat, but he said nothing. Not at first anyway. The silence spun out between them, thick, pulsing, filling the plush limousine like a dense fog rolling off the river. His hand remained curled around her wrist, his body coiled inches from hers.

"Tell me, angel," he said at last, and his voice dipped low. His eyes were gleaming, almost amused. "Was this part of your dream, too?"

She yanked her wrist from the manacle of his hand and narrowed her eyes, reminded herself not to let emotion interfere. "No."

"You sure about that?" he asked lazily. A slow smile curved his mouth. "I mean, I may be a bit woozy, but I don't recall you fighting to get my hands off you." He paused, prosecuted her with his eyes. "Not this time."

It took effort, but she kept her temper from leaking through. "I was trying to help you." Trying to do the impossible.

He scooted closer, lifted a hand to her face. "I want more," he murmured, and his eyes, hard, forbidding, such a dark, primitive green they were almost black, met hers. "About this dream of yours." Slowly, deliberately, he dragged a finger along her cheekbone. "I want details."

The heat of his hand soaked into her, through her. She felt the tip of his finger skim the side of her face, felt her heart kick a little harder. Felt heat chase away the chill.

This man wanted, all right. Wanted with a raw intensity that could never be satisfied. She saw that truth in every rigid line of his body, felt it in his touch, saw it glowing in his eyes. But he wanted more than words, more than images from her dreams. He wanted something indefinable, something long denied.

Something she could not give him.

But, God, for a fleeting moment, a disturbing moment, she wanted, too. Her body tingled from it, melted. Reached.

"There's a beach," she said, careful to keep her voice bland.

Ethan Carrington was a man of cold hard fact and irrefutable evidence. He would never believe her without details. "The water is an incredible shade of turquoise." Like a painting, so vivid it could hardly be real, glimmering like jewels in the hot afternoon sun. "The sand is like sugar."

Against her face, his hand went still. "Mexico." No sound came with the word, just the movement of his mouth. "More."

The word hung there between them, thicker than the night. It took effort, but Brenna forced her gaze from his, instinctively realizing how easy it would be to lose herself in the illusion of this man and give him more. Give him too much.

The prosecutor was interrogating her, she reminded herself. That was all. There was nothing intimate about the way he spoke to her, looked at her. Touched her.

Limousines were not part of her world. She glanced around her posh prison, noted the ivory seats were cushy enough to serve as couches. The bucket of champagne still waited. Next to it, there was a small blank screen.

"Go on," Ethan said, turning her face back to his.

"There's some sort of compound," she said, watching shadows play across his cheek. "There's a huge room with everything in white." The color of purity—and deception. "A wall of windows overlooking the ocean."

"What else?"

"Hatred." The word shot out by itself. "So much hate it's palpable."

"I'm there?"

"Yes." She closed her eyes, invited the unfathomable image to return. The hard lines of his face, the edge of defiance. "I can see you in a mirror." Oval and ornate, a silver-filigree frame. "There's a glass table below and on it there's a jaguar. A sculpture," she clarified. "The animal is running, cast in pewter."

Ethan swore softly. "And Jorak Zhukov?"

Slowly, she opened her eyes. "And others, with guns." Guns that would soon be used.

"What else?"

For five nights in a row she'd had the dream, each time the same, only more intense. She never saw more, never gleaned more detail. "He wants something from you."

"What?" There was no real curiosity in the question, only a mocking insolence. "What does Jorak Zhukov want from me?"

Something he was willing to kill for. Something Ethan was willing to die for. She'd held herself in the dream as long as possible the night before, refusing to let herself surface even when she gasped for breath. "Something only you can give him."

His mouth twisted. "Why am I the only one who can give it to him?"

"Because you're the one who betrayed him."

Ethan went very still, all but his eyes. They burned. His hand fell from the side of her face. He looked deceptively harmless in the faded VMI T-shirt and running shorts, but the energy humming beneath the surface of his skin warned Brenna otherwise. This man was dangerous to her in ways she'd never encountered before.

"Is that a fact?" he asked silkily, and even though he no longer touched her, the words feathered deep. "Just how is it you think I betrayed him?"

Warning flashed through her, but she couldn't back away now, couldn't back down, not when Ethan Carrington looked at her as if she'd just kicked him in the gut. "I don't know," she said honestly. But, God, how she wished that she did. That was the answer, she knew. The key to the riddle.

His face was a study in hard lines and punishing angles, his eyes penetrating, his mouth, no longer soft and full, but a thin line. She could imagine him like this in a courtroom, staring down the one accused, hoping the force of his glare would intimidate into a confession. "Tell me what you do know."

Not enough. Not nearly, nearly enough. Somehow, some way, she'd slipped beneath Ethan Carrington's impregnable defenses and hit a nerve. She'd delivered a morsel of information that fell too close to home. This man, this man who dominated courtrooms like a fierce gladiator dominated an arena, had finally lost the tight grip he kept on the world around him. She'd seen the slash of fury in his eyes, the hatred.

But he'd caught himself. Like a rogue wave frozen before it could crash against the rocks, he'd forcefully cut off the emotion that had gripped him.

She stared at him now, at the glint in his ridiculously green eyes, the shadow of dark whiskers covering the hard line of his jaw, and wondered what in God's name she'd stumbled into.

"There's going to be a confrontation." That much she could tell him. And if he knew, if he was warned, maybe he stood a chance. Maybe he would be the last man standing, not the one who lay in a pool of blood on the beach.

The future isn't etched in stone.

God, how she hoped. Foolishly, naively, and yet still she hoped.

"In the compound?" The harshness of moments before no longer laced his voice, just idle curiosity.

"On the beach." With the sun shining and the surf gently crashing. "You and Jorak, and the woman." Flora?

Everything changed. From the moment she'd mentioned betrayal, Ethan had been tense, on guard, almost bracing himself. Now the harsh lines of his face softened, the planes of his body relaxed, the glitter of his eyes turned to a gleam. "The woman?"

The question was simple, a mere request for clarification, but Brenna was beginning to realize nothing was simple with Ethan Carrington. He lived in a world of complexity and strategy. Taking anything he said or did at face value would be a grave mistake.

Still, she let the images roll back, tried to bring the woman into focus. They'd been painfully vivid the night before, etched with precision into the fabric of the dream, but the second she'd yanked herself awake, everything had faded from vibrant color to whitewashed pastel. It was all muted now, tattered, more sensation than concrete image.

"The one you love," she murmured, and her heart clenched on the words. That much she knew. That much she remembered. The strength of the emotion did cruel, cruel things to her heart. What would it be like, she couldn't help but wonder, to be loved by this man. To be wanted. To be possessed. "You'll die before you let Jorak touch her."

For a moment Ethan just watched her, very carefully, very pointedly, using silence as she imagined he would leverage it in a courtroom, as a commodity, to make a point or intimidate a witness. But she held quiet, waiting, knowing no matter how frenetically her heart beat, no matter how hotly emotion streamed through her, the ball now lay in his court.

And then he laughed. It was a rich sound, deep and animated and oddly seductive, and it reverberated through the luxurious limousine. His eyes, hard and focused fragile moments before, crinkled in amusement. "You're good," he muttered. "I'll hand you that, angel. You're good."

Reality looped around her throat, tightened. He didn't believe her. She didn't need to hear the actual words to know the truth. Ethan Carrington was laughing at her, just like so many before him. So many others she'd tried to warn.

So many others who had died anyway.

"Trust me," she said, squeezing the words past the knot of inevitability. She looked into his face, but saw only the man lying facedown on the beach, the sand no longer pristine white, but stained by his blood. "There's nothing good about this."

"They're *your* dreams," he reminded quietly. "Not mine."

She ignored the scrape against her heart. "But it's your life," she countered, "whether you believe me or not."

He shook his head. "You almost had me," he muttered. With a frown, he shoved a hand through his closely cut hair. "Right up until the bit about the woman, you almost had me."

There was a note of regret in his voice, an edge she didn't understand. She held his gaze, looked deep, couldn't fathom what she saw. Something glimmered in those green depths, a faint light in the darkness, almost like pain.

"You're wrong," she said, but knew he would not believe.

"I saw what I saw, felt what I felt." And even now, more than twelve hours later, the intensity jammed in her throat like an army of needles. "There is a woman, and you'll die before you let Jorak Zhukov touch her."

What would it be like, she thought again, but aborted the question before it could fully form. What it would be like didn't matter, because it wouldn't happen.

He didn't laugh this time, didn't react with anger or incredulity, just a bone-deep weariness. "You and my sisters," he said, shaking his head. "These silly romantic notions."

The sense of time moving forward, slowly, unstoppable, tightened through her chest. She watched him, focused on those intelligent, commanding green eyes. He was a man easy to admire despite the cynicism that hummed through his blood. He was a prosecutor, after all. Disbelief was his job, doubt the commodity that kept him sharp. She couldn't blame him for not believing her, and yet frustration ripped at her.

She knew better than to care, than to let herself become personally involved. She knew what lay in store. And it wasn't as though Ethan Carrington had any desire to be involved with her. The truth of that screamed from every hard, unyielding line of his body. But Brenna couldn't suppress the thought that a pivotal line had already been violated.

"Z hasn't changed at all," he muttered, glancing at the bucket of champagne. "Sending a beautiful woman to do his dirty work." He reached across the seats and grabbed the bottle, the two glasses. "Care for a drink, angel? Might help the time go by faster."

Brenna blinked. "This is all some kind of game to you, isn't it?" A game in which there could be no winners, not when he thought she was affiliated with Jorak Zhukov. On a rush the enormity of her mistake came back to her, the details he'd coerced her into providing. Not coerced, she corrected. She'd supplied them readily enough, never realizing how easily he'd twist them to use against her. "For a man of facts you sure do have a vivid imagination."

The light in his eyes burned with an intensity she'd never

seen before. "So what's your role in all this, Brenna Scott?" He popped the top on the champagne, and the sweet liquid fizzled free. "My escort? A companion? Someone for me to cozy up to and trust, reveal all?" Smiling now, as though he was enjoying himself, he poured a glass and handed it to her. "How far are you willing to take this, angel? How far are you willing to go to earn my trust?"

Incredulity gripped her, even as heat licked deep. She knew the gleam in his eyes, the dare, had seen it before. "The truth is what it is," she said quietly. "Whether you choose to believe it is your problem, not mine."

He poured champagne into his glass then stuck the bottle between his knees and lifted his flute toward her. "To us," he said in a silky voice, heavy with just a hint of an old-south drawl. "And the woman on the beach."

Brenna watched him lift the glass to his mouth, watched his lips part, watched him drink deeply.

"What's the matter?" he asked, meeting her eyes. "Not thirsty?"

Her throat went tight. "No."

He started to respond, but a shrill sound cut off his words. A panel in the side of the door slid open, and a phone emerged.

Ethan grabbed for it, clicked it on. "And so it begins," he drawled by way of greeting. His eyes narrowed into deadly chips of glittering emerald. "Jorak."

Chapter 3

"How nice of you to remember."

The voice, deep, cultured, quietly amused, turned everything inside Ethan as hard and cold as stone. He remembered the voice, all right, had never been able to erase it from his memory, not when it poisoned his dreams on a nightly basis.

"Your voice isn't all I remember, you sorry son of a bitch."

Laughter rumbled through the receiver, low, ridiculously refined. "Now, now. Is that any way to greet an old friend?"

Ethan clenched his jaw, his fingers curling tightly around the small black phone. Years of bottled animosity burned deep. "Don't worry. You'll get the greeting you deserve."

"Soon," Jorak promised. "Soon." He paused, chuckled once more. "Until then, I wanted to let you know the rumors of my death have been greatly exaggerated. I hated the thought of you wasting any time mourning."

As if there'd been any doubt. Ethan looked from Brenna's expressionless face to the back of the luxurious limousine. A dark shield separated him from the men in front, no doubt bulletproof. Not that he had a gun. Not that he wanted one.

Not yet.

"Too bad. Guess I'll have to cancel the spray of flowers I ordered. They were your favorites, too." The memory slammed in, the tall woman with the thick, glossy blond hair, the stunning white dress, the gorgeous pink bell-shaped flowers. And the fragrance. God. He'd never forget the fragrance. "Lilies."

Jorak clipped out a phrase in a language Ethan didn't understand but recognized as the other man's native tongue.

"Ah," Ethan said, ignoring the wave of emotion. "I see you remember, too."

A low clucking sound came across the phone line. "She's quite beautiful, isn't she?"

With cutting clarity Ethan saw her as he'd seen her that night, lying on the floor, broken, bleeding.

"It's always the innocent who suffer," Jorak added. "Always the innocent who pay for our crimes."

Somewhere deep inside Ethan, something snapped, and the rage roared back, dark, violent, as punishing as if seven years had collapsed into seven minutes. "Not always."

"You should be thanking me," Jorak retorted. "I could have brought you in alone."

Ethan narrowed his eyes, but the past kept pushing, pushing. "What the hell are you talking about?"

"The woman, of course," Jorak said in an enormously pleased voice. "I thought you'd appreciate some company."

Everything crashed into focus, and Ethan realized his mistake. This conversation wasn't about Allison but the woman sitting next to him, with her chin at a defiant angle and her fairy eyes shining from an unnaturally pale face. Her tangled blond hair stood in stark contrast to her black leather jacket.

Brenna. She'd called herself Brenna.

"She is striking," Ethan muttered, and the sickness spread. He'd almost believed her. She'd reeled him in, skillfully, diligently, until she'd made that one crucial mistake, and everything Ethan had taught himself came rushing back. Facts never lied. People did.

"I'm sure we'll find some way to pass the time," he added,

looking directly into her eyes. She didn't look away the way most accomplices did, just lifted her chin higher.

"Enjoy her while you can," Jorak advised. "Obey and she won't be hurt," he added, then the line went dead, and Ethan was left staring through the limo's dim lighting at the woman who knew far too much. "How much is he paying you?"

Finally she reacted to something he said. Her eyes widened; her mouth slipped open. "Paying me?"

"Is it strictly a business arrangement?" His imagination tortured him with images he didn't want to see. Of Brenna and Jorak, the many forms of payment a man could provide. "Or is he giving you something else?" Because he wanted to frown, he forced a slow smile to form. "Something more addictive than cold hard cash?"

For a moment she just looked at him, through him. Her eyes, usually an eerie calm, went turbulent, as though she were witnessing a heinous act of brutality. And when she spoke, her voice was no longer accepting, but laden with a scorn that punched deep. "You're not the man I thought you were."

"The one from your dreams?" he shot back silkily. God help him, he didn't want to enjoy this, enjoy her, but the game seduced. "The one who's in grave danger?"

"The danger is real."

That was true. But Ethan knew something she did not, something Jorak did not. Ethan knew this so-called abduction was no abduction at all, but a long-awaited invitation. The other man thought he was in control, but the ace belonged to Ethan.

She handed him her glass of champagne, untouched by her mouth. "I believed what I read about you," she said. "I believed the bit about dedicating your life to truth and justice."

"And now?" he asked, sipping from her glass.

She pushed the hair from her face. "The man I thought you were wouldn't attack without justification." She paused, swallowed. "He wouldn't condemn me, pronounce me guilty, before announcing the charge, giving me a chance to defend myself."

Her words, quietly spoken as always, landed hard. Admiration bled through. "You're right," he said, ignoring the twisting deep inside. "I'm a prosecutor. I deal in fact and evidence, how the pieces fit together to create the truth."

"And just what is the truth?" she asked. "What it is you think I've done?"

"You call me for days, requesting a meeting, telling me it's important. You show up tonight, knowing things you shouldn't—" The limousine's speed slowed. Ethan swung toward one of the darkly tinted windows, saw no lights on either side. Wherever the men were taking them, it wasn't populated. "You tell me Jorak is alive when the government thinks he's dead." He checked his watch, found the hour well after ten. "You tell me the vendetta is personal. That something bad is about to happen."

"Something bad is," she said quietly.

He made a sound low in his throat, the laugh his sister Lizzie called dangerous. "Depends upon how you define *bad*," he muttered as the limo turned right and rapidly accelerated. "The bit about the detective was especially brilliant."

Through the dim lighting, she blinked. "Dave?"

He sipped deeply from her champagne. "I didn't recognize the name, not at first." Just a low buzz of familiarity, the mosquitolike gnawing that he was forgetting something important. "But while I was running I remembered."

He had her attention now. She'd even scooted closer, leaving little of the cushy leather seat separating her black jeans-covered thigh from his loosely fitting shorts. "Remembered what?"

In a courtroom, this is when he would smile, let his appreciation of victory shine through. But he could find no pleasure in what he'd remembered. "Brinker, right? Dave Brinker."

Brenna did smile. It was a slow transformation, all the grim lines and dire warnings washed away by a suffusion of warmth. Like a sunrise, he thought in some ridiculous corner of his mind. Subtle, unstoppable, seductive as hell.

"You know him?" The question came out on a rush, and when Ethan said nothing, just watched her, her eyes went wide.

Dark. Anticipation thickened the cool air blowing against them. "What? What aren't you telling me?"

Ethan let out a rough breath, not at all sure why he suddenly felt like a man about to utter the death sentence in front of a criminal's entire family. "I know him," he said, and the hoarseness to his voice caught him by surprise. "I knew him."

The light, the color and vitality, the hope, drained from her face. "Knew?"

That twist inside, the one he'd felt earlier, the one he was working to ignore, tightened another notch. "Are you saying you don't know?"

"Know what?"

"That your good detective swallowed the barrel of his service revolver six months ago." The second the words left his mouth, sickness slid from the back of his throat to his stomach. He'd spat the words like a skillful counterattack, but shame quickly filled the void. He found no glory in recounting the other man's tragic death.

Her lips parted. "No," she whispered. "That can't be."

"Why would I lie?" Compassion welled up, pushed hard, but he shoved it aside. Truth came in facts. Not emotions. "According to courthouse gossip, Brinker resigned the force then went to Florida, killed himself a week later."

For a moment Brenna did nothing, said nothing. She just stared at him through the darkness, her fairy blue eyes horribly dark against her face. Tangled hair fell against her cheeks, but she made no move to push it back. She just stared, like he'd reached inside her chest and crushed her heart.

Her hand moved first, her right hand, slowly lifting to trace a sign of the cross, from her forehead down to her chest, to her left side, then right. Then her fingers returned to close around the weathered cross dangling between her breasts, and her eyes, still dark but no longer empty, drenched in an emotion that looked damningly real, slowly closed.

"No." The word didn't even qualify as a whisper. The sound was too raw. Too broken. "It wasn't his fault."

He touched her without thinking. His hand found her face,

eased the hair from her alarmingly cold, impossibly soft cheek. She opened her eyes, pierced him with a look of such intensity it zapped him somewhere deep inside.

That should have made him pull back. He knew it was a mistake even as he slid his index finger toward the bruised flesh beneath her eye, even as he swiped the single tear.

"What, Brenna?" He tried for the prosecutor's voice, but found only that of the man. "What wasn't his fault?"

She couldn't breathe. Brenna braced herself for the onslaught, the blinding rush, but found only the voice, quieter than before. Not the prosecutor's voice, but the man's voice.

The man from her dreams.

Through the semidarkness of the limousine, the longing swept in. The drowning sensation curled through her like one of those evocative mists rolling off the river, seeping clear through to her heart. She knew she should push him away, end his touch, dismiss the sensation. But for a moment, God, just for a moment, she sat there with her eyes closed, breathing deeply.

From the second Ethan Carrington had regained consciousness, his voice had been hard, accusing. But now his touch was soft, and in it she felt a humanity at odds with the accusations he'd hurled at her. His fingers whispered across the soft flesh beneath her eyes, rubbing away the evidence of her grief.

Six months. She couldn't believe it. *Six months.* That would have been April. The two-year anniversary. She'd thought about calling him that week, touching base. But she hadn't. She'd decided to leave the past in the past, not drag up memories best left dead and buried.

Another wave of emotion rolled over her, but she fought it. Detective Dave Brinker had believed in her when no one else had, trusted her when no one else would. In return, she'd helped him locate missing children, track a killer. Months had passed since she'd talked to the man. Years. She could still see him as he'd stood that last day, a solitary figure in a black trench coat beneath the leafy branches of an old oak.

"Brenna?" Ethan's voice, warm, quiet. "Do you know why Detective Brinker committed suicide?"

Emotion knotted her throat. What would it be like, she wondered, to just let go. To quit trying to hold all those broken edges jammed together, to trust the subtle persuasion she felt in Ethan's touch?

Trust me, Brenna, baby. Trust me.

She stiffened at the memory. "Adam." The name stuck in the back of her throat, like bile.

Recognition flared in Ethan's eyes. The warmth of his breath fanned over her, but no longer did it fight the chill. The truth drilled too deeply. "The partner?"

"Some people called him that." And Brenna, God, she'd called him so much more.

The old rage stabbed deep, the frustration of being convicted without a trial. She looked into Ethan's eyes, drenched with a concern she knew better than to trust, not after the way he'd been grilling her. Not after the accusations he'd launched. And she knew. God help her, she knew she'd been a fool to turn to a man of fact again, when all she had was feeling. She'd made that mistake before with Adam.

Very efficiently she lifted a hand to Ethan's wrist and moved his arm away from her. If her body mourned for his touch, his warmth, she ignored that.

"You think I'm working for Jorak Zhukov," she reminded and disappointment lashed like the willow branch her grandpappy had once used to punish her.

"You think he paid me to lure you into a trap."

"What else am I to think?" Weariness stained Ethan's voice, a note of frustration at odds with his normal confidence. "The evidence speaks for itself."

Evidence. God, how she hated evidence. So many people believed only what they saw, what they felt, never realizing things of the flesh could be manufactured.

Things of the heart could not.

After everything she'd been through with Dave and Adam, all the lessons her grandmother had tried to teach, the confirmation of Ethan's thoughts should not have hurt. She should have been immune. It should have slid off her like ice pellets against glass.

Instead, the truth penetrated the surface and stung.

Ethan Carrington saw only what he wanted to see, only what he let himself see. For him the world was black or it was white. There was no room for gray. For possibility.

For her.

"You could have believed *me*," she said quietly, pulling away from him. She didn't want to feel his heat. Didn't want to wonder what it would feel like to put her hand to his thigh, see if his body was still as hot as before. Because deep inside, where all those broken edges sliced to the bone, she knew the truth. This man would never believe her. Never trust her.

Men like him, who needed to see the brilliant colors of a sunrise before they believed in dawn, never did.

You could have believed me.

Ethan shoved the softly spoken words aside, refused to dwell on the lingering sting. As a prosecutor he'd trained himself to pick up subtle signs. He knew the mouth could speak lies, but the body could not keep them. An eye would twitch or the nose flare, lips might open slightly before speaking, a tongue would dart out for a nervous lick. Sometimes it was the hands that gave away the truth, a slight twist, the tapping of a finger, clenched fists.

But through the limousine's dim lighting, he saw none of that. Easy to miss, he told himself. Lighting could be used to play amazing tricks.

Her voice, though. There was no accounting for her voice, low and throaty, disturbing him on a level he didn't trust.

She'd cried when she learned of Brinker's death. He'd felt the hot sting of her tears for himself. He'd put a finger to her face, needing to know if the catch he'd heard in her voice had been real or just another act. Another lie.

Her skin had been so cool he'd been unable to take his hand away, not when she'd barely felt alive.

He'd long been a man who prided himself on his instincts. Rarely was he wrong. Only once, actually.

His jaw clenched as the memory rolled over him. The innocence and trust. The betrayal. The aftermath. Lives had been destroyed, some reshaped forever, others snuffed out.

And Ethan had learned. Brutally. Completely. He knew how to discern truth from lies. He knew better than to lower his guard, let a pair of bottomless blue eyes get to him.

But Zhukov wouldn't know that. He would think Ethan was the same trusting fool he'd been five years before, when the two of them had played chess deep, deep into the night.

"How long have you known him?" His gut twisted on the question, but he ignored it. He lived for cross—examinations, that moment when the suspect cracked. He knew what it took. Compassion, softness, weren't part of the game. But, God, never before had he felt this tickle of disgust.

So he pushed it aside.

"Did you just meet him?" he asked, when she said nothing. "Or did you know him before, when he called himself Dimetri?" When he'd lived in the United States, pretending to be an Eastern European war orphan, a man who'd come to the country of freedom in search of the best education possible.

He'd fooled them all.

The limo swerved, throwing Ethan against the door before coming to an abrupt stop. The window didn't reveal a traffic light as before, but the inside of a brightly lit warehouse. A line of men moved toward the car, all bearing assault rifles.

Adrenaline surged. This was it. He heard the car doors slam, the low rumble of conversation in a language he recognized but didn't understand, the shuffle of footsteps.

But Brenna Scott said nothing. No sharp intakes of air, no noises low in her throat, not even a change to her breathing.

"What did he promise you?" he asked silkily. Frustration pushed him on. He needed a reaction, damn it. He needed the truth now, before he stood face-to-face with Jorak. "Did he seduce you with promises of riches or with his body?"

Nothing.

Nothing from her, that is. His own body went tight, his breathing hard. He knew what Jorak Zhukov did with women like Brenna, how he manipulated and lied, violated. Sweet words of seduction. Heated looks. Skillful touches.

Revulsion spit through him so fiercely, he almost gagged. The thought of that man putting his finely manicured hands on her soft skin, poisoning her with empty promises, filled Ethan with dark urges he didn't understand.

Or maybe he did.

I love him, Eth. I love him with all my heart.

"Damn it," he roared, realizing too late he'd fallen into his own trap. He was the one who'd cracked, who'd lost control. Not Brenna. "Tell me—"

The door swung open and one of the guards shoved a gun in Ethan's face. "Get out."

He squinted against the rush of light. He slid his legs to the concrete, just as the guard grabbed his arms and jerked them behind his back. They thought he was going to put up a fight. They were wrong. Escape would not get him what he wanted.

"Your turn, sweet thang," one of the guards bit out in a heavily accented voice, and Ethan swung around to find the big man reaching for Brenna. She sat against the far door, frozen, like a small child in front of an oncoming freight train. Blond hair tangled against her face, drawing his attention to the bruise at her jaw. Her eyes, those bottomless pools of pale blue, were huge and dark, sickeningly vacant.

Ethan reacted without thinking. "Brenna—"

The guard shoved him back.

"Don't touch me," he heard her say in a voice that sounded nothing at all like that of the woman he'd met alongside the banks of the James.

Something inside Ethan snapped. His plan, his restraint, he wasn't quite sure. He spun from the guard and charged toward the open door, but got only two steps before a third guard slashed his submachine gun against the back of Ethan's knees. They buckled, and he went down hard.

"Don't hurt him!" she shouted, but the men only laughed.

Ethan pushed to his knees and blinked to clear his vision, tasted blood. Through the foggy haze he saw the far door swing open and Brenna tumble onto the concrete. Just as quickly, another guard yanked her to her feet.

The sound she made barely sounded human. She staggered, tried to pull away, but the man grabbed her wrists and pulled them behind her back, forcing her breasts to thrust outward.

"Leave her alone," Ethan growled, a command which earned a swift kick in the gut. He sagged, fought the crippling rush of pain. He didn't know who Brenna Scott was or how she fitted into Zhukov's plan, but he couldn't sit back and watch her suffer. Even if she did work for Zhukov.

"It's me you want," he insisted. "Zhukov said she wouldn't be hurt."

"And you believed him?" This from a fourth voice, one that rang with authority. Ethan twisted and found a man standing at the front of the limo, bright light spilling around him. He wore army fatigues, with his green pants tucked into high black boots. A beret sat slightly askew on his head.

"The woman is of no value to Zhukov."

The man, clearly the one in charge, laughed. "Since when is a woman of no value? A man can always find a reason to keep a woman around."

Ethan's blood ran cold. If Brenna was who she claimed to be, a woman guilty only of the crime of trying to help a stranger, then she should have no further role in this vendetta. But if she'd lied, if she really was connected to Jorak, on his payroll or an occupant of his bed, then her purpose was far from over.

He swung back toward her, stared at her frozen expression. He'd seen that look before, on the mother of an eighteen-year-old who'd been brutally raped and murdered. She'd sat in the courtroom and listened to testimony day after day, listened to the officer describe her daughter's apartment when they'd found her, the blood, the stench, the position of the nude body. She'd listened to Ethan as he'd grilled the defendant, recounting in excruciating detail what must have gone on that night, when the punk had broken into his ex-girlfriend's apartment and decided to teach her a lesson about breaking up.

It was an expression Ethan had never forgotten, one that had been etched into his psyche. One he'd hoped never to see again. An expression he'd understood from the mother, but not from this woman who'd stepped from behind an ancient sycamore and plied him with dire warnings of a future yet to come.

"We must go now," the man in charge barked.

Brenna's gaze met Ethan's, stark, isolated, as powerful as though she'd reached out a hand, grabbed his wrist, held on tight, and deep inside, something twisted. Hard. He lunged to his feet and again moved toward her, but again two of the guards jerked him back. This time he was shoved away from the limo and into the bright light of what appeared to be a hangar. Two small planes—Cessnas, he thought—sat to the right. To the left, cool night air spilled in from a huge open door.

He saw the plane first, the sleek little private jet waiting on the tarmac. A Gulfstream, he thought. Top-of-the-line. Fast. Long range. Then he saw the men, the circle of heavily armed guards surrounding the jet. And without doubt he knew they were about to change their mode of transportation.

Stars. They surrounded him. Brilliant pinpricks of light glowing against a sky so pure and dark and endless it looked like a tapestry of black velvet. The moon hung like a suspended sickle. Venus glowed blindingly bright.

"Where are they taking us?"

The question was soft, emotionless. He resisted the urge to turn and look at her, didn't trust what he might find in the disturbing blue of her eyes.

You tell me, he wanted to say. But didn't. "South."

He felt her lean closer, out of the corner of his eye saw her face move near his. She didn't look at him, though, just peered by him through the small airplane window. Her seat belt prevented her from getting much closer. "How do you know?"

He thought about saying nothing, letting the question just

hang there. But he needed answers from Brenna Scott, information she would not give him if he gave her nothing in return.

"See back there?" A rope bound his left wrist to her right, leaving one hand free. He gestured toward the darkness trailing behind them, where stars glimmered like diamonds.

She leaned closer, bringing with her a subtle scent he didn't recognize. Perfume, maybe, but nothing commercial. "They're bright."

"Do you see the Big Dipper?"

"I think…" The ends of her hair brushed his shoulder. "There, right? Low on the horizon behind us."

He suppressed a faint smile. Carly had never been able to make out the constellations, never seen the point. "It's in the northern hemisphere," he said, "which we're moving away from." He turned toward the front of the plane, not realizing how close her face was to his. Skin brushed, cheek to cheek, hers soft, his rough, mouths alarmingly close. Their eyes met.

She pulled away.

He tensed, and deep inside something thrummed in a way he recognized as trouble. "Up there," he indicated, again gesturing with his hand. "The stars ahead of us aren't as bright, meaning we're traveling south."

She leaned forward, squinted against the night. Jorak's men had dimmed the lights in the luxurious cabin, but track lighting ran up and down the aisle between the leather seats. They sat toward the back, just in front of a row of munitions crates. Two guards stood outside the locked cockpit door, assault weapons ready.

It had yet to dawn on them that Ethan wasn't putting up a fight.

"Away from the United States," Brenna muttered.

To Mexico. Just as she'd predicted.

"How'd you learn to do that?" she asked. "Read the sky like a map."

This time Ethan didn't fight the smile. It formed by itself, seeping from his chest and curving his lips. "My grandfather." As a young boy, his father's father, the distinguished senator, had taken his namesake on weekend camping trips. The two of them had played soldier, the elder Ethan providing an early glimpse of hard lessons his grandson would one day learn at the Virginia Military Institute. And from Jorak Zhukov.

"Senator Carrington?"

Incredulity softened her voice. He glanced toward her, found curiosity glowing in those eerie fairy eyes. It was the first spark of life he'd seen since the guards had touched her. "That surprises you?"

Her lips quirked. "Intrigues is more like it." She tilted her head, allowing tangled blond hair to fall back from her face. "I remember seeing him on TV during campaigns. He hardly seemed like the outdoorsy type."

True enough. To the world, Grandfather Carrington had been an icon of propriety and dignity, of stuffy committee rooms and formal cocktail parties. With his tailored suits and thick head of white hair, his bushy eyebrows and that deep commanding voice, his senate colleagues had insisted he could debate a nun out of her virtue. But to Ethan his grandfather was the man with the baggy old jeans and worn flannel shirts, the one with a wicked sense of humor and a thirst for adventure.

"People aren't always what they seem," Ethan said, and the words jammed against his throat on the way out. He shoved the reaction aside, reminding himself there was a difference between appearances and evidence.

The evidence against Brenna spoke a language all its own. She knew too much, facts and details that could only have come from one source. One man.

"I grew up in a house with three sisters. My grandfather insisted I needed good, quality, boy time." Time away from drama and perfume, from giggling and hair ribbons and fights over who took whose earrings. "He'd take me camping, just the two of us." And there, alone, deep in the Virginia woods, his grandfather had taught him how to bait a hook and snag a trout, how to build a fire from rock and stone, which berries would sustain and which would poison, how to track a wild animal, when to shoot and when to wait. "That's when he taught me to read the sky."

Brenna's smile grew distant. "My grandmother taught me a lot, too."

There was an odd note to her voice, one that niggled like the kind of comment made by a witness that often led to a goldmine. "Such as?"

Not so with Brenna. Not now. "It doesn't matter anymore."

The urge to reach for her, to feather a finger against the nasty bruise along her jaw had him curling the fingers of his free hand into a fist. "I think that it does."

She blinked, narrowed her eyes. "Why did your grandfather teach you what he did? He could have rescued you from your sisters lots of other ways."

That was easy. "Survival," Ethan said. "Grandfather Carrington believed every man needed to know how to stand on his own two feet, how to survive."

Her gaze almost seemed to glow. "Survive what?"

The question threw him back in time, to a night a quarter of a century before, when he'd sat shivering on a boulder in subfreezing temperatures, scraping two stones against each other.

"I'm cold," he'd said. "Can't *you* just do it?"

His grandfather's face had fallen into a gentle frown. "At some point in your life, Ethan Douglas, you'll find the only person you can depend on is yourself. You need to be prepared."

The prophecy of those long-ago words blasted through him now, as hot and intense as the floor furnace in his grandfather's old house. "This," he said. Everything inside him went hard, but the word came out soft. "Deceit. Betrayal." He paused, held her gaze. "You."

Chapter 4

Brenna's eyes, those fascinating pools of whitewashed sapphire, went dark. "You're wrong about me, you know. Dead wrong."

Dead. Wrong. The words twisted through Ethan, wrung him out. He *didn't* know, that was the problem. And for a man accustomed to clarity, the uncertainty grated at him. Every time he thought he'd secured a handle on her, on the truth, she managed to erase that clarity with nothing more than a few quietly spoken words or a distant, knowing smile.

"Tell me about the compound," he said, refusing to affirm or deny her claim. "You said Mexico, right?" He waited a charged heartbeat before pointing out the obvious. "That's south."

A soft sound broke from her throat. "And because we're headed south, you think that means I work for Zhukov."

It was the obvious answer. "You said it's on a beach? Something about a room all in white and a sculpture of a jaguar." Automatically, his jaw tensed. He knew that sculpture, damn it. More than knew it, he was the one who'd picked out the exquisite piece of pewter.

It's perfect, Eth! Absolutely perfect! God, I love you.

The memory stabbed deep.

"You asked what my grandmother taught me," Brenna said, and he forced himself back from the landmine of the past.

"You told me it didn't matter," he reminded.

"I was wrong. It does matter." She paused, pulled her bottom lip into her mouth. "She taught me the same thing your grandfather taught you. She taught me about survival."

Ethan stared at the bruise on her jaw, the scratch along her neck, and wondered just how far Jorak would go to lay a trap. How many lies he would tell. How many innocents he would destroy.

"You think *I'm* the threat?" he asked quietly. The thought left a bitter taste in his mouth.

Her gaze met his. "You want to believe the worst about me. You refuse to consider the possibility I have nothing to do with what's happening. Is your world that jaded, Ethan? Is it really so hard to believe that someone you don't know might try to help?"

The jolt went through him like unexpected turbulence. Her eyes—normally such a translucent blue you could see truths too painful to acknowledge—burned with an accusation that scorched to the bone. It was as if she'd picked up his grandfather's hunting knife and skinned him in one swift stroke.

"Give me something, then." The words ripped out of him. Proof. Evidence. Anything. "Something to believe."

"That's just it," she said, and the glow returned to her eyes. "I can't give you what you want. Belief has to come from inside of you, not from me."

Ethan just stared. In all his years grilling suspects and coaxing witnesses, rarely had anyone turned the tables on him. She refused to look away, just kept watching him through those burning eyes, with her chin at a defiant angle and her tangled hair falling against her shoulders. She reminded him of a movie he'd once seen, where a woman accused of witchcraft had refused to break, refused to recant, even as she'd been tied to a tree with flames licking at her legs.

"Christ," he muttered, then turned toward the night. Clouds whizzed by now, high, thin, obscuring the faint glow of the southern stars. She was a complication he hadn't counted on, a kink in his plan he hadn't expected. He understood the vendetta between him and Jorak. He knew what was at stake. He knew how to bring the other man down.

But Brenna...her involvement disturbed him in a way he didn't understand. All signs pointed to her involvement. A messenger, maybe, someone sent by Jorak to warn Ethan what would happen if he didn't cooperate, to intimidate him prior to the face-to-face meeting. Maybe that's why they'd bruised her jaw, to prove Jorak gave mercy to no one, not even those in his employ. Or maybe he only meant her as a distraction, a beautiful woman to muddy the waters and blur Ethan's focus.

The evidence was clear, the facts compelling. Those were the commodities Ethan trusted, the touchstones on which he thrived. But God help him, for one of the few times in his life, he didn't want to believe.

He smiled bitterly, reminding himself it would take more than a pair of fascinating blue eyes and dire warnings to make him forget the betrayal that had forged him into the man he now was, and the thirst for justice that had consumed him ever since.

"Tell me something."

The three words reached out of the darkness and lured him back toward her. He turned to find her watching him, just watching, her eyes glowing with the expectation of a defense attorney about to lay a trap. "What would you like me to tell you?"

"Why you didn't put up a fight."

He was a man who trained himself for all possibilities, but the gustiness of her request caught him by surprise.

"Back by the river," she clarified. "You saw the limousine before the men saw you. I was watching. You could have slipped back into the woods, gone the other direction."

And missed his chance at Jorak, the invitation he'd been carefully engineering for weeks. Months. Years.

"Cowards run," he said simply. His grandfather had taught him that. VMI had reinforced it. Jorak Zhukov had proved it.

Brenna's eyes took on that unnatural glow he'd come to recognize. And dread. "And real men stand and fight? Is that it?"

"You tell me," he said, mirroring her quiet words. He glanced toward the two guards blocking the cockpit door, the MP-5Ns slung across their shoulders, then back at Brenna. "Didn't you say you could see what's going to happen?"

She surprised him by laughing. "I'm not a witness you're cross-examining, Ethan. I'm not a suspect on the ropes. You can't block my questions through questions of your own."

All by itself his mouth curved into a smile. "Touché." He'd have to be more careful around her, more aware. She saw too much, shone a spotlight into dark corners he didn't want illuminated. "Maybe I already have enough blood on my hands. Maybe I'm not interested in amassing more. Too sticky."

The light in her eyes dimmed. "In other words, if Jorak has you, he'll leave your family alone."

The truth, the fact she'd gleaned it from words purposefully vague, proved he had to keep his guard high. "It's me he wants. It's me he'll have."

"What about your own blood?" she shot back. "Don't you think your family will care if it's spilled?"

"It won't be." Of that he was sure. He'd worked too hard, planned too long. Nothing would stop him now. No one. Not Jorak, not this woman—with her claims of precognition and those unnerving fairy eyes that seemed to see right through him—and, God help him, especially not the niggle deep inside, the ridiculous whisper that sometimes evidence didn't mean a damn. "Not so long as I have what he wants."

"And do you?" she asked. "Have what he wants?"

"He thinks he wants it." The truth, he knew. That's what Jorak claimed to want. But Ethan had long since learned the truth could be a gift beyond compare, or a weapon of destruction.

"You think otherwise," Brenna observed.

He lifted his gaze to hers, let his eyes look directly into the swirling blue that dared him to look deeper. "Sometimes our focus can become so singular it turns into an obsession. All we see is what we want. It defines us, drives us, blinds us to the world around us…and the consequences."

"Who are you talking about, Ethan?" She tilted her head, letting the tangled blond hair fall against her cheekbone. "Jorak Zhukov?" She paused like a skillful attorney, let the silence pulse and thicken between them. "Or yourself?"

Ethan just smiled. This woman may have been sent by Jorak and she sure as hell was a distraction, but it had been a long time since anyone had so boldly held a mirror up to his face. He knew better than to enjoy her, the challenge she posed, but like so many other times, knowing better rarely stopped him.

It was like playing chess, one calculated move at a time. The mystery, the anticipation, was all part of the pleasure.

"Does it matter?" he asked.

"Very much." Her quiet voice resonated with a strength and conviction that nudged against those defenses he'd hammered into place. "If you've let Jorak blind you to the world around you, if you've let whatever this thing is between the two of you shape you, define you, then he's already won."

They sat side by side in thick, luxurious airline seats, their wrists bound together, their ankles joined. He couldn't get away from her or she from him. Neither of them could charge the guards in front of the cockpit door. Somehow, though, somehow, with a few well-chosen words, with a penetrating stare that stripped him to the bone, she'd just backed him into a sharp and shrinking corner.

The admiration trickled deeper. "Don't talk to me about winning, angel. Not after what happened with you and your detective."

It was just a query, a probe, a test, but in the space of a

fractured second the color drained from her face. Even the bruise, that nasty smear of green and purple and black, faded.

He knew that look, had seen it countless times in the courtroom, when he leveled a point-blank question at a witness or defendant, a carefully worded query that forced them to dredge up ugliness they'd worked hard to sequester.

"Whose fault was it?" he continued, despite the sudden sickness swarming his throat. His gut. "Whose fault was it the good detective ate his service revolver for dinner?"

Brenna went very still. Absolutely, horribly still. One minute she'd had the cunning attorney on the ropes, but in a heartbeat he'd turned the tables. His softly spoken question sliced through the defenses she'd stapled and glued and tacked into place, through the hardened layers of scar tissue, down deep, to that cold, dark place she kept hidden from the world.

Dave Brinker. Young, hardworking, strong. A man capable of great devotion and driving passion, but of incredible acts of generosity and tenderness, as well. He'd been a good cop. Solid. Thorough. It was true he'd cared more than he should have, but victims hadn't been mere case files to him, they'd been people, with lives and loves, hopes and sorrows, futures. Each one that fell took a piece of Dave Brinker with them.

The edges of her vision blurred. She felt herself start to sway, the dimly lit, obscenely luxurious cabin around her rotate. The vertigo sucked at her like the cold vacuum of time and space, allowing the sludge of the past to bleed through. The punishing rhythm of her heart drummed in her ears. The breath she tried so hard to pull deep stalled in her chest. Her eyes slid shut, revealing the gun, the Glock Dave had always carried but rarely pulled, all shiny and well cared for.

The report of a single shot threw her back against the seat.

"Brenna?"

The sound of her name came at her through a hazy tunnel, distant, warbled, but the image wouldn't let go. The bitter smell of sulfur crowded in on her, the coppery taste of blood pooled in the back of the mouth. Everything started fading then, the vibrancy, the passion, melding into nothingness.

"Jesus, Brenna. Stop it!"

Light, pure and white and blinding. Seducing. The warmth of it surrounded like a shroud, welcomed.

"Open your eyes, damn it!" The words assaulted the cocoon, reverberating with a life force that rivaled the one slipping away. Something nudged her then, something hard, and with stunning speed the sleek little jet came back into focus, revealing a broad masculine shoulder rammed up against hers. "Ethan?"

He struggled against the restraints that prevented him from reaching her. "What the hell was that all about?"

She blinked, brought him into focus. The lines of his face were harder than before, tighter. More severe. His tan seemed several shades lighter. "What happened?"

"What happened?" Something hot and unreadable flashed in his eyes. "You mean besides the fact that you just checked out of the land of the living for a few minutes?"

It all came back to her then, on a horrible, relentless wave. Dave. His death. She hadn't sensed it at the time, hadn't known. No one had bothered to tell her. Certainly not Adam.

She could see it all now, though. Feel it. The punishing hopelessness. The relentless guilt. The bottomless despair. He'd never forgiven himself.

Neither had she.

"My fault," she whispered. The rhythm of her heart slowed, echoing through her, one painful beat at a time. "Mine."

Ethan twisted closer. "What was your fault?"

The dizziness swirled closer, but this time she fought it, fought the past. Fought the future. Fought the ridiculous desire to feel Ethan's arms close around her and hold her tight, hear his deep Virginia voice whisper words she'd long since quit believing. From deep inside came the strength, the sheer force of will, to use the intense, glowing green of Ethan's eyes to ground her. He was a hard, cynical man, she reminded herself. The events that had shaped him, molded him, didn't matter.

"The last time I saw him was at my grandmother's funeral." He'd stood alone that day, beneath a ridiculously gorgeous oak, whereas the day before he'd stood surrounded by friends and family who'd gathered to say goodbye to his wife of thirteen years. They'd stopped trying for children after three miscarriages, and she'd become his world. The week before her death, her murder, they'd begun investigating international adoption.

"I'll never forget the sky," she said. "So sharply blue it hurt to look at it, stretching on forever." Like an endless swath of sapphire velvet, she remembered thinking. The familiar ache rose up in her chest, curled like a vise, constricted. "Only a few clouds." Floating aimlessly. Foolishly. "Those big fat fluffy puffs of cotton Grandma called shape-shifters."

"Shape-shifters?"

"Magical." Mystical. "The kind you could stretch out on the grass and stare up at, let your mind drift. I might see castles and dragons, but those same clouds would shift shapes for you, and in them you'd find something altogether different."

His gaze took on a slow burn. "What would I see?"

A sailboat. That was the first image that came to her. Tall and powerful, with its sail billowed out by a blast of wind, barreling across the sea of the sky. "You tell me," she said instead. She felt her voice pitch low, didn't understand why. "What do you see when you look into the sky?"

Did he even look?

Abruptly he turned from her, toward the oval window, to the night beyond. The stars, once so intense and vibrant and plentiful, now blurred into faint swirls of distant light. Clouds whizzed past them, not the shape-shifting kind, but a dense mist that somehow seemed sinister.

"I don't see anything," Ethan muttered, and deep inside, Brenna felt a little protest rise up.

"When was the last time you looked?" The question slipped out before she could think better of it, and in the silence that ensued, seconds passed before she realized she was holding her breath.

Slowly Ethan turned to face her. She didn't need him to

speak to know his answer, the truth glowed in his eyes, the same faraway look he'd had when speaking of his grandfather. "When I was a kid I saw sailboats."

This time when her breath caught, it was for a very different reason.

Time hung there between them, elongated, stretched to the breaking point. Silence drowned out the silky hum of the jet engine, the low murmur of the guards talking up front. Instinct demanded that she look away from Ethan, break the moment, but curiosity refused to let her. The man…fascinated her. In so very, very many ways he reminded her of Dave, but in other ways he was unlike anyone she'd ever met.

Touch her, and it will be the last mistake you make.

She recoiled from the memory, the dream, the strobe-light image of Ethan running down the beach, shouting. Of the woman, her torn white sundress flapping in the breeze. The surging, crashing wave of red. The flash of white.

The darkness.

"Brenna?"

She blinked, focused on the angles of his harshly handsome face, absorbed the sight of him now, sitting inches from her, with his eyes all concentrated and glowing, whiskers darkening his jaw. *Alive.* "What?"

"Are you o—" He broke off the question, launched another. "Why was Detective Brinker at your grandmother's funeral?"

She didn't know whether to laugh or clench her fists in frustration. For a moment she'd successfully ripped away something between them, that invisible barrier Ethan used to hold himself apart from others. The doubt that had throbbed between had vanished, and he'd been just a man, she just a woman, comparing notes from a simpler time.

Now the prosecutor waited.

"Because," she answered quite simply, quite honestly, "he held himself responsible for her death."

But simple was never good enough for men like Ethan Carrington, and he immediately dug for more. "Why?"

Brenna looked away from him and stared down at her hands,

her nails short and unpainted, her fingers curled against her palm. When she opened them, she knew she'd find small crescents dug into the flesh, deep and red, rimmed by bloodless white.

Two years. Two years since the lies and the betrayal, the consequences. The aftermath. Two years since she'd held a gun on a man she'd once trusted, a man who stood before her naked and leering, laughing. Two years since she'd raced through the night, run from her car and onto the porch, burst into the house, the darkness, knowing even as she did that it was too late. That she was too late.

Two years since her world had caught up with her.

Two years since she'd quit living.

"When I was growing up, I had a knack for finding things." Back then, it had seemed like a game, an adventure. A gift. Only later did she learn the truth. "Stuffed animals, jewelry, neighborhood pets." She closed her eyes, drifted back in time. "My grandmother had a cat. She was a tiny little white angel, with slanted green eyes and little pink ears…only problem was she was deaf. One day we couldn't find her anywhere—calling wouldn't work—and realized she'd managed to get outside. Gran was sick with worry. Little Elsie was completely defenseless. We looked and looked and looked, and then I had the strongest feeling to venture out back to an old abandoned shed. Inside I found a broken floorboard, and down below, little Elsie sat, cold and scared and shivering."

Brenna opened her eyes but didn't look at Ethan. "I'd never been inside it before that day. I didn't even know it was there."

Nothing. Just silence, the thick, heavy kind that spoke a language of its own.

"When I was seventeen a girl in my class disappeared." Gretchen. A cheerleader, a beautiful, precocious, I-can-take-on-the-world blonde. "That night when I went to bed, I saw her. By the river. Tied to a tree, bleeding and beaten. But alive."

"You saw her?" Ethan repeated. "Don't you mean you had a nightmare?"

Brenna forced a breath, refused to let herself slip too far

away. "I went to the cops, told them what I'd seen, told them they had to get to her fast or it would be too late."

"And?"

"They laughed, thanked me ever so politely and told me to leave crime solving to the professionals." Bitterness squeezed from her throat, tightened her voice. "It was ten days later that they found her by the river, tied to a tree, dead of excessive blood loss."

Ethan swore softly. "What happened then?"

"They brought me in for questioning." The memory sickened. "Put me in one of those interrogation rooms and spent the next several hours throwing heinous scenarios at me. That I was jealous. In need of attention. That I'd staged the whole scene—that I'd brutally assaulted my classmate—just so I could play hero and lead the cops to her."

A moment of silence passed before Ethan said anything. "Look at me, Brenna."

She didn't want to, but slowly she did.

He watched her through those penetrating eyes, but the dark green depths didn't burn with prosecution as they had before. Instead she found the embers of a horror she knew better than to trust. "They were doing their job. You know that, don't you?"

The jab of pain was quick and efficient. "I know." She knew it now and she'd known it then. To the cops her warning looked more like a confession.

"You weren't arrested?"

"Not enough evidence." But not for lack of trying. "After that it was hard to go back to school. Gretchen was dead, and suddenly I was a freak. The crowd she ran with never believed my story." Never missed an opportunity to intimidate and harass. "Thank God we graduated a few weeks later."

"Is that when you met Brinker?"

Brenna shook her head. "That was later. He was working on a case, the disappearance of a professor at the local college I was attending." Stick to the facts, she reminded herself. Recount the story without the crippling emotion. "It was the same thing all over again—I had a dream and saw Professor Little, knew she was still alive.''

Ethan's gaze narrowed. "So you went to the police?"

"I didn't want to." God, how she'd wanted to erase the dream, the knowledge, but every time she'd closed her eyes, she'd seen her professor, alone in a cellar, desperate, and she'd known she had to try. "The detective I talked to blew me off, patted me on my head like a good little puppy dog and sent me on my way, but another detective caught up with me outside."

"Brinker?"

"Brinker." And instantly she'd known he was different. There'd been a strength to him, not ugly and twisted like the first detective, but brimming with integrity and compassion. "He listened to me. He asked questions, took notes." The emotion she'd been fighting swarmed her throat, thickened her voice. "Twelve hours later he found Professor Little, badly beaten and repeatedly raped, but alive."

Ethan's mouth flattened into a hard line. "He believed you."

"He believed me." Moisture stung the backs of her eyes, but she refused to let it fall, refused to let this hard, unyielding man know how much it hurt just to remember. "We worked together for several years after that. Mostly missing children, one serial killer just getting started."

"What went wrong?"

The question startled her. "What?"

"Something went wrong," he repeated. His voice was softer than before, warmer, and deep inside she had to wonder if it was a ploy. "I can see it in your eyes."

Instinctively she blinked. "He was assigned a new partner. Adam Gerritson." She didn't need to close her eyes to see him as he'd been that first day, all tall and well built, with a deep gold Florida tan and the most fascinating blue eyes she'd ever seen. He'd smiled, a razor sharp, hundred watt smile, and Brenna had felt the zing clear down to her toes. "Three months later we were working on a case, a killer who was abducting women from grocery store parking lots and taking them out to the woods, where he brutally assaulted them, sometimes for days at a time, before leaving them to die.''

"The suburb slayer," Ethan muttered.

The sound of the press's nickname, after all this time, was enough to unleash the horror. Her stomach churned. She turned toward Ethan, saw the memory etched in his face. "You remember the case."

The lines of his face tightened. "I wouldn't let my sisters go grocery shopping alone until that bastard was caught."

Brenna fought the surge of warmth, the glimpse of Ethan Carrington the man, the protective brother, the son who loved his family so deeply he was willing to shed his own blood to preserve theirs.

"I woke up one night with this cold certainty drilling through me. I'd seen the killer. Knew where to find him." The slippery slope beckoned, but she resisted, knowing if she let herself go, even an inch, this time she might never claw her way back. "I tried to reach Dave but got Adam instead. I gave him the information, and he promised to check things out."

"Did he?"

"I thought he did," she said. "For three days I fed him information, and for three days he lied to me."

Ethan muttered something unintelligible under his breath. "What happened?"

For two years she'd worked hard to lock the memory away, somewhere deep, somewhere safe, somewhere it couldn't destroy on a daily basis. Now it slid through, cold and dank and slimy. "I was with Adam when this horrible sensation washed over me. It was like the world had just stopped spinning, like everything had slammed to a halt." A cruel, punishing halt. "And I knew. I knew something horrible had happened." That's when she'd pulled the gun. That's when she'd demanded the truth. "I was too late," she whispered. "Too late."

"Damn it, Brenna," Ethan growled, and with his free hand grabbed a blue blanket from the seat pocket in front of him and draped it over her body. The warmth was immediate, but nowhere near as intense as the press of his fingers to her jaw. Slowly he turned her face toward his. "Too late for what?"

She didn't want to look at him. She didn't want to see the strength in his face, the juxtaposition of hard lines and impossibly soft lips. The glow in his eyes that she foolishly wanted to label compassion.

"Too late for what?" he asked again, and this time his voice, the subtle urging in it, crushed her resolve. She lifted her eyes to his face and almost drowned.

"'I ran.'" Her voice cracked on the words, the memory. She wanted to run now, not to or from anything, just to run, change things somehow, undo the past. "Home. To Grandma." But even as she'd leaped from her car, she'd known it was too late. There'd been a stillness inside her, a vacuum she'd never experienced, like the lifeless, empty confines of space. "There was blood on the porch." And the house had been cold, unnaturally cold for a gorgeous spring day. "She was in the kitchen, on the floor in front of the stove." Blood, so much blood. "There was a fresh blueberry pie," she whispered. Her favorite. "Untouched."

Against the side of her face, Ethan's fingers, so big and strong, inched higher. "I'm sorry."

Brenna tried to bring him into focus, but saw only her grandmother sprawled on the kitchen floor. "The bastard got her. He knew I was on to him and got her before we could get him."

Ethan's mouth twisted. "He was a cop, wasn't he?"

Brenna felt the glow move into her eyes, the hatred stream through her body. "Adam had told him about my visions over beer, and he realized we were closing in."

"He killed Brinker's wife, too."

"On the same day," she confirmed. "Hoping to teach us a lesson, force us to back off."

Ethan's hand fell away. "Brinker shot him dead three hours later."

"Dave was never the same man. Never forgave himself for

trusting his partner, never forgave himself for relying on Adam to pass on crucial information.''

''And you?'' Ethan asked, and again there was a warmth to his voice, a gentle coaxing that brushed up against that dark place inside of her. A prosecutor, she reminded herself. A man skilled at choosing just the right angle to secure the information he needed.

A man not to be trusted, no matter how much she wondered what it would feel like, for just one fraction of one second, to have those strong arms of his close around her and hold on tight. That was just loneliness talking, she reminded. Longing. The basic human need for companionship.

This man was not the man to fill that need or any others.

She looked at him, careful to wipe away the longing, careful to keep her voice strong. ''I'm afraid you'll have to decide that for yourself, prosecutor. If you can't see the answer to that question for yourself, there's no point in me saying anything further.''

Chapter 5

The sun boiled over the turquoise waters of the ocean in an angry display of reds and pinks and oranges. Violent slashes of light streaked through the lingering gray of dawn. Sensing land, craving the coming confrontation, Ethan watched high, thin clouds whipping by the small window of the jet. His ears tightened and popped with the gradual descent of the aircraft.

Beside him, Brenna slept.

He refused to look at her. Not again, not anymore. He'd done that enough. Through the deep, dark hours of the night, with only dim lighting illuminating the cabin and two guards glaring at him with weapons poised and ready, he'd been unable to turn from her, unable to look away from the way her slight, black-clad body melted into the thick leather seat. With any other woman he might have called it relaxation but not with Brenna. He'd literally seen the wall of exhaustion collapse around her. She'd fought it, just as she'd fought him, but in the end she'd succumbed.

And now she slept.

Christ. No wonder she was exhausted. Her performance had been spectacular. And that's what it had to be, he'd told himself as he'd watched the shadows play against the soft lines of her face. A performance. Her voice had been pitched perfectly singsong, distant, stretched to the breaking point. Her eyes, stunning. Eerie as always, but glowing with a hard light he'd rarely seen. And her body language. Even now, hours later, the tension she'd radiated tightened through his chest.

A performance.

The plane bucked through a pocket of turbulence, continuing its steady descent. And yet beside him he felt no movement, no conscious awareness of the disturbance.

Ethan felt his jaw clench, his body go tight with frustration. For a man accustomed to sorting through lies and exaggerations, excuses and alibis, a man accustomed to zeroing in on the truth, the lack of clarity grated like a riddle he couldn't wrap his mind around. He'd faced a lot of adversaries, hardened criminals and slippery defense attorneys, but now, intuitively, he realized he faced the most dangerous demon of all.

Himself.

He, the man who'd lived up close and personal in the aftermath of Jorak's deceptions, a federal prosecutor and member of the antiterror task force, a man who'd long since learned to never, never believe in anything that couldn't be seen or touched, Christ, he *wanted* to believe her. That was the real kicker, the bitter pill that jammed in his throat. Everything he knew about Jorak, everything he'd learned about deception and trickery, urged him to see through her lies, but something deep inside him responded to her, to those whitewashed fairy eyes, tempting him to forget everything he knew, everything he'd learned, and trust her.

Over the years he'd lost count of the number of suspects he'd interrogated, the witnesses he'd cross-examined. He was good at his job. He knew how to scrape aside emotion and focus on that which could be trusted—facts. Because facts didn't lie. But the cruel fact of the matter was that during those dark, dark moments when Brenna Scott had looked at him through remote eyes, with tangled hair falling against her pale face, telling him the most ludicrous, impossible story in the world, he'd almost believed her. He'd wanted to believe her.

Wanting. God. He had no business thinking of Brenna Scott and wanting in the same sentence.

Another bump, this one more violent, and there in the shimmering blue distance, the first sight of land on the horizon. An island. Small, green, beckoning.

Ethan used the island and a fresh surge of anticipation to block her story, the way it had slipped past his suspicions, like a soft hand easing beneath the fabric of clothing, sliding beyond what he knew to be real and true. The desire—the need—had stunned him. Bothered him. He'd sat inches away from her, watching the play of shadows against her face, hearing them thicken her voice, all the while fighting the urge to pull her into his arms and comfort her, chase away the demons, the darkness.

Now, long hours later, he found himself grateful in a sick way for the constraints that prevented him from making such a stupid mistake. He didn't know who this woman was, didn't understand how she knew what she claimed to know. The more she'd talked, the deeper the night had grown, the more he'd found his certainty that she worked for Zhukov crumbling. And that made her dangerous. Very, very dangerous.

Jorak Zhukov was a master of deception. Ethan, better than anyone, knew that. Z knew what buttons to push, what ropes to pull. A woman like Brenna Scott was the perfect weapon.

"Where are we?"

The sleep-roughened words cruised through him like a shot of early-morning whiskey. He knew better than to look at her, but turned anyway, found her face inches from his, her eyes darker than usual, heavy with sleep.

The urge to streak a finger along the side of her face, to slide the tangled blond hair back from her bruised cheek, had him closing his hand into a tight fist.

"The Gulf of Mexico or the Caribbean, I'm guessing," he said, and the thickness to his voice surprised him. The whisper deep inside grew more insistent, the disturbing trickle, the unwanted draw.

He had to find out, damn it. Once and for all, he needed to know just who this woman was, on whose side she stood.

She peered around him, toward the increasingly turquoise water below. The faint scent of something spicy and exotic taunted. "Are we landing?"

You tell me, he wanted to say but didn't. "Looks that way."

She watched the water a moment longer, then let her head loll back against the thick leather of her seat. "It's not like me to sleep so deeply."

"Your story tired you out." He saw it all the time, from people called to testify.

Her eyes took on the same glow from the night before, her mouth hardening into neither a smile nor a frown, just grim acceptance. "You think that's what I was doing? Telling a story?"

Again he resisted the urge to swipe a strand of blond hair from her face. It was bad enough that he was looking at her. He didn't need to touch.

Might never be able to stop.

"Time will tell," he muttered gruffly. Soon, too. Very, very soon. Time would tell and, unlike people, time didn't lie.

There was no airport, only an airstrip, all but deserted. The plane touched down with the smoothness expected from a top-of-the-line private jet, gliding to a seamless halt at the end of the surprisingly well-maintained runway.

No attendants greeted them. No other planes flanked them. No tourists or employees milled about the small, decrepit building through which they were led, ankles no longer bound together, but hands still secured behind their backs. No gift shops or rest rooms or food courts, no customs officers, though through a darkened hallway Ethan saw signs of what looked to have once been a formal passenger processing area.

Two armed guards walked in front of them, two behind, one on each side. No one spoke, not even Brenna. She just looked straight ahead, with her soft blond hair blowing in the warm tropical breeze. The sun assaulted them, telling Ethan they had indeed traveled south. He was grateful he still wore his running gear from the night before. The black outfit that hugged Brenna's lithe little body would undoubtedly hold the heat.

A battered gray Hummer whisked them into the dense vegetation of the jungle. Vines of green tangled up palm trees in various stages of growth. Considerable debris lay alongside the bumpy road.

Adrenaline pumped through him. He looked at the woman seated beside him, her thigh brushing his, and couldn't help but notice the moisture beading along her face. "Maybe you should have dressed for the occasion, huh, angel?"

The second the words left his mouth, regret swarmed him, but he ignored it. He had to know, he reminded himself. He had a plan, had to execute.

But Brenna didn't rise to his bait. She just sat there, quietly, staring straight ahead.

The vehicle slowed near an arched entryway, reminiscent of an elaborate resort he'd once visited along the Mayan Yucatan. Three armed guards, clearly Latino, strolled from within a small windowed station. A moment later, after a conference with the driver, a wrought-iron gate ambled to the side, granting them access to the heavily tree-lined road.

The compound came into sight five minutes later. Large, Mediterranean in design, shockingly white against the vivid azure sky. Just like Brenna had predicted. The massive structure sprawled like a damning nail in an unwanted coffin.

"Home sweet home?" he asked quietly.

This time she looked at him, pierced him with those eerie blue eyes of hers, but rather than condemning, they glowed with a pity that pricked somewhere deep.

"Time will tell," she answered in that remote voice he was growing to detest. The parody of his own words stung.

"Out," they were instructed after the Hummer stopped in front of a massive, whitewashed stucco entryway.

Ethan maneuvered from the back seat, instinctively turning to offer Brenna a hand, even though the cuffs prevented him from doing so. She glanced at him and slid past him, stepping into a wash of hot morning sunshine.

Silently they were led through a white marble entryway, columns flanking them on each side, toward the back of the house.

"Wait here." The cuffs binding their wrists behind their

backs were released, two double doors thrown open, and they were pushed inside the sanctuary.

Ethan took only two steps before stopping cold. He saw the wall of windows first, massive, overlooking the beach below, the turquoise waves swishing against sugar-fine sand. Slowly he turned to take in the rest of the room, and a chill quickened through him.

White. The entire room was white—walls, marble flooring, ultra-chic modern furniture, even a sleek baby grand piano. On the wall hung an ornate, filigree mirror. And on a glass table below sat a pewter statue of a jaguar frozen in motion.

And all that hope he'd been denying, the hope that beat against his chest like an endangered bird trapped in a cage too small, shattered.

I can see you in a mirror, he remembered her saying. He moved across the room now, drawn by the object he didn't want to see. *"There's a glass table below it, and on the table there's a jaguar. A sculpture.* He put his hand to the animal and ran his palm and fingers along the familiar smooth lines, fought the memory. Fought the truth.

She felt the second the change washed over him. She didn't need to look at him, didn't need to see those intelligent green eyes to know he saw what she saw. The room from her dreams. The room she'd told him about. The room he would now take as further proof that she'd been here before, that she was involved with Jorak Zhukov.

"Well, well, well," he said in that slow, dangerously seductive Virginia drawl of his. In a lightning-quick move he tore away from the statue and returned to her, tucked a single finger beneath her chin to tilt her face toward his. "You have an impressive eye for detail, angel."

The burn singed through her. She squared her shoulders and tilted her chin, refusing to let the hurt, the stinging disappointment, glimmer through. There was no point defending herself. She'd known men like Ethan Carrington before, so hardened by the life he'd lived, so cynical and jaded that he trusted only that which could be seen or felt.

Right now, both condemned.

"You should have listened to me," she said, and the strength to her words was not forced. "You should never have let them bring you here."

"And miss an opportunity like this?" His eyes were on fire, not so much with anger or scorn, but with the thrill of the chase. "Do you have any idea how long I've been waiting for this moment?"

Brenna blinked, but the image didn't fade. The tall raven-haired man watched her with a gleam of excitement in his eyes. He reminded her of an eager kid on Christmas morning. "You won't have to wait much longer."

"You know what the kicker is?" he asked, and this time the slightest trace of harshness twisted his voice. "I almost believed you."

The words landed hard, kicked deep. She staggered back from their force, his touch, not at all understanding the slide of disappointment through her chest. "That's because you've taught yourself to see the truth," she shot back. "Even when you don't want to."

That got him. His eyes flared, then narrowed in on her. Then, God help her, he laughed. It was a deep and rich sound, echoing through the cavernous room. "A man could come to enjoy you, Brenna Scott."

The flash of heat was immediate, zinging like an arrow down low in her stomach, spreading, pooling between her legs. "I'm not here for your enjoyment."

Smiling now, a slow and sensuous tilt of his lips, he streaked a finger down the side of her cheek. "That, angel, remains to be seen."

Again she stepped from his touch, but the image remained, gossamerlike, just out of reach, a yearning she neither understood nor trusted. "Some things can't be seen," she said very softly, very pointedly. "Some things just are."

He said nothing to that, not at first, just continued to watch her through those burning green eyes. For some crazy reason she couldn't shake the sense he was enjoying this. "And some things aren't," he said finally.

"Pardon the intrusion," came a cultured voice from behind them. They spun toward the open doorway, found a young man with white clothes and dark skin standing just inside the room. "You'll need to come with me now."

Ethan started toward him. "Where's Zhukov?"

"He sends his regrets, but he's been detained."

Ethan stopped abruptly. "I want to see him now."

"I'm afraid that's impossible." The young man glanced at Brenna, then Ethan. "If you'll come with me, I'll lead you to your quarters where you can freshen up, rest if you like."

Brenna worked hard to keep her face expressionless, devoid of the confusion twisting through her. They were like actors, she realized, on a cardboard stage. All these fake manners and courtesies, the house staff treating them as though they were guests rather than detainees.

"Follow me," the dark man in white said.

For a moment Brenna thought Ethan was going to refuse the offer, but then he turned to Brenna and extended his hand. A slow smile curved his lips. "Angel?"

She looked at his hand outstretched toward her, the square palm and strong fingers, the tanned flesh, and didn't want to take it. Didn't want to touch him again. That's how everything had started, after all. With a simple touch between strangers. He'd yet to make the connection, yet to remember the night they'd brushed, flesh to flesh, in the vet clinic where she worked. She was nothing more than a stranger to him, and even were she to remind him, he still wouldn't believe.

It wasn't in his blood.

She brushed by him, toward the open doorway. "Freshening up sounds wonderful," she said. Pointedly she turned and scorched him with her eyes, let her gaze linger on his ratty running clothes. With great effort she wrinkled her nose, pretended the masculine smell offended. "Something around here stinks more by the minute."

The room stole her breath. Large and spacious, with a stunning wall of windows and a verandah overlooking the beach, high windows open to allow the crosswinds to feather through the tropical warmth, several wicker fans whooshing lazily from high on the ceiling. Not much furniture adorned the room, but then, not much was needed. The wood was surprisingly dark, mahogany maybe, reminiscent of that found in the old sugar plantations. A dresser, an armoire, a chest and a bed. A big, beautiful, four-poster bed with netting dangling around all four sides.

Brenna ignored the quickening deep inside and tried not to look at the white covers, pulled crisply back. At the pillows, fluffed and waiting.

"These must be for you," Ethan said, and she spun toward him, relieved not to look at the bed, not at all prepared for the sight of him standing by the armoire with a pair of dusty rose panties and bra dangling from his fingers.

She swallowed hard. "I certainly hope they're not for you."

He glanced toward a pile of clothing by his feet, a pair of khaki cargo shorts and black knit shirt, a pair of gray boxers. "Not unless you'd rather wear these."

The room started to spin, but she fought the sensation, fought the odd vertigo whirring through her. It was like falling down the rabbit hole, she thought dizzily, and discovering a strange new world where nothing made sense. She'd seen the dream, after all. She knew what was coming.

The elegant room and fresh supply of clothing didn't fit.

"Would you like to clean up first?" Ethan asked.

There was a gleam in his eyes, a gleam that matched the thickness of his voice. Pretending she noticed neither, she crossed to the armoire and looked inside, selected a simple white sundress. There was no simple underwear. It was all in sets, all provocative. There was a black combo with a lacy bra and a matching thong, a crimson set in silk. The pink set in Ethan's hands. The most discreet was a set of pale yellow, a demicup bra and matching bikini panties.

An odd rush feathered through her as she picked up the garments under Ethan's watchful eye. When she returned from the shower, he'd know what she had on beneath her dress, a reality that left her feeling as exposed as if she stood before him naked.

"I won't be long," she said with a breeziness she didn't come close to feeling, then forced herself to walk casually to the bathroom.

She'd never seen anything like it. Sprawling, definitely. Elegant, for sure. All white marble. A sunken tub large enough for two, with blood-red rose petals sprinkled liberally, even though no water waited inside. Jacuzzi jets. A shower encased in erotic glass blocks. Dual vanities, each stocked with shampoos and lotions and powders, toothpastes, the works. An entire wall of windows, with no curtains or shutters, open and exposing tropical foliage just beyond; the beach below. The tide washed lazily against the beach of glowing white sand.

The beach soon to be drenched in red.

Blocking the images, the memories and visions she wanted no part of, she stripped out of the stifling black clothes and stepped into the shower, welcomed the blast of lukewarm water washing away the dirt and grime from the night before. Arching her back, she turned up to the rainlike spray, let it run down her head and face, trickle over her chest and slide down her body.

"Feel better?"

The roughly masculine voice jolted through her, prompting her to draw her arms across her chest. Through the glass blocks she could see the outline of his body, tall, broad, but no detail. Pray to God he saw the same.

"I'd feel better if you left me alone," she said, and like so many other times, he treated her to one of those slow, dark laughs. Predatory, almost. The sound swirled around her, much like the warm water against her naked flesh, but quietly he turned and walked out the door.

For a few minutes Brenna didn't move, just stood beneath the spray, waiting, not at all convinced he wouldn't be back. She didn't take him for the kind of man to force himself on a woman, but nothing was as it seemed in the rabbit hole, and too well she knew men with their backs against the wall knew no limits. She'd walked into some kind of odd chess game, and if she wasn't careful, she could easily get caught in the crossfire.

Cautiously she reached for the bottle of liquid soap. Hibiscus scented, she noted, squeezing a blob into her palm. Trying not to think about Ethan, or the fact that she stood naked and all that separated them was a door and his honor, she slid her hands along her body.

The flash froze her. The heat electrified. It was only her hands splayed against her body, but too easily she felt those square palms and strong fingers, the calluses that made no sense for a polished city lawyer.

Not a premonition, she told herself. Dear heaven, not a premonition.

She let the water wash away the lather, the unwanted images, and quickly shampooed and conditioned her hair. She kept her mind blank, refusing to allow thoughts of Ethan Carrington and those fascinating hands of his seep through. She didn't need to imagine them on her body, tangled in her hair. Even if he didn't believe she was on Jorak Zhukov's payroll, there was no room for a man like him in her life. She'd learned the price of loving, the price of letting herself care. She'd felt the sting of betrayal, cried the tears, attended the funerals.

Ethan Carrington would be no different.

Abruptly she turned off the water and glanced through the thick glass blocks to make sure he'd not slipped back into the bathroom. When she saw nothing, she opened the door and reached for a thick peach towel, wrapped it around her body, secured her wet hair in a smaller towel. Through the foggy bathroom mirror she caught sight of her face, noted the deep flush to her cheeks, the darkness to her normally pale eyes and damned her body for betraying her.

Brenna wasn't a woman for primping and pampering, but she couldn't resist squeezing rich, hibiscus-scented lotion into her palm and smoothing it over arms and legs, her chest and stomach. Then she brushed her teeth and dried her hair, stepped into the lemon-yellow panties and secured the bra, pulled on the soft cotton sundress.

A wide assortment of makeup lay scattered on a mirrored tray, but she ignored it all, reminding herself she was not here to look good for Ethan Carrington.

"It's all yours," she said, opening the bathroom door and letting the steam roll into the surprisingly cool room.

Nothing prepared her for the sight of him sprawled on the big bed, his deep tan and raven hair a stark contrast to the crisp white linens and netting. He looked even more imposing lying down than he did standing up, with his chest and shoulders dominating a ridiculous display of frilly pillows, his long legs bent and crooked open.

Slowly his lips curved into a breathtakingly sensuous smile. "Angel, I've heard people compared to a breath of fresh air before, but until this moment I've never seen it with my own eyes."

The words rushed through her, softening the hard edges she'd tacked into place while showering. "Maybe I should slip back into the black."

"Can't," he said with a devilish grin, and Brenna abruptly swung toward the bathroom, where her jeans and top no longer lay in a heap on the floor. "Don't look so upset, angel. It's just clothes."

She grabbed the edges of her control and knotted them together. "I'm beginning to wonder why I saved hot water for you."

She realized her mistake too late. A gleam moved into his eyes, darkened them into a primeval glow. "Trust me, angel," he said, swinging to the side of the bed. His bare feet came down on the white tile floor. "I don't need to be any hotter than I am." He crossed toward her with an easy masculine grace, a man clearly comfortable with his own body, even though he wore loose-fitting running shorts and a torn and dirty VMI T-shirt. "I'm thinking a cold shower will do just the trick."

Pausing beside her, close enough to touch, he took in first her eyes, then let his gaze slide lower, down along the scoop neck of the sundress, along the bodice, to her legs and bare feet. He didn't touch her this time, not physically, not with his hands, and yet everywhere his gaze skimmed, her body burned. "Your toes aren't painted."

Her throat tightened. "Why would they be?"

"I've never known a woman who didn't paint her toenails."

At that, Brenna found she could smile. "And I've never seen the point." Almost never, that was. There'd been a brief period there, a couple of shattering weeks, when she'd put pink on her toes and black around her eyes, mauve on her lips. She'd wanted to feel womanly, had thought it would make a difference.

"Christ," Ethan swore softly, but sounded more fascinated than angered. "Another time, another place, another circumstance, and who the hell knows?"

She did. She knew. No matter the time, the place, the circumstance, she could have no relationship, no future, with this man. She'd left that part of her life behind. She trusted her dreams, her visions of what would come to pass in other people's lives, but her mind went dark when it came to her own emotions. Her own future.

With one last heated look, Ethan strolled past her and into the opulent bathroom but didn't shut the door. Instinctively she looked after him, stood frozen when he pulled off his T-shirt and tossed it to the ground.

She'd seen a man naked before. She'd seen a muscular, well-built man without clothes. But then she'd wanted to run. Then she'd scrambled back across the bed, grabbed a gun.

Now she just wanted to stare. The deep bronze of his arms extended across his shoulders and down his chest, lower still to a stomach of finely corded muscle. Dark gold hair curled along his pecs and swirled around flat mauve nipples, trickled like an arrow down toward his shorts...

...which he was reaching for.

Brenna spun away, refused to watch, to stare, to wonder. She didn't understand what kind of game he was playing. She knew he didn't trust her, that he thought she was on Zhukov's payroll.

How far are you willing to take this, angel?

The shower came on, and fleetingly she wondered if he was really going to take it cold. Didn't matter, she told herself. All that mattered was staying alert. Surviving. She had no allies on this island. If she was going to make it off alive, she had no one to trust but herself.

The temptation to turn toward the open bathroom door was strong, but she resisted, wandering instead to the wall of windows overlooking the beach below. The sun glimmered on the sugary sand, the waves, gentle now, swishing against the shore.

"All better?"

The voice, deep and slightly rough, rushed through her, like the warm breeze rustling the palms lining the beach. She turned to find Ethan striding toward her, wearing the khaki shorts she'd seen on the floor, but nothing else. His closely cut hair was damp, the whiskers still darkened his jaw.

Because her heart beat much too fast, she wrinkled her nose, drew in the unmistakable scent of man and soap. "Much," she said.

"Do you have any idea?" he asked, and the words sounded rough, torn from some place deep inside. He strolled closer, not stopping until he'd invaded her personal space. "Any idea at all, what it does to a man to stand in a shower and know that only a few minutes before a beautiful woman stood in that very same place, naked, running her hands along her body?"

Brenna's mouth went dry. She tried to swallow, couldn't. To breathe, couldn't. To think, understand, prepare...couldn't. "Ethan—"

His eyes heated, slid to the enormous poster bed, with both the netting and crisp white sheets pulled back. "Now that we're all fresh and clean, why don't we put each other out of our misery?" He lifted a hand and gently slid the hair behind her ear. Then his fingers feathered over the swirl of purple and green left by Zhukov's men. "Who knows what this evening will bring? Maybe we should make the most of the time we do have." He paused, let his thumb slide to her lower lip. "I've always found a little afternoon delight an unbeatable distraction."

Deep inside, something broke and gave way. She stared at him, at his impossibly full mouth, lips that had no business being moist but were, eyes that glowed not with their customary fierce intelligence but a desire that heated her blood.

And in that place inside, the one she'd turned her back on, had taught herself not to trust, she started to bleed. "What happened to you, Ethan?" The question broke on the way out, smashed to smithereens by the emotion jammed in her throat. "What turned you into such a hard, cynical man?"

His eyes narrowed in on her face, locked on her, reducing the world to one man, one woman, one moment. "No matter who you are or why you walked into my life, we may never leave this island alive." He slid his thumb along her lower lip. "What's so hard and cynical about a man wanting to spend what could be his last moments making love to a beautiful woman?"

The question did cruel, cruel things to her heart. The yearnings it unleashed, shattered. "You don't want to make love to me."

"Are you sure about that?" he asked in a thick drawl that sent her bones into meltdown.

Slowly she looked from his mouth to his eyes, found them hot and burning. Instinct demanded that she turn away from him, run into the bathroom and lock the door, but no power on earth could make her move, not when he lowered his face toward hers. Then his mouth was on hers, and for a blinding heartbeat nothing else mattered.

Chapter 6

Sensation assaulted her. Not the cruel, suffocating kind that had once prompted her to draw a gun on the man she'd thought she loved, but the whirring, bone-melting kind that jumbled every protest hammering through her. She tried to rip herself from the dream, as she'd trained herself to do, but this was no dream, and her body refused to obey. Ethan's arms came around her and pulled her to his chest, still warm and damp from his shower. She braced herself for the onslaught that inevitably came with intimate touches, but found only a longing that stole her breath.

"Kiss me back, damn it," he murmured, and through the haze of passion, she heard an edge to his voice, a razor-fine desperation, completely at odds with the smooth, always-in-control attorney.

His hands cruised up her back, one of them tangling in her hair, just like she'd imagined while standing naked under the spray of warm water. For a gossamer moment time slowed, and she could no longer just stand there, not when the need to respond swamped her. She opened to him, accepted him, let herself taste that which she knew would ultimately destroy.

His lips were amazingly soft for such a hard man—persuasive, urging her mouth to open to him, yield, give back all that he was giving her. Whiskers scraped her jaw but didn't hurt. Need, hot and boiling, drenched, drowning out sanity.

He muttered something under his breath, a jumbled sound of male frustration, and deepened the kiss, pulling her farther into his embrace. His body surrounded her, engulfed her, and before she realized her intent, she'd lifted her arms to curl around his back. The hard, smooth planes she found there had her fingers digging deeper, loving the hot male feel of him.

Time, still for a delirious heartbeat, lurched violently. Liquid heat pooled between her legs. She'd known this man less than twenty-four hours, but in his arms, with his mouth roughly claiming hers, hours felt like eternity. Because of the dreams, she knew. Their intensity. The nighttime images had bound their lives together, long before she'd stepped from behind the tree and tried to warn him of the danger lying ahead.

Now she arched into the kiss, welcomed the feel of his lips moving against hers, his tongue sweeping into her mouth. The truth stunned her. She wanted him. Despite everything, the circumstances that brought them together and the distrust that kept them apart, she wanted to know this man intimately. To run her hands not just along the hard planes of his back but all of him. To have him do the same to her, to feel his roughened palms slide along her arms and chest, caress her breasts, slide along her stomach, lower still.

That knowledge gave her the strength to twist away.

She staggered from him, brought the back of her hand to her mouth and wiped away the evidence of what they'd just shared.

"Someone hurt you," she said, and barely recognized the ragged edge to her voice. Emotion clogged her throat, but she refused to let it invade her eyes. In his kiss, the gentle intensity of his embrace, she'd found a truth she'd not seen before, one that changed everything. "Someone you trusted." And because of that he would never trust again. "I'm not that person."

* * *

Ethan felt his nostrils flare but refused to let any other trace of reaction break through. He stood very still, watching her in a puddle of early-afternoon sun, pale hair falling with a hint of curl, cheeks and lips flushed without the aid of makeup, the look of pure, stricken horror in her eyes. They weren't white-washed now, but dark and haunted.

Swearing softly, he shoved a hand through his hair. "Are you sure about that, angel?" he asked, careful to keep all the hard edges from his voice.

She lifted her chin. "I'm sure."

Sure of what, he wanted to demand but didn't dare. Sure that someone he'd trusted had betrayed him, or sure she wouldn't share his bed. The answer didn't matter, he told himself. She was just chasing shadows, knitting together loose ends he'd carelessly shared with her during the long hours of the night, to come up with an obvious conclusion.

Or, he reminded himself, Jorak had told her the truth.

He spun from her and stalked across the room, slammed his hand against the doorknob, not at all surprised to find it locked. He'd decided to make the most of the game, but now he felt like an animal in a cage grossly too small, and the urge to do something intense and physical ground through him.

She'd kissed him back, damn it. Hotly. Explosively. Just as he'd expected. Jorak only hired the best. Anyone in his employ would be willing to go the distance for their boss. A woman sent by Jorak to masquerade as his companion, to slip through his defenses and earn his trust, would be eager to slip between the sheets and twist in his arms, making him so mindless with need that he'd slip up and reveal something he shouldn't.

But she'd stopped. She'd thrown on the brakes like a freaking bucket of cold water. And then she'd lanced him with her quiet statement about hurt and betrayal.

He spun back toward her and stalked across the cold tile. He saw her eyes go wide, saw her take a step back, but neither stopped him. "Who the hell *are* you?" he demanded in a rough voice that appalled him. "And what do you want with me?"

He expected her to turn from him or retort with some vague, cutting words. He didn't expect her eyes to go soft. He sure as hell didn't expect her to lift a hand to his face and gently cradle his jaw.

"You already know," she said softly, and he refused to believe it was pain he heard in her voice. Slowly she slid her index finger to his lower lip. "Whether or not you let yourself believe is entirely up to you."

He tore away from her, refused to look, refused to see. She was wrong. He didn't know who she was. Didn't know what she wanted. Didn't know what he wanted. If he believed her, if he ignored the facts and accepted her riddles as truth, then the implications would violate everything he'd ever believed.

"I'm not the problem here, Ethan," she added in an eerily quiet voice. "I'm not the one you need to trust."

"No?" he asked. "Who, then? Who do I need to trust?"

Standing by the bed in the damningly soft sundress, backlit by the afternoon sun streaming through the windows, she looked more ethereal than real. But she *was* real, damn it. And beneath that white cotton, she wore pale-yellow panties and a flimsy bra. And beneath the slinky fabric, her skin was damnably soft.

"When was the last time you looked into the mirror?" she asked, derailing his thoughts. "Really looked?"

The question zinged into him. The frustration he'd been holding in check shoved a little harder. "What is that supposed to mean?"

"I think you know."

More riddles. "Answer my question."

She glanced toward a dark wood table beside the bed, where a pale but sharply beautiful orchid arched, fragile yet somehow strong. Enduring.

Damn the flower for reminding him of her.

"Haven't you ever wondered why facts and evidence are so important to you?" she asked, glancing back toward him. Her voice was soft, but a cutting precision lanced the question. "If you relied more on yourself, your instincts and what you feel, you wouldn't need those crutches anymore.''

Crutches. The word, and all that it implied, stung. ''Is that what you've done, angel? Is that why you're here with me, because you trust yourself so much?''

Her mouth, those beautiful soft pink lips he'd tasted and claimed not five minutes before, dropped into a frown. ''I'm here with you because I couldn't let you walk into danger without trying to warn you.''

''Why? Why was warning me so important?'' Why did she just keep looking at him like that, with wisdom and sorrow clashing in her eyes? And, God help him, why did the need to pull her back into his arms, pick up where they'd left off, burn through him? Still. As it had from the moment he'd first laid eyes on her. Hell, from the moment he'd first heard her throaty voice. ''I'm a complete stranger.''

She held his gaze a heartbeat before answering. ''Are you? Are you sure? Is that why you want to make love to me, because we're strangers?''

No, he wanted to make love to her because—

The answer stopped him cold.

He didn't answer her question. He didn't continue the conversation. He broke it off as abruptly as a brittle twig snapped in two. Silence poured into the room, thick and stifling like the hot humid air outside. He turned from her, paced the spacious room like it was a cramped cage, shoved his hand through closely cropped raven hair, but didn't look her way, didn't speak.

She had no business being fascinated. Brenna knew that. She had no business being intrigued by this man haunted by demons he refused to see or admit. But her body still tingled from the force of his kiss. Not a physical force, but threatening all the same. His mouth had moved against hers with a hunger and urgency that rocked her, even now.

She'd never been kissed so thoroughly before, as though something grave depended upon her response.

Not even by the man she'd once thought herself in love with. The man who had betrayed her. The man who had taught her the folly of exposing herself to emotions that blotted out everything else, even the senses and images she trusted above all else.

Detective Adam Gerritson.

Chest obscenely tight, Brenna turned from Ethan and stared out the window, watched the sun blaze from high in its perch against the azure sky. The temptation to let down, to slip between the sheets and close her eyes, let herself drift, pulled at her, but she knew what would happen if she surrendered. Alone in this room, she'd be vulnerable in ways against which there were no defenses. Not with a man like Ethan Carrington.

What would he do if the dreams struck? What would he do if she cried out? What would *she* do if he slid beside her in the bed and drew her close, used that deep Virginia drawl to coax her into telling him what she saw?

He wouldn't believe her. She already knew that. Anything she said, any response she gave him, would only deepen his mistrust.

Why then, why did the thought of being in that bed with him make everything inside her go soft and liquid?

Because the question didn't bear answering, she didn't even try. She just stood there watching the sun pass the time. Shadows announced the arrival of early evening, stretching and dancing across the sand, the worn, winding dirt pathway leading to the beach.

And then suddenly Ethan was there, standing between her and the rest of the room. His presence zinged through her, but before she could say anything, he drew a finger to his lips. "Shhh."

She heard it then, heavy footfalls coming toward the room. They stopped outside the door, and a series of clicking noises preceded the appearance of one of the guards from the airport. He strode into the room, his hand ready on the automatic weapon slung across his shoulder.

Ethan lowered his arm to Brenna's waist and pulled her closer.

"You'll come with me now," the man said in his heavily accented voice.

"Come where?" Ethan demanded.

"That doesn't matter."

"It does to me."

"You can obey," the man said, reaching for Brenna, "or we can do this my way."

The darkness slammed in the second the beefy hand curled around her wrist. She felt herself recoil, heard the sharp gasp break from her throat. Ugliness. So much ugliness. Depravity. A complete lack of remorse. Force.

"She begged," she murmured, and the chill cut clear to the bone. Somewhere deep inside, she started to shake. The woman had begged, for her life, her children, clear up to her last shallow breath. This man had still been buried deep inside her.

"Brenna?"

Her knees went out from under her. She felt herself sway, felt strong arms close around her. "Brenna!"

Fighting the fog, the ugliness, she blinked and brought the hard lines of his face into focus, staring down at her in abject horror. "Listen to him," she managed through the sickness swarming inside her. "Don't...test him."

The guard, so deceptively, disgustingly handsome, grunted his approval. "Your friend is smart."

Ethan smoothed the hair back from her face. His hand was warm, his palm gentle. "What in God's name is going on?"

She absorbed the feel of his touch, the quick rush of concern, the razor-fine slice of confusion. The infusion of strength. Light then, not blinding, but welcoming, pushing away the darkness of moments before.

"I'm okay," she said, and was. The man with the gun no longer touched her. Images from his life no longer slithered through her. "Please. Let's just go."

And please, please don't leave me alone with this man.

The lines of Ethan's face tightened. "You said she begged. Who, Brenna? Who begged?"

The woman. The woman's whose only mistake was trusting this man. Loving him.

Wincing, Brenna pushed the memory aside, having no desire to linger in the filth. "It doesn't matter."

"I think that it does," Ethan said quietly, reaching for her hand. His palm was wide, his touch gentle, his fingers so thick she couldn't comfortably slide hers between his. She clenched his palm instead, instinctively held on.

Leering with self-satisfaction, the guard led them from the bedroom down the cool, dimly lit hall, retracing their path from earlier in the day. A shiver ran through her as they approached the massive doors leading to the white room, and then they were there, inside the sanctuary.

Ethan never let go of her hand.

She saw the man immediately, reclining in a deeply cushioned, white leather chair. He wore all white, a linen summer suit against his dark, Mediterranean skin. He held the tumbler in his hands up to a ray of sunshine cutting in from the wall of windows. The light reflected off the amber liquid inside.

And she knew. She knew this man. Knew this moment.

Ethan knew, too. Beside her, she felt him go very still. Absolutely, completely, deathly still. His fingers, curled around the back of her palm, tightened. It was a sharp contrast to the frustrated pacing of earlier in the afternoon, but as she glanced at him, instinct told her this was the real Ethan Carrington. He was not a man of wild, jerky movements. He wasn't a man to release his tight grip on control. He was a man of unyielding iron, unbendable determination. He played every scenario in his mind prior to execution. There were no accidents. No mistakes. Nothing was left to chance.

That's why he'd agreed to meet her, had arrived without the security detail she'd expected to be flanking him. That's why he'd stood in the open along the banks of the James, making himself the perfect target. That's why he hadn't tried to run when he'd seen the limo.

He wanted to be here. She saw it in the slow burn in his eyes, every hard, etched line of his face. The subtle flare of his nostrils. The tightness of his jaw, made more menacing by a shadow of whiskers completely at odds with the image the cool, refined federal prosecutor usually showed his adversaries.

This was the real man, the man he concealed from the world, the quietly dangerous, cunning predator. The man who knew no fear, who would walk into the line of fire to protect his family.

And the woman he loved.

The thought, the memory of what was to come, wrapped around her heart and squeezed. What happened next? she couldn't help but wonder. What happened when those tightly bound chains of constraint broke?

Excitement hummed beneath the hard surface of his body, radiating from him like the hot summer sun baking through an exposed plate-glass window. Brenna absorbed it, looked slowly from Ethan to the man in the chair, the man who just watched them, lazily swirling the amber liquid in his glass.

"Ethan," he said in a richly cultured voice, one that sounded as if it belonged in some exotic European destination, like Cannes. He smiled slowly, revealing a row of white teeth. "How kind of you to join me."

Brenna hadn't thought it possible, but Ethan's body went even more tense. "Jorak," he said, his voice betraying none of the simmering animosity that practically choked her. "Or should I say Dimetri?"

There was an edge of menace to the second name he spoke, an edge she remembered from the night before, when he'd tossed out snippets of Jorak Zhukov's life in the States. Snippets she was no doubt supposed to recognize.

Jorak unfolded his large body from the chair and stood. "It's been a long time, my friend."

"Seven years."

A shadow crossed the other man's face, briefly, fleetingly. "And three months, two days."

The breath jammed in Brenna's throat. Something had gone

down between these two men, something horrible, something unimaginable. The aftermath, the residue, still throbbed between them.

"Here I am," Ethan said, finally releasing her hand. He stepped forward, extending his arms downward in a false gesture of surrender.

"Ah, yes," the other man said, smiling. He strolled to a glass-and-pewter bar and poured another tumbler of Scotch, extended it toward Ethan. "I take it you found your room accommodating?"

Ethan stunned Brenna by crossing to Jorak Zhukov and taking the heavily cut crystal glass from his hands, throwing back the amber liquid. "Glenmorangie," he muttered. "Single malt."

Satisfaction gleamed in Jorak's dark, dark eyes. "Your favorite."

Ethan smiled lazily. "You remember."

"I have forgotten nothing, my friend." The words sounded innocent, almost kind, but beneath them slithered a current of animosity. "Not one single detail."

Ethan poured more Scotch, but didn't drink. "Neither have I."

"That's what I'm counting on." He held Ethan's gaze a long moment, then glanced toward Brenna. She bit back a wince at the sudden contact, the sensation of being caught in the sights of a sniper's rifle.

"You know what I want," he murmured, and his eyes, cold moments before, heated.

Ethan's jaw went tight. "She can't help you," he gritted out, and for a second, there, Brenna's heart foolishly swelled.

"Oh," Jorak crooned, strolling toward her, "but she already has."

Disgust crammed into her throat, a dread unlike anything she'd ever known. He was going to touch her. She saw it in his eyes. But even worse was what she saw in Ethan's eyes, the splinters of accusation. And worse, confirmation.

"Has she now?" he asked in that deceptively quiet voice of his. "Has she really?"

Jorak lifted a hand toward her face. "Immensely," he murmured, but rather than putting finger to flesh, he streaked an imaginary line down her cheek. "I am sorry about the bruise," he said. "One so valuable should never be hurt."

Somehow Ethan kept himself from moving. Yet it was hard, damn hard, when his blood pounded a battle cry through his body. He'd learned, though. Learned to hide emotion, hide reaction. Because both damned. He forced himself to just stand there in the whitewashed room, with the glass of fine Scotch in his hand, and not move a muscle. Just watch.

The sight of Jorak and Brenna together sickened.

Seven years had passed since he'd last seen the man he'd once called friend. The man he'd invited into his home and his family, the man who'd married the woman Ethan had once dreamed of making his wife, the man who'd betrayed them all. Time had spiraled relentlessly forward, but little had changed. Life on the run, hands drenched in blood, had done nothing to mute the chiseled dark looks of Jorak's Mediterranean ancestry. Standing there in the kind of trademark white suit his father had always worn, the man looked as though he should be attending an opera in Barcelona, rather than holed up in a compound on some hot, sweaty island.

It was no wonder women fell so easily under his spell.

"You know what they say about intentions," Ethan muttered with a casualness completely at odds with the fury of his heart rate. Brenna had yet to move. She just stood there with her chin angled and her eyes unusually dark, pale blond hair falling loosely around her face.

The surge of protectiveness made no sense. The evidence spoke for itself. And yet…the thought of Jorak touching her, of all the ways in which he could use her, hurt her, twisted through Ethan like barbed wire.

"You seem to have a habit of catching women in the crossfire, don't you?" he reminded Jorak, forcibly loosening his grip on the glass. If it shattered, he would have a weapon. And a simple shard of glass was all it would take, all he would need, to turn his quest for justice into revenge.

Jorak's expression darkened. Lips tight, he turned his attention from Brenna, to Ethan. "And you seem to have a habit of letting the good ones slip away," he taunted. Then smiled. "My men tell me you did not make love to your woman this afternoon, despite the beautiful bed I provided. Was there a problem?"

Ethan saw Brenna's eyes flare. It was almost as though she hadn't known about the three strategically placed cameras in the big bedroom. He'd found and destroyed five listening devices during her shower. If others existed, they hadn't been close enough to pick up the highlights of their conversation.

"I don't perform on command," he shot back.

Jorak laughed. "Really? Since when?"

The burn started low, spread fast. He'd prepared himself for this moment, played it out in his mind hundreds of times, but the contempt slicing through him dwarfed anything he'd imagined. Because Jorak was right. He had performed on command. Brilliantly. Stupidly.

And because of him, because of his mistake, men had died. So had a child.

"It's not a problem," Jorak said, turning back toward her. Appreciation warmed his voice. And this time he touched. A hand to her face, the gentle caress of lover to lover.

Brenna reacted so swiftly, so violently, Ethan never saw it coming. She slapped Jorak's hand away and shoved back from him, spun away and positioned herself behind one of the big white chairs. "Don't touch me," she ground out in a voice Ethan had never heard her use before, low and throaty, but laced with deadly intent.

Out of nowhere three guards materialized and closed in on her.

Ethan was across the room before his heart could beat. He pulled Brenna toward him, inserting his body between her and the men with the guns. "Leave her out of this."

Amusement sparked in Jorak's dark eyes. He barked out a command in his native tongue and lifted his hand. "I will deal with her personally," he added in English, and the guards stopped dead in their tracks.

Ethan expected Brenna to be trembling, but in his arms she held herself completely still. So still she barely felt human. He wanted to turn her toward him, to look into her fairy eyes and feather a finger down her face, check the temperature of her skin. But didn't dare. Wasn't about to show Jorak an ounce of vulnerability.

"Feisty, isn't she?" the other man commented, strolling closer. His eyes met Ethan's. "Maybe I should just dispose of the pretenses and get rid of her now."

It made no sense, but Ethan pulled her tighter. "This is between you and me," he reminded, detesting how readily he performed on command. But he couldn't help it, damn it. He couldn't just stand there while Jorak Zhukov used and discarded another woman. "Why do you insist of dragging innocents into the line of fire?"

"You know the answer to that," Jorak chided. "It's the same reason my father went after your sister."

Ethan's jaw tightened, and he knew. He just didn't understand. "Leverage."

Jorak smiled. "It's all very simple, my friend, not all that different from the chess we used to play. The choice is yours. Give me what I want, and the lady walks out of here alive."

The farce almost made Ethan laugh. Almost. No one was walking out of here alive, not if Jorak had his way. And even if Ethan believed the lie, why would he compromise himself, his family, the information he'd been protecting for years, for a woman he didn't even know? Didn't even care ab—

He broke off the thought. "And if I don't?"

Another shrug. "Then you missed your last chance to get naked with the lovely lady."

He would kill her. She would serve no more purpose to Jorak, and he would find some creative way to execute her, staining Ethan's hands with more blood.

He looked from the cold triumph in Jorak's black eyes to
the blank stare in Brenna's, and without warning all the pieces,
all those misshapen, jagged edges, came crashing into place.
And he knew. God help him, he knew. Standing there in the
fading light of the late evening, with lengthening shadows
creeping across the white carpet and darkening the white walls,
the truth doused like a bucket of acid, and blinded.

Adrenaline let loose with a violent surge. "I'm not going to
let you hurt her."

"That's what I was hoping you would say." Jorak smiled.
"Let's dispense with the games, then, and get down to business. The name, Ethan. I want the name."

Somehow Ethan kept everything he felt, all the hot, virulent
loathing, off his face. For years he'd been looking forward to
this moment, savoring just the thought of once again standing
face-to-face with this man, and bringing him down. But now,
God, now he wanted to shout "Time out," and wipe away the
past twenty-four hours, find some way to erase Brenna from
the picture. She didn't belong here. She was in way over her
head.

*I'm here with you because I couldn't let you walk into dan-
ger without trying to warn you.*

God.

It took effort, but he said nothing, just let a hard smile curve
his lips and invited the hated memory to return. Already he
saw its embers burning in Jorak's eyes. The other man knew
only of the outcome, the night the FBI had busted into the
apartment he'd shared with his wife, and a volley of gunfire
had shattered the lie, the life, he'd been building.

Ethan knew the beginning, the night a few weeks before,
when a hooded figure had met him by the banks of the James
River. The scene played before him in vivid detail, the half-
moon hanging in the sky, the brutal cut of the sharp March
wind through the sycamores and elms. The frozen moment he
learned that the man he'd called friend had betrayed them all.

The moment when he'd realized what had to be done.

The moment he'd set into motion a chain of events that

extended well beyond those crucial weeks, traveling years into the future and touching so many innocent lives. He'd put a fist through the window of his town home when his father had called with news of his baby sister, Miranda's, kidnapping, and the sick piece of information that Jorak's father was responsible.

The moment that was culminating here, now, in this bright whitewashed room, with yet another women caught in the line of fire.

Exhaling roughly, he glanced at Brenna, who watched through those mystical blue eyes of hers, not calm now, but sparking with mistrust. She didn't look scared, though. Didn't look frightened. It was as if she'd watched this movie hundreds of times before, knew how events would play out, knew the ending, and was merely waiting for the pages of the script to be turned.

"Brenna?" he asked, ignoring the strange observation.

She pulled back from him, his touch, and hugged her arms around her middle. "You know what you have to do."

Yes, he did. He just didn't like it. "I'm not the same naive kid I was all those years ago," he said to Jorak. Wasn't one to trust something as flimsy as words and feelings. Both misled. "The second I give you the name, the second you have what you want from me, I serve no further purpose."

"That's hardly my problem," Jorak mused.

Oh, but it was. He just didn't know it yet. "I'll give you what you want," Ethan promised. "But you've got to give me something in return."

Jorak lifted a single brow. "Do I?" he mused. "And just what is it you would like, my friend? What means so much to you?"

Ethan didn't even hesitate. "Another night with Brenna." Out of the corner of his eyes he saw hers darken, saw the confusion shadow her expression, but he didn't let himself react. "Give me tonight and, come the morning, I'll give you my decision."

Jorak glanced toward the wall of windows, where the shadows of evening replaced the mellow light of dusk. Fading streaks of crimson shot up like arrows from the dark sea beyond. "You think one night will change anything?"

No, but one second had. One amazing, blinding second had changed everything.

"Not necessarily, but I can tell you this." Slowly Ethan smiled, not a nice smile, but one he knew Jorak would recognize. "If you hurt her now, you'll never get what you want from me." He shoved free of the figurative corner Jorak had tried to put him in and steadily backed the other man toward a stalemate. "If you want me to talk, the lady stays with me."

Brenna splashed cold water against her face, then looked into the mirror and watched it drip down her cheeks. The color had finally returned, the warmth that had drained the second Jorak Zhukov had touched her. But the images lingered, dark and dank and slimy. The man had lived a dirty life. He had no conscience, no moral compass. He lived only for himself.

And his thirst for revenge.

Turning off the water, Brenna looked at the nightgown hanging from her shoulders. Ivory silk. From thin straps it fell gracefully down her body, draping over her breasts and curving at her waist, falling over her hips. It was long, almost clear to the floor. But in it she felt naked.

Give me tonight and, come the morning, I'll give you my decision.

The roughened words whispered through her, much as they had when Ethan had first issued the ultimatum. He hadn't been touching her when he'd spoken, but she'd felt the caress of his voice, his implication.

And now he waited in the bedroom. For her.

One more night.

Warmth. Excitement. Anticipation. Uncertainty. They clashed, creating a hot melting sensation that streaked from her breasts to her belly, lower still, intensifying between her legs. Longing. That's the only way to describe the ache for something she couldn't name, but inherently knew would change her life.

Dangerous.

Despite everything, the past and what she knew still lay ahead, the thought of opening that door and joining Ethan Carrington, a man she'd met in the flesh only twenty-four hours before, in that bed thrilled her in ways she had no business feeling. He was not her friend. Not her ally. Not her lover.

But, heaven help her, some place deep inside wanted to believe he was all of that.

With one last glance in the mirror, she wiped the edginess from her face and strolled across the tiled bathroom floor, turned the knob and forgot to breathe.

He lay sprawled on top of the floral comforter, wearing only a pair of loose-fitting gym shorts that did nothing to conceal what lay beneath. He might as well have been naked. A deep bronze tan graced his entire body, even low on his stomach, where a trail of dark golden hair arrowed downward. His legs were thick and well muscled, covered by the same wiry hair as his chest.

"Brenna," he said, and slowly his eyes warmed. "I've been waiting for you."

Her mouth went dry. Because she'd been waiting, too. But until this moment, she'd never known for what. "It's not like I could go anywhere," she pointed out.

"I know. I checked the windows."

Her heart kicked hard against the confines of her chest. She didn't really think he would force himself on her, but clearly he expected her to join him in that big bed. "Ethan—"

"Shh," he said with a tenderness that staggered her. "Don't fight me on this, angel. I need you in this bed with me." Very blatantly he took in the sight of her standing barefoot in the silk nightgown that hugged all the right places, and a slow, lazy smile curved his lips. "Right. Now."

Chapter 7

No one had ever spoken to her like that before. No one had ever used a rough voice that sounded smoother than the Virginia whiskey her grandmother had given her to chase away a fright. No one had ever looked at her with such raw desire. It streamed through her like a potent drug, stroking deep.

Tomorrow she might die. In all likelihood she would. This night could be all she had left. It would be easy, so easy, to forget about survival and just let go, let Ethan take her to a place where she didn't care what would happen with the sunrise. To feel the warm heat of his skin, his lips against hers, roughly, gently, urging and seeking at the same time.

"No." The word came out with surprising strength. She pivoted from him and crossed to the wall of windows, stared out into the night. Stars lit the dark sky, the moon still little more than a sickle.

"Brenna." His hands, warm, wide, settled against her bare shoulders. "I know this has been hard on you, angel. But don't turn away from me. Not now."

She didn't want to. God help her, more than anything, she

wanted to turn toward him and look into those dark green eyes of his, see something other than cunning glinting there.

"What kind of game are you playing?" she asked, then with a strength that pleased her, twisted from his touch and turned to face him, looked into his shadowed face. "We both know what you think of me."

Regret. That was her first impression. Raw regret. And it blurred her determination not to trust this man or the draw she felt toward him.

"Earlier you challenged me to look in the mirror," he said, and his voice rasped low, touched deep. He hesitated, ran his gaze over her face. "But I looked somewhere else and saw all I needed to see."

The breath jammed in her throat. There was something about his voice, a note of sorrow she'd never heard, a sincerity that made her throat go tight. A game player, she reminded herself. The man was a master at getting what he wanted.

And now, for some reason, that seemed to be her. "What was that?"

His eyes heated. "You."

He only mouthed the word, very softly. It shouldn't have hurt. It shouldn't have sliced.

"The way you looked at Zhukov," he continued, never releasing her gaze. "The way you recoiled when he touched you." A muscle in the hollow of his jaw started to pound. He paused, let out a rough breath, then stunned her by taking her upper arms and pulling her against his body. "I don't know who the hell you are," he ground out in a ragged voice so low Brenna barely heard, even though his mouth spoke directly into her ear, "or what you're doing in my life, but you don't work for Jorak."

She went very still. Well-honed instincts demanded that she twist away from him, but shock held her motionless. Her heart hammered hard. The edges of her vision blurred. Ethan held her so close she could feel his every breath, his every heartbeat, every hard line of his body. And despite his words, words she'd been hoping to hear from the moment she'd entered this man's life, relief didn't come. Denial rushed too hard and fast, like a swollen, muddied river demolishing its banks.

"Maybe that's all part of the ploy," she said lazily, angling her chin. "A game, isn't that what you said?"

His mouth twisted. "Maybe."

"We could be acting," she went on, driven by the need to make him stop looking at her as if he'd never seen a woman before. The need to push him away, change his mind, gripped her. And she didn't understand why. "That whole scene back there could have been staged."

"Maybe," he conceded, assessing her through narrowed eyes. Then his expression changed, and the lines of his face relaxed. "I've hurt you," he stunned her by saying, and before she realized his intent, he lifted a hand and slid the hair back from her face.

This time she did jerk away, pull back from his touch, his body. The temptation to lean closer was too strong, to lift her own hand and put it against the warmth of his chest, to see if it could possibly be as hard as it looked. If the dark gold hair would be as soft.

"Why, damn it?" The question ripped from somewhere deep inside him. He stepped toward her, stopped himself before touching. And in his eyes a light burned hot enough to destroy the darkness pushing in from the night. "Why won't you let me touch you except when others are around?"

She swallowed hard, forcing back a surge of questions of her own. Why was he acting this way? Why was he pretending he cared? And, God help her, why did she want to step closer, when instinct warned to keep space between them. She'd avoided human contact for so many years. The desire to try, one more time, staggered. "I told you. I don't like to be touched."

"I know what you told me. I just don't know why."

Because it hurt. The words broke from her heart and scraped against her throat, stayed there, lodged behind a knot of emotion. It hurt when Ethan touched her. It hurt to feel the warmth of his skin, the tenderness of his touch, to feel the longing unfurl through her, when she knew nothing could ever come of it. Even if they weren't from different worlds, even if she didn't stand to be killed the following day, even then, nothing would come of it.

Because she wouldn't let it.

And neither would he.

Something had hardened this man beyond the point of repair. He'd been jaded, his soul darkened by a betrayal so heinous he no longer knew how to trust. He wasn't a man who believed in things he couldn't touch or feel, and emotion, the kind she'd once longed to share with a man, fell into that realm.

"Not everything in life is as simple as you want it to be," she said, careful to keep her voice from breaking.

"Simple? Who said I thought life was simple?"

She wrapped her arms around her middle, but the growing chill didn't lessen. "You and Jorak, your quest for justice and revenge." She inhaled deeply, let the breath out slowly. "Sometimes things aren't so clear."

A hard sound broke from low in his throat. "Trust me. There's nothing clear or simple about this."

That much they agreed on. Frowning, she turned to the night beyond, concentrated on the sound of the surf swishing against the beach. She had a CD of nature sounds at home, of waves crashing and wind blowing, and whenever she needed to pull back from the world, the ugliness, she'd sit in a dark room with a candle lit, turn her stereo on very softly, and concentrate on her breathing, let it carry her away. Even her regal, constantly alert Great Dane, Gryphon, relaxed when she turned on the music and off the lights.

Gryphon.

The thought stabbed in, unearthed a wave of sadness. She'd rescued the dog, malnourished and abused, from an animal shelter when he'd been little more than a bag of bones. In the eighteen months since, they'd never spent a night apart. What would he think now, with Brenna gone? Leanne, her cousin and roommate, would take care of him, but inherently she knew her companion would again feel abandoned, this time by her, the one human he'd grown to trust.

"Brenna."

The voice, quiet, intense, jarred her back into the softly lit room, with the big bed only a few feet away, the big man even closer.

"Please," he said. "You have to trust me on this."

She wanted to. Oh, how she wanted to. "Why?" she asked, spinning toward him. The blast of anger felt good. "From the moment I walked into your life, mine has been turned upside down. And now you want me to trust you? You, the man who—"

He moved so quickly she didn't have time to prepare. In a heartbeat he destroyed the distance between them and pulled her back into his arms. His hands splayed wide against the cool silk of her nightgown, one grabbing a fistful and holding on tight while the other cruised up to claim her shoulders.

"Not another word," he rasped into her ear. "Not if you want to stay alive."

The threat lanced through her like a broken needle. She shoved against his hold on her, shoved harder when he wouldn't let go. "You son of a bitch," she said, curling her hands around the hard muscles of his upper arms and digging her nails into his flesh. Hurt gave her strength. "How dare you—"

"Stop it," he hissed, sliding his hand to the back of her head. With just the slightest pressure he had her gazing up into the intensity of his green, green eyes.

"Don't you get it?" he asked, his face moving closer to hers. She could do nothing but stare at his mouth, his lips, as they formed words, moving closer to hers. "I'm not the enemy," he said, and once again his mouth was on hers.

She wanted to feel shock. She wanted to feel rage. Revulsion would have helped. Instead there was only the sharp, sudden draw of danger, the tight curl of longing. Against his biceps her fingers dug deeper, and though she told herself she sought to wound, some wicked place deep inside pointed out that she was holding on tight.

His mouth slanted against hers, not soft and persuasive as it had been earlier in the day, but hard and demanding. His increasingly thick whiskers scraped her jaw. She hadn't thought it possible for his body to become even harder, but flush against her, she could feel the ridge pressed into her belly.

"Ethan," she tried, but in opening her mouth, she only gave him better access. His tongue swept in, shimmied along her teeth, explored deep.

And her body caught fire.

Colors exploded through her mind, a prism of swirling, intense reds and greens and blues, yellows and purples. All the darkness she lived with, the oppressive shades of black, vanished.

Then he was gone. His mouth was anyway. His lips no longer claimed hers, but were sliding to her ear. "Don't you understand?" he murmured roughly. "Jorak thinks he can get to me by threatening you. He thinks we're involved. That's why you're here."

And suddenly it all made an ugly, unwanted sense. She'd never understood why Jorak's men had grabbed her, but now she knew. She understood the abrupt turnaround. She understood the heat in his eyes, the intensity of his kiss.

None of it was real.

Ethan Carrington was a man of principle and integrity. So long as he had a breath in his body, he would never let those he cared about come to harm. His family was under intense protection. There was no way Jorak could get to them, no way Jorak could use a parent or a sister as the leverage he needed.

But in Brenna he thought he had the perfect weapon.

"Then tell him he's wrong," she gritted into his ear. "Tell him I mean nothing to you."

Ethan swore softly. "Are you out of your mind?" He pulled back to pierce her with his eyes. They burned darker than the night. "Don't you know what would happen if I did that?"

She did. She would become disposable. "Your family is well protected. He can't get to any of them."

"But he would get to you, damn it. He would kill you without thinking twice."

A shiver ran through her. "But he wouldn't have his so-called leverage, and you would have no reason to give him what he wants."

Ethan's grip tightened. "What kind of man do you think I am?"

The question was hard, angry, and it stole her breath. She knew what kind of man he was, that was the problem. "This isn't about what kind of man you are. It's about justice, right?"

"Jesus." He held silent a moment, burned her with his gaze. "You don't belong here, Brenna. You're not disposable. I'm not just going to toss you aside like an empty soda can."

Her throat tightened. "Then what are you going to do?"

For a moment he said nothing, just looked at her. The sounds of the night drowned out the uncomfortable silence, the screech of an egret somewhere not too far beyond the window. The wind blowing off the water and through the open slats in the windows perched high on the walls. The rhythmic sway of the surf.

"This," he said at last.

She never had a chance to fight him. She never had a chance to prepare. He lifted her into his arms and carried her to the bed, like a scene ripped straight from a romantic movie. A man dressed only in revealing gym shorts, his flesh hot and hard; a woman in a sexy silk nightgown clinging to the curves of her body, her hair loose and flowing. Her eyes wide and seeking.

Instinctively her arms lifted to curl around his neck. "Ethan—"

Still holding her, he pulled back the floral comforter and soft peach sheet, then sat, positioning her in his lap. "The cameras," he whispered, brushing his mouth along the side of her face. "They're watching."

And suddenly it all made sense—why he was kissing her, holding her, carrying her to the bed. Because Jorak thought they were lovers, and Ethan, for some ridiculously noble reason, was letting the farce continue.

Her heart thudded hard against her rib cage, adrenaline streaming dizzily.

"Trust me," he murmured, nibbling on her earlobe.

Little tendrils of heat licked through her, giving rise to a wave of panic. "I can't."

"Yes," he said very quietly, very persuasively, "you can."

She stared into his eyes, those dark, burning swatches of green, like a primeval forest, and for a fleeting heartbeat, imagined what it would be like if this moment were real, if he'd carried her to the bed out of desire, not a cunning plan. If he touched her because of want. If he made love to her slowly, deliberately, thoroughly, with the lights on. The other time—

The other time had been fast, sudden, unbearably dark.

"Brenna," he murmured, again lifting a hand to the side of her face. His touch was punishingly gentle. Her gaze focused on his mouth, those lips that could appear hard and unyielding but now looked surprisingly soft. Soon they would be on hers.

"Do you have any idea?" he ground out. "Any idea at all how much I want to make love to you?"

The quiet words stopped her heart. And her breath. Any trace of coherent thought. It was cruel, so horribly cruel, to have to act out her sweetest fantasy.

"To feel you in my arms," he went on, feathering his fingers along her face. She waited for the bite of dread, the flood of darkness, but found only yearning. "Show you just how sorry I am about everything that's happened."

She looked away from his eyes, realized her mistake too late. Away from his face she found his chest, lower still to his abdomen, where the arrow of dark blond springy hair vanished beneath his shorts, which weren't quite so loose anymore.

A finger to her chin, the tilt of her face back to his. "But I know you're tired," he said, more loudly this time, and just like that she realized another truth, that he spoke softly when he spoke of the truth, more loudly when he voiced a lie. If cameras watched the room, then bugs could be recording their conversations. "You need to sleep more than I need to be inside of you."

Her mouth went dry. My God, she thought maniacally. My God. Ethan the hard, driven prosecutor hid more behind his sharp suits than just a mouthwatering body. The man packed a seductive punch she'd never seen coming.

"It might be our only chance," she stunned herself by saying. Acting, she told herself. She was just playing the game.

He went very still. "Not if I have a damn thing to say about it."

Her heart beat cruelly against the confines of her chest. "I'll hold you to that," she said, lifting a hand to his face. She'd never touched like this before, never skimmed her fingers along a firm jaw and soft whiskers. She'd never let herself.

He grabbed her wrist. "You're killing me," he said, and his smile looked pained. "Just sleep, angel." He patted the pillow.

Heart in her throat, she slid back against the cool, crisp sheets and watched him pull the covers over her chest. "I'm here if you need me," he said, feathering a kiss across her lips.

And then he was gone. He strolled from her side of the big poster bed to the switch by the door, flicked it and immersed the room in darkness. She blinked, opened her eyes to the wash of soft moonlight, saw the shadowy form of his body move to the other side of the bed. He yanked the covers back and lay down, made no move to pull the sheet over himself.

Brenna lay there a long time, listening to the heavy, irregular rhythm of his breathing. He shifted back and forth from his left side to his right, periodically punching his pillow. Even all the way across the big bed, she felt the heat of his body wash over her.

She'd never shared a bed with a man before. Never shared her body. Once, she'd come close. Once, she'd gotten naked for a man, let him cover her body with his. Once, she'd seen the darkness too late.

For as long as she lived, she'd never forget the broken moments that followed, the desperate groping for the gun, the frantic run for the door, the endless drive back to her house.

The blood waiting on her porch.

"Come here."

The rough words startled her. She blinked against the darkness, turned to see Ethan facing her. "You're restless," he said. "Maybe if you let me hold you, you can go to sleep."

God. She didn't want that. Didn't want him to hold her, lull her to sleep. Didn't want to play the game one second longer than she had to. But she found herself sliding toward him anyway, drawn by a need she neither understood nor trusted.

"Like this," he said, pulling her closer, so close her head rested on his chest. "I'm not going to let anything happen to you."

She wanted to believe that, but she'd seen the truth in her dreams. She wasn't the one in danger. Ethan was. And if anyone in this bed carried the role of protector, it was her, not him.

But she said nothing, knew that just because he believed she didn't work for Jorak didn't mean he believed what she'd seen in the darkness. Didn't mean he trusted the dark light she saw in his eyes. Something had happened to this man. Something had hardened him, twisted him. Something had robbed him of his fundamental ability to trust, not in the world around him, but the world within him.

And that, Brenna knew, was more dangerous than any prophecy she could voice.

Throat tight, she lay against his body and resisted the urge to tangle her legs with his, concentrating instead on the steady thrum of his heart, the feel of his chest hairs tickling the side of her face.

She didn't want to sleep. She didn't want to let go. She knew what would happen if she did. But gradually, with the feel of his hand stroking her back and playing lazily with her hair, lethargy overcame her, and she began to drift.

How long, Eth? How long since you've slept through the night?

He lay there in the smothering darkness, with Brenna's impossibly soft body sprawled over his, and concentrated on the answer he'd refused to give his sister, Elizabeth. His twin, she knew him inside out. She'd shared a special bond with her sisters, that was true, but nothing compared to the unspoken understanding the two of them had always shared. When their older sister, Kristina, had died, Ethan had mourned the loss of two sisters, because he'd lost part of Elizabeth that brutally cold night, as well.

Until bold, brash, fly-by-the-seat-of-his-pants Wesley "Hawk" Monroe stormed into her life and turned it upside down, bringing her back to the land of the living.

No one had brought Ethan back.

Through the darkness he felt a dark smile curve his lips. He let his hand explore Brenna's back, absently keeping time with the gentle swishing of the surf beyond. The open slats of the high windows let in sound as well as the cool evening breeze.

Seven years. Eight months. Two days. That's how long it had been since he'd slept the night through. Before then he'd never had a problem sleeping, had, in fact, frequently found himself facing his father's gruff stare at nine in the morning when he would rip open Ethan's curtains and let in a swath of sunlight. Military school had been brutal. Not only had they had to rise early, but frequently the upper classmen got their kicks by tormenting the green-bellies at all hours of the night.

But it wasn't until that cold night seven years before that Ethan had quit being able to sleep. It had started out innocently enough. A phone call. A deep, garbled voice. A request for a twilight meeting along the shores of the James.

Now he stared up at the ceiling, watched the lazy swish of the ceiling fan and realized the truth. That's why he'd been so certain Brenna worked for Jorak. Because she'd replicated, down to the detail, the phone call, the request, the meeting, that had started this game all those years ago.

That night he'd driven to the river, ready for a long run, with absolutely no idea his life, the world as it he knew it, was about to end.

This time he'd driven to the river filled with a hot, pulsing anticipation.

And in the process he'd dragged an innocent woman into the darkness he'd lived with for seven years.

She shifted against him, the open fingers of her hand closing to tighten around a fistful of chest hair. He winced at the tug, but made no move to stop her.

"Don't," she muttered, and the broken sound of her voice cut right through him. He looked down at the shadows playing across her face, as he'd done so often for the past two hours, but no longer saw soft lines of relaxation. Her mouth and jaw were tight. Her eyes were squeezed shut.

"No," she ground out, and this time, she started to thrash. Her legs kicked against his body with surprising force. Her hand, curled around his chest hair, pulled viciously. The other scratched. "No!"

"Brenna." He slid from beneath her and hovered over her, put a hand to her face. The blast of heat staggered him. She'd been resting on his chest, but he hadn't realized how hot she'd become, that her hair had become damp and plastered to the sides of her face.

"Stand down!" The words were hard, violent, and she bucked beneath him, jammed a knee into his thigh. "Never…let…you…win…"

Fighting her, fighting himself, he held her against the bed, but she thrashed harder, twisting against his hold.

"Brenna, baby," he said, pushing the hair back from her face. "Come on, angel. You're scaring me."

The scream stopped his heart. It split the night, tore into some place deep inside.

"Jesus," he swore, pulling her upright and giving her shoulders a gentle shake. "Brenna." He said her name firmly, stripped all the emotion from his voice. "It's just a dream."

She jerked violently, and her lids flew open, revealing eyes drenched in absolute horror. "Kill…you…"

Ethan reacted without thinking, just pulled her into his arms and started to rock. She crawled into his lap and stunned him by wrapping her hot, sweaty body around his and holding him back, holding on tight. They stayed that way for a long, long time, shock waves lingering as they rocked in the darkness.

Music. Aching. Dramatic. The haunting sounds drifted from the parted doors at the end of the interior hallway, echoed off the walls and floor of misshapen tiles of gray slate. Piano, Brenna recognized. Classical. Familiar. Drenched with emotion. Beethoven, maybe. Perhaps Copland. She concentrated on the melody, grateful for a reprieve from the oppressive silence that had settled between her and Ethan the moment she'd awoken sprawled all over his hot, hard body.

Dear God. Dear. God. She'd slept with the man. Not sexually, not in the sense of body joined to body, but she'd shared another kind of intimacy with him, one that penetrated beyond the confines of the flesh to that dark place she'd walled away two years before.

The music grew louder, crashing now, resounding with a raw edge she recognized too easily. The two armed guards leading them down the hall pushed open the massive double doors, then a third nudged Ethan and Brenna inside.

The glare of the bright morning sunshine, after the shadows of the hallway, momentarily blinded her. She blinked rapidly, brought the room of all white into focus. It looked just as it had the night before, not even the bright wash of daylight able to chase away the aura of darkness.

Her heart tattooed a frenetic rhythm. Familiarity drilled through her. This was it. Not just the room but the moment. The moment from her dreams. The moment of choice, when the man she'd shared a bed with the night before, the man who'd honored the cameras in the room by holding her against his body, who'd murmured words of comfort, the man who was willing to put his own life on the line to protect his family, would have to throw someone to the wolves. Her or the informant who'd betrayed Jorak all those years ago.

She turned to look at him now, as she'd not let herself do since opening her eyes to the sight of dark gold chest hair and one flat nipple resting beneath her fingertips. She'd excused herself to the shower with a curtness she hadn't come close to feeling, not when her body still tingled from his touch. Standing naked beneath the warm spray of water had been torture. Every time she'd touched herself, slid a bar of soap along her stomach or rubbed the shampoo into her hair, she'd imagined another pair of hands, stronger fingers.

The sight of him now, standing next to her in Jorak Zhukov's whitewashed room, made her heart bleed in a way she instinctively mistrusted. He'd showered but not shaven, dressed in a pair of khaki shorts and a black knit shirt. His raven hair was damp, but not long enough to curl. The subtle aroma of musk and citrus drifted toward her.

But none of that masked the truth she saw etched into every hard line of his body, the fact he'd not slept for more than a minute the night before. Neither had she. Not after the dream.

She followed his gaze to the right, where the white baby grand dominated a corner of the room. She saw the picture first, a picture she hadn't noticed the night before. A silver frame embraced the black-and-white image of a woman. She was smiling, her long, blond hair soft and wavy around a face aglow with what could only be love.

Then she saw Jorak Zhukov.

He sat on the bench before the baby grand, his eyes closed, his long, tanned fingers dancing gracefully along the ivory keys. The music came from him. The dramatic, aching sounds that touched some place deep inside her came from this man in the suit of spotless white but with a heart of pure darkness.

The tempo swelled, crashed, like the frothy white waves visible through the wall of windows.

Throat tight, she looked up at Ethan again, standing rigidly by her side, and saw the shadows in his eyes, the hard clench of his jaw. The emotion emanating from this man who pretended to feel none nearly choked her.

With one final crescendo, the music stopped, and Jorak sat there a moment, shoulders erect, fingers on the keys. His breathing was heavy, choppy. The lines of his face were hard.

"Don't stop on my account," Ethan drawled with an insolence she'd rarely heard from him.

Jorak's coal-black eyes snapped open, but they weren't as razor sharp as they'd been the night before. There was a haze there, the noncomprehending blur of someone jarred from a deep sleep.

"Music won't bring her back."

Chapter 8

The words were soft, quiet, but they cut through Brenna with an eerie precision. She saw Jorak's eyes clear, sharpen, saw the change consume him. He wasn't a man lost anymore. Not a man driven by music. The monster was back, the man she'd seen in the still of the night.

"I can still hear her voice," he murmured, rising. Eyes trained on Ethan, he walked toward them. "I can see the look in her eyes when she went down. I can hear the way she cried out." He paused a few feet away, pierced Ethan with a look of pure hatred. "Can you?"

Brenna's heart was pounding so hard she could barely breathe. She looked at Ethan, saw the shadows had deepened. "She deserved better."

Jorak laughed, a dark sound ripped from somewhere deep. "I would have given her the world."

"But you didn't, did you?" Ethan shot back. "You gave her something entirely different."

Jorak's eyes went wild for just a heartbeat, then he banked

the emotion, brought himself under control. With a slow, degrading smile, he turned his attention to Brenna.

"You look lovely this morning," he murmured in his rich Mediterranean voice. His gaze skimmed the length of the skimpy sundress she'd slipped into after showering. She preferred jeans and T-shirts, but Jorak had only provided scant slips of fabric that clung provocatively to her curves. This was the simplest she could find—a soft white cotton with a scoop neck, a line of tiny buttons extending down the fitted torso and flared at the hip.

The urge to wrap her arms around her body was strong, but she refused to show even a sliver of fear or intimidation.

Jorak's smile widened, revealing his gleaming white teeth. "My men tell me the two of you didn't get much sleep last night."

Ethan reached for her hand, the first contact since she'd rolled from his arms, and curled his fingers around hers. "What went on in that bed last night is none of your business."

"Tsk-tsk," Jorak chided, pursing his lips. "Don't tell me my adventurous friend has grown prudish in his old age."

My adventurous friend. *Friend.* The word fell softly into place, another piece to the puzzle Brenna didn't understand.

"We're both men," Jorak continued. "We both know what a man wants from a woman like this."

Ethan urged Brenna closer to his side. "I highly doubt we have the same appetite."

"We'll see," Jorak murmured, lifting a hand to Brenna's face.

She never had a chance to brace herself. Never had a chance to prepare. The images came at her like a fractured prism, cutting, blinding, distorting. Darkness. Rage. An unquenchable thirst for revenge.

"Take your hands off her."

Ethan. His voice. Quiet. Deadly. Far away. So far away. His hand, curled around hers, gone. She blinked dizzily, brought the room back into a hazy focus, saw Ethan struggling against two dark-skinned guards in fatigues. They each had one of his arms, but still he fought like an untamed animal.

"So lovely," Jorak murmured, feathering a hand down her throat. "Such a waste. Maybe I should enjoy her first."

Panic sliced in fast and raw. She twisted against him, swung her elbows. "I'd rather die," she gritted out.

"Touch her, and it will be the last mistake you make."

Those words. The lethal vehemence of his voice. She stopped struggling, stopped breathing, looked at Ethan standing there through a distorted window of time and space, blurred but horribly clear. She'd seen him like this before. So many times. She'd heard his voice, heard those words. And God, she'd fought. Fought so hard to prevent this moment from arriving.

Never before had she lived through one of her visions. She'd always been a witness, an observer suspended on the sidelines, unable to participate, to prevent, only to discover the aftermath. She didn't belong here in this glaring room of white. She should never have made contact with Ethan Carrington. Never have tangled their lives.

But that was a lie, and she knew it.

The late-morning sun cut through the expansive wall of windows, falling like a spotlight on Jorak Zhukov. He no longer touched her, instead had his hands curled around a sleek, black semiautomatic. And just as she knew he would, he laughed.

"Look at you." He swept an arm toward the far side of the spacious room, where armed guards stood ready and waiting. "You're hardly in a position to be making threats."

Instinctively Brenna glanced toward the ornate mirror, where she knew what she would see—a tall raven-haired man surrounded by a semicircle of guards with guns she recognized from her dreams as MP-5Ns. One of the men had secured rope around Ethan's wrists to keep his arms behind his back. Still, he looked defiant, his eyes hard, his jaw a firm line, and she knew he welcomed the bite of the rope digging into flesh. It meant he was alive. And so long as he was alive, the man with the suit of white but smile of darkness would not be allowed to win.

The man who called Ethan friend.

"I have what you want," Ethan said in a dangerously quiet voice. "Killing me leaves you with nothing."

Contempt flashed in Jorak's coal black eyes. "Death doesn't always involve the body, my friend. Only if you're lucky."

The threat echoed silkily through the sun-drenched room. White walls, white furniture, white carpet. But not white lies. The lies were black, and they had destroyed.

But not again.

With punishing clarity, Brenna knew that as long as Ethan Carrington had a breath in his body, he would not allow Jorak Zhukov to hurt another, not ever, ever again.

Frowning, she glanced at the silver frame embracing the photo of the woman, and finally she knew. Finally she understand. The hatred that simmered between these two men was personal, and before too many more suns sank beneath the horizon of the ocean, the vendetta was going to end in a spray of gunfire.

"The choice is yours," Jorak announced, reaching out to slide the barrel of the gun along her throat. "The power has always been in your hands."

Somehow Ethan kept himself from lunging. Somehow Ethan kept himself from slamming his body against Jorak's and severing the contact between the vile man and Brenna. She stood there so unnaturally still, looking breathtakingly beautiful in a simple white cotton sundress. He didn't want Jorak putting his manicured hands on her, touching her, making the color drain from her face. He didn't even want him looking at her.

But acting prematurely would ruin everything.

So he forced himself to stand there, with his body rigid and his jaw tight, and tried to communicate to her with his eyes. To assure her everything would be okay. That Jorak would not hurt her. That he would not let him.

God help him, she was amazing. Jorak Zhukov held a gun

to her throat. In less than a second, he could end her life. But she wasn't screaming or crying, wasn't fighting. She just stood there, staring at him through hard, challenging eyes, with her chin tilted and her blond hair, still damp from her shower, falling against stiff shoulders.

Jorak was right. The power was in Ethan's hands. That's what this whole charade was about. That's why he'd dropped his security detail, why he'd gone to the river that night, convinced Brenna was luring him into a trap. *Hoping* that she was.

Now… Christ, now the gravity of his mistake burned, and he knew he had to play his cards even more carefully. She wasn't part of his plan. She was a complication, a danger he could neither afford nor risk.

Refusing to take the bait, knowing Jorak would never hurt her until he was sure he had the information he needed from Ethan, he wiped the emotion from his expression and stared beyond the weapons trained on him and through the window to the beach beyond, where a turquoise surf swished lazily against a carpet of sand so white, so sugary, it defied logic and possibility.

"So what's it going to be?" Jorak slid the barrel of the gun along Brenna's throat. Ethan saw her wince, felt it deep. "The name?" He dragged the gun between her breasts. "Or the woman."

This was it. The moment he'd been waiting for, planning for, since Jorak escaped custody. He looked at Brenna, found her eyes locked on him, felt the punch in his gut. "Jordan Cutter."

Jorak swung toward Ethan. His eyes were narrow, mistrusting. "Cutter? The name means nothing to me."

"Actually, it means everything to you," he said with a casualness he knew would infuriate the other man. "Cutter is the one you want. The one who betrayed you. Bring Cutter here and all your questions will be answered."

And then some. In devastating ways Jorak couldn't even begin to foresee.

Holding his face expressionless, Ethan watched the other

man process the information, saw the doubt, the fledgling hope. "Why should I believe you?"

"You mean, besides the fact you're holding a gun on the woman I share my bed with?"

Jorak returned his attention to a motionless Brenna, sliding the barrel of the gun along the swell of her breasts.

Ethan had never wanted to kill so badly in his life.

"It could be a trap," Jorak mused.

"It could be," Ethan agreed, and still Brenna showed no reaction. It was as though she'd seen this movie before, knew the ending.

"She'll die if it is," Jorak pointed out.

"She'll die anyway."

"Miguel!" Jorak snapped, and another man pushed through the circle of guards, this one small and Latino. "Find this Jordan Cutter and bring him here."

The other man nodded, turned to leave.

"Last-known address was Baltimore," Ethan tossed out, trying damn hard not to smile. It was like fishing, just as Grandfather Carrington had taught. Bait the hook, dangle it, then wait. Patience truly was a man's best friend. "In case that helps."

Jorak's eyes hardened. "I was going to be gentle with her, make it fast. But if you've lied to me, if you're trying to trick me, stall for time, there will be nothing gentle or fast about what I have in store for her." With a self-satisfied smile, he shoved her toward Ethan. "Until then she's yours."

Only a few nights before, along the bank of the James River, the first hint of fall had whispered through the stately old sycamores and oaks. Not here. Summer held the island firmly in a death grip, with the sun, closer this far south, beating down relentlessly. Ethan stripped off his shirt and stood, reminded himself to breathe.

She stood on the sugary-fine sand at the water's edge, with the warm breeze blowing her blond hair and tropical water surging around her ankles. With a hand lifted to shield her eyes from the sun, she looked down the beach, where a long-haired black-and-white dog raced after the ball she'd just thrown.

He couldn't remember the last time he'd seen a more damning sight.

She didn't belong here. She didn't belong on this island, in Jorak's foolishly elegant compound, in this charade. She didn't belong in his life. She was a rare combination of strength and vulnerability, alluring yet aloof. Sometimes he caught a look in those whitewashed sapphire eyes of hers, a faraway, haunted look that jammed in his gut and made him wonder why she held herself apart from those around her, why she recoiled from a simple touch.

The further she held herself apart from the world, from Ethan, the closer he wanted to pull her.

They'd returned to their room to find beach clothes laid out on the bed, accompanied by a note informing them of the afternoon they were to spend enjoying a picnic—and their last moments together. For months he'd been looking forward to again standing face-to-face with Jorak. Once he would have been amused by this farce, the way Jorak was treating them as houseguests, fattening them for the kill. But now the game sickened him.

Because now Brenna was involved.

The dog ran toward her at a full gallop, splashing through the surf. Laughing, she bent and rubbed his head, took the red ball and threw it again, this time into the water, toward a rickety pier at the end of which bobbed two speed boats. The dog took off, running at first, soon breaking into a paddle.

Laughing. Dear God, it hit him with the jolt of the walls of water he craved while rafting through level-four rapids. She was laughing. The soft sound carried on the breeze, above the din of the seagulls, to stab into his gut. From the moment he'd met her she'd been tense and rigid, guarded, all except for those broken hours the night before, when she'd clung to him in the darkness. But now she was laughing, more relaxed with the dog than he'd ever seen her around people.

Desire sliced hard and fast. He wanted to be the one to make her laugh. He wanted to be the one to soften the tight lines of her body. He wanted to touch her and bring a smile to her mouth, not the hard lines she usually gave him. He wanted her to wrap her body around his out of desire, not horror.

But more than anything he wanted to stop wanting. Wanting only led one place. He knew that. Had learned not to trust the cravings that blotted out logic and caution.

Focus, he told himself. Put aside the want, and focus on the need, not for her body, but for the answers she continued to deny him. The truth. He'd tried to be patient. He'd tried to respect the walls she'd erected between them with the first light of the morning, when she'd awoken to find his hand tangled in her hair, their legs intertwined. She'd bolted from the bed and locked herself in the bathroom, torturing him with thoughts of her standing naked beneath the warm spray of water.

Aside from the time with Jorak, she'd not said a single freaking word. It was spooky how completely she could withdraw from the world.

No more. He was done lurking on the sidelines, sulking like a schoolboy. He'd waited long enough. The need for answers burned too hot. Time ran too short.

The sand burned the bottoms of his feet, but he welcomed the sensation. He approached her quietly, careful to stay out of her line of vision. He didn't want to give her a chance to prepare.

The dog, a Border collie mix of some sorts, swam back to shore, brought his prize to Brenna and shook the water from his drenched coat, and again she laughed.

"Such a good boy," she cooed, rubbing his head. The mutt's eyes glowed with eagerness and warmth. His tongue lolled in anticipation.

The fact Ethan could relate frayed his patience even more.

"Here you go," she said, and launched the ball farther into the surf. With an excited bark, the dog took off.

She stood with her back to him, sunlight streaming off her golden hair. He took a step closer and put his arms around her waist, urged her back against his chest. "How long are you going to pretend I don't exist?"

He didn't mean for the question to come out husky, but damned if it didn't. He felt her stiffen, all that fluidity and grace coalescing into cold, hard stone, and resented the loss.

"I know you exist."

The words were curt, matter-of-fact. "That's why you won't even look at me?"

He'd wanted to catch her off guard, but somehow she turned the tables on him. Nothing prepared him for her to turn in the circle of his arms. He'd expected her to keep staring off toward the glimmering turquoise water, where the black-and-white dog paddled toward the bobbing red ball. But she turned. She turned and looked up at him, bringing her face only inches from his.

"I'll look at you."

It was like a swift kick to the gut, the feel of her in his arms, her breasts pressing against his chest. "That's a start."

Her mouth twisted and she started to pull away, but he locked his hands together and held her closer. "They're watching," he reminded, brushing his lips over hers. He meant to leave it at that. Stop, pull away. But then a soft sound rasped from her throat, and he felt himself leaning in for more. He'd already kissed her several times, but this was different. This time was soft not hard, slow not demanding, leisurely, like a long rainy Sunday morning spent in bed.

Another sound then, deeper, ragged, and he didn't know whether it tore from her throat or his own. The haze gripped him harder, and he lifted a hand to her face, cradled the side of her cheek.

She pulled back and looked beyond him, to where three armed guards stood beneath a frayed, yellowing palm at the edge of the beach. "What do you want from me?" she asked, returning her gaze to Ethan. Her eyes were dark, turbulent like the sea beyond. "Why won't you just leave me alone?"

The question grated, the answer condemned.

Because he couldn't.

Their lives had tangled. Their futures were intertwined. He couldn't ignore her, not when he had to share a bed with her, not when every time he closed his eyes, she was there waiting. "I think you know what I want." He watched her eyes flare, wondered just what she thought he meant. To taste her again? Yes, he did want that, God help him. God help them both. But he wanted more. "The truth."

The wind whipped long, blond hair into her face, which she jerkily pushed back. "The truth?" she returned, but then the dog was there, soaking wet and nudging against her legs. She cut Ethan a hard look and turned her attention to the mutt.

"Good boy," she cooed again, reaching down to lovingly stroke its muzzle, and he couldn't help but wonder what it would be like to be willingly touched by her. "More?" he asked, and Ethan could only think yes. God, yes.

The thought ground through him. He wasn't some lovesick schoolboy, damn it, and Brenna was not the object of his latest fantasy.

"Here you go." She launched the ball back into the water toward the pier, and again the besotted dog took off.

"I'm waiting," he said more roughly than he'd intended.

She spun back to face him, her eyes aglow with an emotion he couldn't name. "The truth?" she asked. "You want the truth?" Her voice was hard, almost angry. "Tell me something," she said, and for a moment he could see her in a courtroom, turning the tables on the most skilled prosecutors. "What is the truth? How do you know when it's real?"

"I'll know." Because he always knew.

Liar, chided a nasty little voice deep inside, but he ignored it.

The wind returned the hair to her face, and this time a strand stuck to the soft pink of her lips. "Let me tell you something about the truth," she said. "It's nothing more than those clouds I told you about, the ones my grandmother called shape shifters."

The ones he'd long since quit seeing.

"Nothing is concrete," she said. "Nothing is etched in

The Silhouette Reader Service™ — Here's how it works:

Accepting your 2 free books and gift places you under no obligation to buy anything. You may keep the books and gift and return the shipping statement marked "cancel." If you do not cancel, about a month later we'll send you 6 additional books and bill you just $3.99 each in the U.S., or $4.74 each in Canada, plus 25¢ shipping & handling per book and applicable taxes if any.* That's the complete price and — compared to cover prices of $4.75 each in the U.S. and $5.75 each in Canada — it's quite a bargain! You may cancel at any time, but if you choose to continue, every month we'll send you 6 more books, which you may either purchase at the discount price or return to us and cancel your subscription.

*Terms and prices subject to change without notice. Sales tax applicable in N.Y. Canadian residents will be charged applicable provincial taxes and GST.

If offer card is missing write to: Silhouette Reader Service, 3010 Walden Ave., P.O. Box 1867, Buffalo NY 14240-1867

NO POSTAGE
NECESSARY
IF MAILED
IN THE
UNITED STATES

BUSINESS REPLY MAIL
FIRST-CLASS MAIL   PERMIT NO. 717-003   BUFFALO, NY

POSTAGE WILL BE PAID BY ADDRESSEE

SILHOUETTE READER SERVICE
3010 WALDEN AVE
PO BOX 1867
BUFFALO NY 14240-9952

PLAY 7 Lucky

and get 2 FREE BOOKS and a FREE GIFT

Scratch off the gold area with a coin. Then check below to see the gifts you get!

NO COST! NO OBLIGATION TO BUY! NO PURCHASE NECESSARY!

DETACH AND MAIL CARD TODAY!

YES!

I have scratched off the gold area. Please send me the **2 FREE BOOKS AND GIFT** for which I qualify. I understand I am under no obligation to purchase any books as explained on the back of this card.

345 SDL DZ4Y   245 SDL DZ5F

FIRST NAME | LAST NAME

ADDRESS

APT.# | CITY

STATE/PROV. | ZIP/POSTAL CODE   (S-IM-04/04)

7 7 7   Worth **2 FREE BOOKS** plus a **FREE GIFT!**

Worth **2 FREE BOOKS!**

Worth **1 FREE BOOK!**

Try Again!

stone. That's all an illusion, a matter of the lens you use. One man's truth is another man's lie.''

Ethan just stared. He felt as if he'd been thrown onto the stand to be prosecuted and wasn't quite sure how it had happened. ''What the hell is that supposed to mean?''

She twisted out of his arms, but didn't put distance between them, just balled her hands into fists and glared up at him. ''You and Jorak. You say you want to bring him to justice. He says he wants revenge against you.

The shaggy wet dog raced toward them, but before he could interrupt, Ethan relieved him of the ball and pitched it again, as far as he could.

''What you both fail to see,'' she said, ''is that one man's justice is another's revenge. They're the same thing, Ethan. They both seek to punish for some perceived hurt.''

Something inside him snapped. ''Perceived hurt?'' She made it sound as if they were fighting over spilled milk. ''Do you have any idea what that man did?''

She pushed the hair back from her mouth. ''He hurt you,'' she said quietly. ''He hurt you bad.''

Ethan felt himself go very still, felt the glare of the sun, the warm breeze whipping sand against his legs and chest. She couldn't know. ''Is that what you saw in your dream?''

''No. It's what I see in your eyes.''

The soft words cut through him, bringing a surge of denial. This wasn't about hurt. This wasn't about betrayal. It was about justice.

''What about last night?'' He retrieved a pair of sunglasses from his khaki shorts and slid them into place. ''Tell me what you saw in the darkness. Tell me what turned your skin colder than ice.'' Why she'd clung to him. ''What made you cry out.''

It was her turn to pull back, pull away. She put distance between them this time, wading deeper into the water. It swirled up around her knees now, not quite warm, but not cold either.

''I thought you didn't have time for dreams,'' she said in

that defiant way of hers, then just like he'd come to expect, she lifted her chin. "Isn't that what you told me by the river?"

God help him, her bravado made him want to laugh. Knowing that would be a severe tactical error, he bit back the urge and waded after her, reached for her shoulders, "Careful, angel," he warned above the roar of the ocean. "I told you I don't like to be played with."

She tensed beneath his hands. "And I," she said very slowly, "told you I don't like to be touched."

He stared down at his hands curled around the pale skin of her upper arms, and wondered why she was lying to herself. "You didn't seem to mind last night," he reminded, lifting his gaze from her arms to her eyes. The denial swimming there almost stopped him. Almost.

"Was it me?" His body braced for the answer. "Were you dreaming of me again?"

He expected her to look away, evade his question. She didn't. "Yes."

The single word rushed through him like a shot of fine, aged whiskey. "And? Was this one any better?"

Now she did look away from him, toward a pair of pelicans flying low over the pier. "No."

Frustration nudged closer. "What then? What did you see?"

"You," she said, returning her gaze to his. "And Jorak."

Before, he'd scoffed at her stories of dreams and visions. Before, he'd discounted everything she'd had to say. But now, now curiosity burned through him. Not because he was starting to believe her claims of precognition, he assured himself, but because he wanted to know why this tough, gutsy woman had come undone in his arms.

"The same dream as before?" Just because she dreamed of him and Jorak didn't mean she knew anything. Hell, as a kid he'd had some damn fine dreams featuring centerfolds, the University of Virginia homecoming queen, a time or two about *Charlie's Angels*. That didn't mean he knew them, and it sure as hell didn't mean what he'd enjoyed with them there in the darkness of his adolescent bed had come true.

"Worse," she said, absently taking the ball from the dog. She patted its head and again sent him running, but her eyes never left Ethan. "More detail."

Detail that had turned her skin cold and clammy like something fragile and precious left out in subfreezing temperatures. "Is that why you almost blacked out when Jorak touched you?"

She frowned. "No."

"Tell me," he said, urging her closer.

This time she didn't resist. "It's...complicated."

"Try me." The need to know, to understand, burned like a white-hot poker.

"Why, Ethan? Why is this suddenly so important to you?"

"Because no matter what you think of me, I'm not a man to stand by and watch others suffering."

"I'm not suffering."

But she was. "Don't lie, angel. Not to me. Not now."

Chapter 9

She didn't want him looking at her like that. She didn't want him speaking to her in that whiskey-smooth, Old-Virginia voice. She preferred the hard edge of the prosecutor. That, she could defend against. That, she could ignore. She could remain detached, safe behind the brick and mortar of self-protection, insulated from the sweet curl of longing.

But Ethan Carrington didn't play fair.

He was a man who played to win, knew how to get what he wanted. He knew when to employ cunning, when to use finesse. And, God help her, standing there with the warm turquoise water swirling around her legs, the roar of the ocean behind her and the endless azure sky above her, she knew she'd met her match. She'd been trying so damn hard to hold herself apart from this man, to ignore the steady draw that pulled her toward him like a full moon seducing the seas, but now she didn't want to fight. Didn't want to deny. Didn't want to pretend.

The pelicans returned, sweeping low over the water and diving for dinner, then arching back up toward the sky. She watched them, not wanting to see Ethan standing in the surf against a backdrop of shape-shifting clouds, a tall man with raven hair and piercing eyes, dressed only in a pair of khaki cargo shorts. Who as a boy saw sailboats but now saw nothing.

"Brenna." A single finger came to rest under her chin, and slowly he turned her to face him.

Her breath caught. This is what she hadn't wanted to see, what she was finding harder and harder to resist. At least he'd slid on sunglasses and she no longer had to see his eyes, those dark, primeval chips of emerald that damned her with insight she didn't want. The pain. The longing. The scorn that would be there the second she told him the truth.

In protecting himself, he'd protected them both.

"Everyone is familiar with the five senses," she said through the tightness in her throat. Images flashed back, of the first fruitless trip to the police station. All those closed, hard faces, brows tight in scorn, eyes quietly mocking. Arms crossed over chests. It was always the same. "Sight and touch and hearing…" The commodities on which this man relied. "Smell—"

"And taste," he finished for her, sliding his index finger to her lower lip and rubbing.

The sun bore down mercilessly, but deep inside, she shivered. Pull away, some voice inside instructed, but the truth held her motionless. He was touching her. Just as he'd done during the fragile hours of the night before when she'd fought the fringes of the dream. And the images, they didn't form. Didn't consume. There was only a quiet strength.

"And taste," she said, remembering how he'd tasted when he'd put his mouth to hers the day before, the sweet combination of whiskey and man. And today the slight salty spray.

The dog bumped into her from behind, rubbing the back of her thigh with his cold nose and wet fur. He'd been on the beach when they came down, almost as though he was waiting for her, and her spirits had immediately lifted.

"Good boy," she cooed, and again took and tossed the ball, this time toward the wide expanse of white sandy beach.

"We're born with other senses," she said, returning her attention to Ethan. He was watching her intently, the lines of his face tight. She could feel his eyes burning into her, despite the dark sunglasses that separated them. "Intuition is the most common."

Gut instinct, people commonly called it, and they trusted it with their lives, even the most jaded, cynical of cops. Even the ones who'd laughed at her.

"Is that why you called me? Because you had a feeling something bad was going to happen?"

She wished it was that simple. "No. My gift is another form of precognition."

Against the glare of the sun, she saw his mouth tighten, and felt the wince cut clear to the bone. "Precognition?"

"Telepathy," she explained. "I..." God, this was the hard part. "I see things that happen to other people." Hear things. Feel things. "Usually before they happen."

Ethan just stood there. He would have looked like a picture, except for the constant motion of the waves swishing against his legs and dampening the bottom of his cargo shorts. "I see."

No, he didn't. And he wouldn't. Men like him never did.

But she had to try.

"I didn't know what it was at first," she said, wrapping her arms around her waist. She'd heard the scream first, there alone in the darkness of her childhood bed. Then she'd seen the blood. The nude and abused body, abandoned beneath a willow tree.

"My mother told me what I'd seen was just a nightmare," she recalled, and though she looked at Ethan, she saw her mom as she'd been that night, in her soft pink floral nightgown, holding a seven-year-old Brenna to her chest, rocking, rocking. "And she was right. It was."

But not in the way Maggie Scott had meant.

"What you saw," Ethan said, then stopped abruptly. "Brenna."

She blinked up at him. "What?"

He swore softly. "Don't do that to me," he ground out, and though the words were rough, they fluttered around her heart like a gentle caress.

"Don't do what?"

His mouth tightened. "Check out on me."

Instinctively she closed her eyes and sucked in a deep breath, fought the tattered remains of darkness. "I'm here."

"And I'm not letting you go anywhere again," he said, then stunned her by taking her hands in his. "What you saw," he said again. "It happened."

Yes. God, yes. Slowly she nodded.

He said nothing, just continued to watch her from behind his sunglasses and hold her hands. The heat staggered her. She'd always had cold hands and feet, had never known anyone's touch could be so warm and vital. So sustaining. For the past twenty years, touching had been her enemy.

"My grandmother was the one who finally figured out what was happening." The one who'd explained the gift, the one from whom she'd inherited it.

"And this…" She could tell he was struggling, the man versus the prosecutor, one wanting to understand, the other wanting to scorn. "This just happens randomly?"

"No." The word shot out of her. Not random, thank heaven. Once she'd learned how and why it happened, she'd been able to control it. To an extent.

"Then how?"

Brenna glanced beyond him to the glowing white beach where the black-and-white dog had given up on her and lay sprawled in the sand, panting and soaking up the sun.

"A touch," she said.

His fingers, wrapped around her hands, squeezed. "A touch?"

She looked up at him and felt her chest tighten. "Everyone is surrounded by an energy field," she explained. "And when I touch someone, or sometimes just something that belonged to a person, I tap into their energy field." She paused, searched for words to make him understand. "It's like shock waves," she said. "Running through me. Little jolts of electricity."

He released her hands, stepped back. "Shock waves."

She heard the doubt in his voice, didn't understand why it cut so deep, not when it was what she'd come to expect. "Yes."

He looked past her shoulder to the ocean beyond, where

turquoise melted into azure. She bit the inside of her lip and waited, scanned the horizon for the pelicans, saw only a lone seagull.

"It doesn't happen all the time," she said. "Sometimes there's nothing there." Those were the blessed times. "But other times it's immediate." Like with Jorak and his men, when death and desecration stained their energy field. "And then there are the times like with you, when the images come to me later." Under the cover of darkness, when her own defenses ebbed low. "That's where the precognition comes into play."

Ethan swore softly. "There's just one problem," he pointed out, and she heard the hard edge of the prosecutor return.

"Just one?"

He took off his sunglasses and let her see his eyes, darker than usual, but still penetrating. Still burning. "We've never met. Never touched until that night by the James."

The memory washed through her of the night in question, when she'd seen him standing alongside the river. She'd sensed the same solitude about him she'd sensed when she'd seen him surrounded by a mob of reporters earlier in the day outside the courthouse. And when he'd touched her—God. When he'd touched her there'd been no ugliness, no dark, hurtful images. Only heat, a low, hot energy curling through her.

That's why she'd jerked away.

"That's not true," she said, and refused to feel the disappointment. There was no reason he should remember her, not when she'd made a habit of fading into the background. "We touched once before, almost two weeks ago."

His eyes narrowed. "That's not possible. I would remember meeting a woman like—" He broke off the words. "I would remember meeting you."

She stared up at him, wondered what kind of woman he thought she was. "But you don't," she said, and this time the blade of disappointment nicked harder. "It was at Doc Magiver's clinic," she explained. "The night you brought in the emaciated Dalmatian you found while running by the river."

A wave crashed around them, but not strong enough to send

Ethan staggering back from her the way he did. "You were there?"

"I'm one of his technicians," she said with a smile that streamed from her heart. "I pull the night shift." That way she slept during the daylight and tended to animals when the darkness pushed close.

Ethan shoved a hand through his hair. "Christ."

"It was almost 10:00 p.m. when you came in," she said to prove her story. "It had been raining, and you were soaking wet. Your tank top was clinging to your body." She'd seen him pacing the small waiting area, and her heart had taken a long, slow freefall through her chest. Even without a touch, his presence had jolted her. "The dog was barely more than skin and bones."

Ethan squeezed his eyes shut, opened them a moment later, said nothing.

She'd gone out of her way to avoid him, instinctively knowing trouble would follow. "You were carrying the dog down the hall, and I tried to get out of your way, but you brushed against me anyway."

"Sweet Mary," he swore. "That was you?"

A little thrill burst through her. "Just a touch," she murmured. "That's all it takes."

Another wave broke against her, this one thrusting her toward him. He caught her, held her by the shoulders. "And then you dreamed of me."

Longing streamed to every nerve ending, punishing her with the desire to step closer, wrap her arms around his waist and see if the flesh there would be as warm as his hands. "That's why I called you. I...knew you were a good man." Emotion knotted in her throat. "I...I couldn't just let you die."

He swore again, this time harder and more creative, a combination of words she'd never heard strung together. He swung toward the beach, where the guards still stood beneath the battered palm, then back to her. "Come on," he growled, taking her hand and practically dragging her toward the shore.

She stumbled after him, fighting the pull of the water returning to the ocean. "Ethan—"

He turned toward her and lifted a hand to her cheek, and though the lines of his face were hard, troubled, his touch was gentle. But still troubled. "I don't want you to burn."

Emotion swarmed her throat. Fighting it, she brought her hand to his, skimmed her fingers along the backs of his. "I'm tougher than I look."

He frowned. "That's what I'm afraid of."

Silence fell between them. They'd not spoken on the way down to the beach, either, but he'd held her hand then. Now he strode through the sugary sand with so much agitation she almost had to jog to keep up with him. One guard led the way, two followed close behind.

Ethan seemed oblivious.

Brenna welcomed the cooling breeze rustling the palms, despite the pinging of sand against her arms and back. Ethan was right. She had been starting to burn. But that wasn't the reason he'd pulled away, and she knew it. She watched him navigating the narrow trail toward the compound, the tension in his darkly tanned back and shoulders, the way his damp cargo shorts hugged his backside, the taut lines of his legs. Runner's legs, she knew. Finely muscled and strong. His feet were bare, but as tanned as his arms and chest.

She wondered if the same golden color graced all his body.

The thought stunned her, the corresponding image disturbed. Her body didn't seem to care. With staggering ease she could imagine what he would look like walking in front of her completely naked, those powerful legs carrying his body with the masculine grace of a big, powerfully built cat, the way his muscles would bunch, the sun-kissed color of his skin.

Dangerous.

Brenna shoved the hair from her face and concentrated on the Mediterranean villa with the red-tiled roof. Emotional attachment led to pain. She knew that, had long realized she was better off, safer, steering clear of intimate relationships.

Relationships. The word almost made her laugh. Almost. Instead it sharpened the pierce of longing.

"This way," one of the guards instructed, opening a door

to the compound. Ethan let Brenna step inside, then followed. She blinked hard, adjusting to the dim lighting after the bright wash of late-afternoon sun. Cool air embraced her.

At the room she and Ethan shared, a guard unlocked the door and shoved it open. She went inside, followed by Ethan, and then the door was shut, and again they stood alone.

Questions streamed through her, questions she'd intended to confront him with on the beach, without the risk of anyone hearing what they were saying. Who was Jordan Cutter and what would happen when he was brought here? Why wasn't Ethan acting more concerned? How could he be so casual about everything, when clearly Jorak did not intend them to leave the island alive?

But he'd derailed her first with a kiss, then with questions of his own, and now here they were, alone in this room dominated by a big bed, with cameras recording their every breath.

"Now what?" she asked, turning toward him. The memory flashed in without warning, of the day before—God, was it only the day before? It seemed more like a lifetime. Ethan had looked at her through those dark, penetrating eyes and let her know in no uncertain terms exactly how he liked to kill time.

"More games?" she asked with a cynicism she wished she still felt. But she didn't, not when every minute she spent with Ethan exposed her to the man he was, not the man he wanted the world to see. The man who'd been hurt and shaped, the man who was driven to stand alone.

"Son of a bitch," he swore softly. He strode toward the small table beside the bed, where a crystal frame embraced a large, black-and-white photo. Of a man and woman. In graduation gowns and caps. Embracing. Laughing. Love shining in their eyes.

Ethan grabbed the frame and pulled it close, shadows consuming his eyes like smoke from an inferno. The couple in the frame was young. Innocent. None of the cares, the trials of the world marred their faces. Only hope and joy, a thirst for the life ahead of them.

Ethan. The man in the picture was a much younger Ethan.

And the woman—it was the same woman Brenna had seen in the photograph sitting atop Jorak's white grand piano.

"Who is she?" she asked, though deep inside she already knew.

The woman. The woman from the beach.

The woman Ethan would die for.

He dropped the picture onto the brightly colored comforter dominated by orange and yellow hibiscus. Then he turned to her, exposing her to the darkest, most hate-filled eyes she'd ever seen. "Jorak's wife."

Two words. Two little words, one piece of information, but they lanced through Brenna like a broken needle. Jorak's wife.

The woman Ethan loved.

"I don't understand—" But Ethan had already strode past her, into the sunny bathroom, where he slammed the door shut. Water shot through the pipes seconds later.

Brenna stepped forward and picked up the picture, looked first at the woman, the light dancing in her eyes, then at Ethan, young and ready to conquer whatever stood in his path, an image captured before he'd lost faith in the world. And then she did something she'd sworn to never, never let herself do again.

She cried.

He hated being played with. He hated being confused. He hated not knowing what the next day, hell, the next minute, would bring.

Ethan stepped from the coldest shower of his life and grabbed a towel, swiped it viciously over his body then slung the terry cloth around his hips and secured a knot. He'd staged the showdown with Jorak. He'd meticulously planned every step along the way. He didn't give a damn about using himself as bait.

But he'd never planned on Brenna.

Frowning, he glanced at the closed bathroom door, but saw only Brenna as she'd been that afternoon, standing up to her knees in the turquoise water, with the wind whispering through her pale hair and the ridiculously blue sky behind her, the sun fighting with the shadows in her eyes. Fairy eyes, he remembered thinking. Now the analogy didn't seem quite so foolish.

He remembered her. He hadn't at first—or at least, drunk on the idea that she was affiliated with Jorak, he'd not let himself remember. But he'd felt a nagging familiarity the first time he'd seen her standing by the James, and now he knew. The clinic. He remembered seeing the woman behind the counter, remembered the way she'd turned from him the second he'd caught her eye. He remembered seeing her in the hall. Remembered how she'd swerved to avoid touching him, a gesture that had only made him all the more determined to brush against her. Touch her.

Now he looked into the mirror and saw his face, not the face of the golden son of Richmond, not the face of the confident, unflappable, celebrated prosecutor, but a collection of hard lines and flat planes, of flintlike eyes and unruly whiskers. But he saw something else, too, a thirst, a hunger, a desire in those narrowed eyes, almost a craving.

It was the face of a man Ethan had not seen in a long, long time, not since the night he'd learned the truth about Jorak Zhukov.

And he didn't understand. He didn't understand why he suddenly felt so damn alive. He didn't understand her story about touching and shock waves. And most of all, worst of all, he didn't understand the way she twisted him up inside, the burning desire to believe her, to accept the wild story she'd told him, the kind of tale he'd raked witnesses over the coals for saying under oath. It was crazy and he knew it, but the need to touch her burned like an obsession; touch all of her, see if he could give her more shock waves. Different shock waves.

See if he would feel them, too.

Swearing softly he strode to the door and grabbed the handle, stepped into the warm bedroom. "Brenna, I'm sor—" He stopped cold. His heart kicked hard.

"Brenna?" His voice was louder this time, harder, edged with a panic that stunned him.

So lovely…maybe I should enjoy her first.

The words, uttered by Jorak just that morning, twisted

through Ethan. He spun toward the far side of the room, hoping she'd just fallen asleep on the chaise lounge.

She hadn't.

"Brenna!" He scanned over to the bed, saw the picture of him and Allison no longer lying atop the comforter, but on the hard tile floor in a puddle of broken glass. Blood pumping, he searched for other places to hide, dropped to his knees and checked under the bed, strode to the armoire and tore open the doors, pulled out the clothes.

Nothing.

She was gone.

"So help me God," he swore, pivoting toward one of the cameras. "You hurt her," he ground out, balling his hands into tight fists, "touch just one hair on her head, and you will regret it."

A sound at the door then, the turn of the locks. Ethan was across the room in a heartbeat, wasn't at all surprised to see a placidly smiling Jorak in the doorway, flanked by two guards.

He lunged. "Where the hell is she?"

"Patience, my friend," Jorak said mildly, as the guards rushed in to restrain Ethan. "Patience."

The urge to fight ripped through him, but he kept himself standing still. Deadly still. "What's the matter?" he taunted. "You can't fight me like a man? You have to recruit others to do your dirty work?"

The man he'd once called friend made a condescending clucking noise. "You've always enjoyed our games in the past, Ethan. What's changed?"

Everything. *Everything.* "If you hurt Brenna—"

"What? If I hurt Brenna, what? You've already given me the information I need, yes? Why should I keep her around?"

Ethan clenched his jaw. The truth burned the back of his throat. If he played this wrong, his whole house of cards went up in smoke, hideous and black, lethal.

"It's always smart to keep an ace in your pocket," he drawled with a laziness he didn't come close to feeling. "Isn't that what you always said?"

Jorak's smile hardened. "So it is." He turned and gestured

behind him, then a young woman came forward and handed Ethan a black garment bag.

"For you," Jorak said. "We'll be back in fifteen minutes."

Then the entourage was gone and the door was slammed shut, the locks clicked into place, leaving Ethan standing with the bag in his hands and rage clouding his vision.

More games. With hands that wanted to shake, he tore at the zipper and opened the bag, saw the tuxedo. It was black, with tails, European in design, much like one he'd seen Jorak wear years before. At his wedding.

He didn't want to put on the damn tuxedo. He didn't want to keep playing, pretending this was nothing more than a high-stakes game of chess, not with Brenna's life on the line. But more than everything he didn't want were the two things he did—to bring Jorak to justice and to touch Brenna again.

"I'm all yours," he drawled when the guard came for him fifteen minutes later. The thin man with the thick crop of dark hair jammed a gun to the small of Ethan's back and led him down an intricate network of dimly lit hallways to a wing of the villa he'd never seen before.

He saw her the second he entered the ballroom. The only light came from an army of flickering candles lining the walls and the long dining table, but he didn't need light to feel relief. She stood in front of a floor-to-ceiling window with her back to him. The fading light of twilight cast her in silhouette, making her blond hair look darker, the slim black dress look sleeker. She was standing so still, unnaturally still for most people but completely natural for her.

The need to touch and hold, to taste, to protect, almost sent him to his knees.

"Have mercy," he half swore, half breathed, then crossed to her, not giving a damn about the guard with the gun or the cameras he was sure were mounted somewhere along the ceiling. "Brenna."

She turned to him slowly, revealing a sweep of soft blond hair falling against her forehead. Her eyes went wide, her lips parted.

Need almost blinded him.

He acted without thinking, touched without caution. He had to have his hands on her, and he did, first her shoulders, slightly red from the glare of the afternoon sun, then down her arms to her waist, around to the small of her back. He was holding her then, pulling her close, running his hands up her back to tangle in her hair. And, God help him, for the first time, she was holding him back.

"If he hurt you," he gritted out, and barely recognized his own voice. "If he put so much as one hand on—"

"No," she murmured against the jacket of his tuxedo. "They didn't touch me."

It hit him then, what he was doing to her, the agony he had to be inflicting, and he pulled back abruptly, severing the contact between them. "Christ." Never in his life had he felt so helpless, and he hated it. But even stronger than that feeling was his desire for her. "I'm sorry."

Her eyes went dark. "It wasn't your fault. You were in the shower."

"I shouldn't have left you alone," he insisted, and knew that he wouldn't again, not for one single second. "And I shouldn't have touched you." Not after what she'd told him, that all it took was a mere brush of flesh to flesh to send her into hell.

Through the glow of candlelight he saw her lips curve into a smile, but it wasn't warm and soft the way he wanted, but hard, bitter. "Isn't that part of the game?"

The question stung, because it was true. "Not if it hurts you," he countered, because God help him, that was true, too.

He saw her swallow, saw her brace herself. "It doesn't hurt me," she said, and her voice was thicker, like the honey he'd ridiculously dreamed about smearing all over her body. "Not like you think."

He tried to do just that, to think, but the haze blurred everything. "You don't feel anything?" he asked, and cursed the blade of disappointment. He didn't want to hurt her, that was true. But he did want to make her feel.

"That's not what I said," she whispered, then did something

she'd never done before. She reached for him, his hand, and drew it to her face. "I only said it didn't hurt."

He stared at the shadows flickering across her face. They stroked, gently, provocatively, brushing along the hollow of her cheek and caressing her lips, making his fingers itch to trace their path. "So I can do this?" he asked, and did just that, skimmed a finger along the soft curve of her face.

Her smile was slow, oddly tremulous. "Yes."

He was a man of stillness and patience. He'd taught himself to plan, to wait, that the sweetest reward came from holding back when he wanted to charge, from denying when he wanted to indulge.

But there was no holding back now, no denying, not when the feel of her mouth beneath his fingers demolished everything he'd ever taught himself. Everything he'd ever believed.

"What about this?" he asked experimentally, lifting a hand to the curve of her collarbone.

A low whimper broke from her throat, not of pain but edged with a pleasure that fired his blood. She looked up and let her head fall back, angling her neck and allowing her hair to fall against his fingers. "Yes."

He told himself to stop. He told himself this was not the right time, not the right woman. But as he stared down into her heavy-lidded eyes, darker now, like sapphires against ivory velvet, he also told himself to shut the hell up.

Then he kissed her. Slowly. Tenderly. A mere brush of mouth to mouth. "Shock waves," he muttered, then went in for more.

Chapter 10

Brenna waited for the tight grip of panic. The wave of revulsion. That desperate, clawing sensation in her throat. The
blind need to push him away, to twist from the prison of his
arms and put space between them. To breathe.

But none of it came.

Instead she did something she never thought she'd do again.
She curled her arms around his waist, held on tight and kissed
him back. Because his arms weren't a prison, and his mouth
didn't punish. In his embrace she didn't feel stifled or dominated. She didn't feel threatened. There was only pleasure, gentle waves rolling through her like the turquoise tide washing
against the glowing white sand.

And God help her, she wanted.

She wanted this kiss, this moment. She wanted this man.
She wanted everything that she'd told herself she couldn't
have, a normal life, a normal relationship, normal intimacies
with a man, not muddied and soiled by the ugliness of touch.

Shock waves, he'd murmured, and she felt them. Not the
dark violent kind that normally ripped through her like the
vicious cut of a sickle, but slow, persuasive. Drugging almost.

Making her ache to feel everything, all those hazy sensations she'd grown not to trust.

His mouth moved against hers with a strength that was both tender and strong. He urged her to open to him, explored her, tentatively at first, then more boldly, as though the same rhythm that drummed through her possessed him, as well.

From somewhere deep inside, she heard the hum, the low sound of pleasure and desire, and it staggered her. She leaned into him, drank of him, wanted…him. Intimate strangers, they were. She'd been sharing her bed with him for weeks, waking with the burning ache, the relentless need to find the man who ruled the dark hours she spent alone in her bed, twisting, turning, crying out when in dreams she saw him go down. Not because he was a good man and didn't deserve to die, but because—

Because what? It made no sense to want a man she didn't know, to burn for him. Not even to her, a woman who lived in a world that made sense to no one around her. She knew things, saw things, felt things that most people called nonsense. Hocus-pocus. Witchcraft.

The draw she felt toward Ethan Carrington defied not only logic but it defied the parameters of her world, the rules she'd tacked into place to prevent the disillusionment from striking again, that bottomless, suffocating feeling of standing on the outside looking in, while life danced on without her, no matter how hard she pounded her fists. No matter how much she bled. No matter how much she hurt. Or wanted.

"Not going to let him hurt you," Ethan murmured against her open mouth. He changed the angle of his, pressing his lips deeper against hers as his hand slid inside the open back of the dress Jorak Zhukov had insisted she wear. It was slinky and skimpy and clung to Brenna's body in a way nothing ever had before. She'd slipped it on then stared at herself in the mirror, cringing the second she'd realized the direction of her thoughts.

Maybe if Ethan Carrington saw her like this, in a sophisticated black dress with her hair combed and a soft blush of makeup on her face, he'd look at her the way he'd looked at the woman in the picture.

She moaned again, low from her throat, where the truth stuck like glue. She wanted Ethan to look at her like that, with that warm glow in his eyes, the reverence that made her heart ache.

The truth she thought again, and this time moisture stung her eyes.

Wanting was dangerous. She knew that, no matter how tempting it felt to have Ethan's roughened hand skim the exposed flesh of her back, to feel his fingertips brush low, to imagine them brushing elsewhere. God help her, she'd learned. And she'd hurt.

But she wouldn't cry. Not again. Not over Ethan, she thought, ignoring the ache in her heart. Not over a life she was better off not wanting.

Because wanting didn't matter. She knew that. She'd wanted her mother to stay in her life, but that hadn't stopped her from leaving. She'd wanted the kids at school to accept her. She'd wanted the police to believe her. She'd wanted Adam to love her.

She'd wanted her grandmother to slip from this world peacefully in her sleep, at the end of a long life, not at the violent tip of a butcher knife.

"No," she said now, pulling back from Ethan even as her heart begged her to stay. "No."

He let her go. Just let her go, didn't try to hold her, didn't try to keep her close. Just let her step back from him. His eyes were dark, his mouth swollen and moist from where he'd possessed hers.

The quick slice of pain made no sense. She was the one who'd ended the kiss. She was the one who'd pulled back. She was the one who'd said no. But standing there looking at him, so tall and commanding in that black tuxedo, with his raven hair mussed from where she'd run her fingers through it and his eyes gleaming, with his expression hard and unyielding, she felt as though something precious and fragile had just shattered.

"I'm sorry," he said, and his voice was rough. "Sometimes relief makes a man do stupid things."

Stupid things. The hurt cut deeper, swirled darker. "Relief?"

He cleared his throat and looked away from her, toward the window, where somewhere out there the wind whipped the surf into a frenzy. It roared louder than the choppy rhythm of her heart, punctuated by the rumble of thunder in the distance.

"When I came out of the shower and you weren't there—"

He broke the words off abruptly, still staring into the darkness beyond her shoulder, and her pulse did a cruel little stutter step.

"You what?"

Something brief and unfathomable flashed through his eyes, gone before Brenna had a chance to see what it was.

"I was worried," he said simply. "I didn't know where you were."

"Games," Brenna told him. Jorak himself had come for her the second the water of Ethan's shower had rumbled through the pipes. She'd turned to find the man all in white standing behind her. He'd snatched the photograph of his wife, muttered something vile under his breath, then dropped the frame and taken Brenna by the wrist. The flash of pain had staggered. The rush of hatred, pure and black and evil, confirmed what she'd known all along. The showdown was coming, and when the smoke cleared, only one man would be left standing. Only one man *could* be left standing.

Someone was going to die. Soon.

Ethan glanced toward the far right corner of the immaculate room of alabaster tile and Corinthian columns, where the unblinking red eye of a camera recorded their every move. "He's not going to win."

Brenna swallowed hard. She hoped not. God, she hoped not.

Still frowning, Ethan turned and took in the rest of the room, for the first time studying the long, gleaming table set with a white cloth, fine china, expensive silver and glimmering crystal. Candles flickered intimately. Domes covered two plates.

"Is this supposed to be my symbolic last supper?" he drawled, returning his glare to the camera.

Brenna moved without thinking, laying a hand on his arm. "No," she said. No. "This isn't how it ends."

He swung back toward her, all hard lines and dark places

again, all that burning passion from moments before completely extinguished. "Ah, that's right," he said, and even his voice was different, not the man's voice, the quiet Virginia drawl that had seeped into her bloodstream, but the hard, bludgeoned edges of the prosecutor. "This is all like some recycled movie to you."

She pulled back from him, physically, emotionally and every other way imaginable. "Not a movie."

"No?" he asked, blasting her with the full focus of his attention. She instinctively took a step back, but he took an equal one toward her. "Then what would you call it?"

A nightmare. His life. Inevitable. "The beach," she said, sidestepping a question that had no answer, not for a man like Ethan Carrington, who was already retreating behind the wall of fact and evidence upon which he relied. For a few minutes, there, a few lethal minutes, there'd been no walls, no defenses, no memories of the past or visions of what was to come, only a man and a woman reaching for each other. Wanting each other.

But that was gone now, leaving the stripped-down truth of who and what they were.

"It happens on the beach," she clarified. "The final showdown."

His jaw hardened. "The beach."

"That's where she is," Brenna added, her heart twisting on the words, the reality. "The woman."

Ethan's eyes went wild, for just one fraction of one heartbeat, as though her words had manufactured a ghost. Then he muttered something hot and hard and broken under his breath and turned from her, stalked to the table and lifted one of the domed lids. Then he laughed. It was a full, rich sound, and it hurt. "You son of a bitch."

Well-honed protective devices insisted that she stay where she was, but Brenna moved forward anyway. She saw the steak first, then she blinked. Tator Tots. There, next to the thick slab of meat, sat a pile of fried Tator Tots.

Ethan swore softly. "He didn't have to ask what I wanted for my last supper, because he already knew."

Brenna didn't know whether to laugh or cry. Untouchable, unyielding Ethan Carrington preferred Tator Tots to the traditional baked potato, and Jorak Zhukov knew. "Peach cobbler?" she asked, gesturing to the small china bowl next to the plate.

Ethan's mouth twisted. "My grandmother used to make it...it was Jorak's favorite."

The meal passed in silence. Brenna tried to enjoy the richly seasoned steak, but her stomach betrayed her. She wasn't hungry. She didn't want to eat. She just wanted—

She broke off the thought, reminded herself of the truth. Wanting only led to heartache.

"How old were you the first time?"

The question, quiet, intense, slipped through the semilit room and hit like a fist she'd not seen coming. She looked up from the three pieces of cut meat she'd been pushing around her ivory china plate with a thin gold line circling the circumference, to find Ethan watching her through those penetrating eyes. The prosecutor's eyes.

"The first time?" Her heart kicked hard. There'd never been a first time, just a sickeningly close call.

"When you had the first dream," he clarified. "What your mother said was a nightmare."

Her fork clattered to the table. She swallowed hard and braced herself, but the swirl started, slow, steady, unstoppable, just like always. "Why?" she asked, but barely recognized the low scratch of her own voice. "Why does it matter? I thought you were done prosecuting me."

"Prosecuting you?" He dropped the Tator Tot he'd been about to pop into his mouth. "Is that what you think I'm doing?"

"Isn't it?" More darkness, swirling faster, pulling harder. "You've already made what you think of me abundantly clear."

I'm a prosecutor. I don't have time for dreams.

"Have I?" He pushed back from his chair and stood, crossed to the other side of the table. She watched him, that leggy masculine grace that reminded her of a big cat. "Then maybe you should enlighten me."

Outside, the sky flashed, casting the room in a brilliant swath of light, then returning them to the flicker of dying candles. "You don't believe me."

His mouth flattened into a hard line, drawing her attention to the whiskers darkening his jaw. "This isn't about believing." He extended an arm toward her. "This is about wanting more."

Everything inside of her went very still. Cruelly, horribly still. All but her heart. It slammed hard, ramming up against her ribs without regard for damage or pain.

"More?" Her blood heated, because God help her, God help them both, she wanted more, too.

"I'm not a man to rush to judgment," he said, reaching for her hand. Slowly, persuasively, he urged her to her feet. "I prefer to gather all the evidence first."

Evidence. The word, the favored tool of the prosecutor, crushed that soft, hazy feeling burgeoning within her. He was just gathering facts, weighing her word, her truth, against that which he could accept.

She stood anyway, determined not to let this man know that he could cut her down so easily, with nothing more than a few words and a simple touch. She was stronger than that, had to be stronger than that. She could play the game as well as he could.

"I was seven," she said, going into his arms. They closed around her, pulled her against that rock-hard chest of his, so close that even through the fabric of his elegant tuxedo, she could hear the steady thrumming of his heart.

"That's awfully young."

She refused to believe she heard compassion in his voice, knew better than to believe she felt it in the way his hands skimmed along her back. The cameras were watching. Jorak thought they were lovers. Ethan was just going along with the guise.

That didn't explain why she curled an arm around his middle

and let her open palm settle against his back, but she refused to analyze.

"What did you see?" His breath, warm, carrying the aroma of the fine Scotch he'd sipped with dinner, caressed the sensitive skin beneath her ear.

The pull increased, the vortex of the past. Closer. Darker. "A woman," she told him. There was no point lying or evading. No point denying. "I saw a woman."

Ethan's hold on her tightened, one hand sliding up to tangle in her hair. "Then what?"

In a flash the night was gone, replaced by a brilliant summer morning. The sky was blue, so impossibly, beautifully blue. There were no clouds, though. No breeze. Only a stillness, stark and punishing. The faint hum of insects. Flies, she would later learn. And the green, the grass and the trees, the lingering stems of irises past their prime and fresh stalks of daylilies that multiplied every year.

"She was just lying there, beneath the shade of a weeping willow. Battered and beaten. Naked." Through the vacuum of sound there'd been only the tinkling of a nearby stream and the sickening buzz, the lingering echo of her screams. Screams for help. For mercy. Screams for the future she would never see, an end that she prayed would come quick.

And the screams of a little girl forced to face the ugliness of the world far too early.

"Who was she?"

Deep inside, something started to tear, threatened to completely give way. Brenna held those shredded ends together tightly but the truth seeped through her clenched fingers, and she started to shake.

"Brenna?" Ethan pulled from her and stared down at her, tilted her face to his. His eyes were no longer hard and condemning, no longer the cynical, fact-thirsty eyes of the prosecutor, but the warm, devastating eyes of the man. "Who was she?"

All the emotion she'd shoved down deep, starting that day so many years ago, when she'd been running barefoot through the woods with her golden retriever, Bambi, burst free, and for a dangerous moment she wanted to sink against this man, let him hold her. Let him make it all go away.

But that couldn't happen, and she knew it. None of this was real. Not the concern she saw in the burn of his eyes or felt in his startlingly gentle touch, not the crazy desire to forget the past and savor only the moment, this moment, not the damning urge to once, just once, let go.

"My mother," she told him, stripping every sliver of emotion from her voice. "She was my mother, and I saw her death a week before it happened." She swallowed hard, tried to bank the flow, but it was strong and it was dark, and no matter how desperately she fought it, it would not be denied. Words that had been jammed inside her, so awful she'd not shared them with anyone, not even her grandmother, who'd found her two days later, rocking in the darkness of her mother's closet, broke free.

"I saw it," she ground out, tearing out of Ethan's arms. She saw the way he was looking at her, the horror in his eyes, and despite how badly she wanted to sink back into his arms, she just kept backing away from him, as though he was somehow to blame.

"And I felt it." All of it. "Her terror, the ropes cutting into her wrists, the warm night air against her naked flesh." Tears filled her eyes and spilled over, but she didn't brush them away, just kept talking. Kept backing away.

"The horrible sense of inevitability," she said, aware that her voice had dropped to barely more than a scratchy whisper, much like her mother's final words. "The filth and pain of each violating thrust." She saw Ethan move toward her, but held up a hand. "Don't," she said, but it sounded more like a screech. "I saw her die. I *felt* her die." She'd let her die. "I cried the tears that she cried when she realized she wouldn't be around to raise her daughter." A maniacal laugh broke free. "Me. I felt her pain over leaving me alone." Even now the memory shattered. "But I couldn't stop it," she whispered through the tightness in her throat. "I couldn't stop it."

And she couldn't stop what was going to happen to Ethan, either, no matter how hard she tried. No matter how much she wanted. The only thing she could stop, the only thing she could control, was the pain, the stabbing vulnerability she allowed into her own life.

"Are you happy now?" The question ripped out of her, harsher than he deserved, especially the way he was standing there staring at her, looking heartbreakingly helpless but unbearably strong. "Is that the evidence you wanted, prosecutor? Does that make you feel better, to have more pieces of the puzzle?"

She didn't wait for him to answer. She spun from him and hurried across the room, to a pair of French doors leading onto a small veranda. The kiss of the warm breeze greeted her, the angry hum of the ocean, the quickening of the sky around her.

She wasn't running, she told herself. That's not what this was about. She didn't run. She'd never run.

This was about the truth, the fact that she and Ethan Carrington were from different worlds. Not just different worlds, but colliding worlds. Incongruous worlds. He was a high-profile man of concrete evidence and cold fact. She was a woman of instinct and intuition. To let herself believe, to let herself fantasize that this intensity between them was real would only lead deeper into the darkness. The absolute worst thing she could do was allow herself to depend on him, want him, trust what she felt for the tall man with the hard eyes but gentle hands.

No matter how badly she wished otherwise, no matter how badly she wanted, this pretense could never be real.

Ethan watched her go. Instinct demanded he go after her, comfort her somehow, pull her into his arms and hold her, take away the pain, but he didn't move. Couldn't. Not when her words continued to lash at him from all directions.

Her mother. Christ. The first death she'd witnessed in the dark confines of her childhood bed, a bed that should have been filled with teddy bears and dolls, had been her mother's.

He closed his eyes, not wanting to see her standing on the patio with her hands curled bloodlessly around the railing, but she was waiting in the darkness of his mind, as well. A little girl of seven, with soft blond hair and shining blue eyes, the youthful glow of innocence. The girl in his mind wore pigtails and dirty overalls, with a smear of mud on her cheek.

Sickness scratched into his throat, and the image changed, twisted, from a mischievous little girl to one thrashing in her bed, crying out with terror, not understanding what she'd just seen. A nightmare, her mother had told her. A nightmare.

Ethan opened his eyes and let out a rough breath, couldn't stand there one second longer, not when the truth pierced deeper by the second. He strode toward the parted doors, stepped into the warm humid air of late evening, and felt the soft ping of rain. Angry clouds blotted out the moon, making the streaky lightning more vivid.

I saw her die. I felt her die.

I *let* her die. She hadn't said the words, hadn't had to. He'd seen them reflected in her dark, unseeing eyes. Felt them somewhere deep inside, somewhere he didn't want to name.

The need to eliminate the distance between them, to pull her against his chest and block out everything, the past and the present, the gently falling rain, shook him. He'd done that to her. He'd sent her into the night, the rain, because in his world two and two always, always had to add to four.

But in her world they didn't.

Lightning split the sky in a network of horizontal and vertical slashes, flaring brightly, then fading into darkness. Thunder rumbled. The truth taunted. If he crossed to her, touched her, that meant he believed what he'd seen in her eyes and heard in her voice, what he'd felt deep inside in that walled-off place he'd quit listening to years ago.

And that violated the core building blocks of the man he'd become.

The cameras were watching, recording, but still he didn't move, just stood there on the edge of the balcony, watching her. *Wanting.* Somewhere along the line, somehow, some way, the facts had blurred. He wasn't sure how it had happened, how she'd slipped under his skin, into his blood, but once again he'd made a crucial mistake. He'd let himself get close, let himself care. Let himself trust something he could neither see nor feel. Again, damn it. Again.

He started toward her, stopped abruptly.

Circumstances, he told himself, the pull of adrenaline and desperation. Good old-fashioned compassion. He felt responsible for her. The disturbing hum that jolted him when he looked at her, heard her voice, put a hand to her body, or worse, his mouth to hers, that was only the result of their circumstances. Nothing more.

The transformation came over him abruptly, the prosecutor he'd become pushing aside the man he'd once been, the man who'd believed, who'd wanted, the same idyllic notions as his sisters, the foolish boy who'd once seen sailboats in the sky.

More comfortable now, he shrugged out of his tuxedo jacket and closed the distance between them, draped it over her shoulders but didn't let himself touch. "It's starting to rain."

In a violent rush of motion she spun toward him, letting the expensive jacket fall to the wet concrete. "Why are we doing this?" she asked, and her voice cracked on the words. Her damp hair stuck to the sides of her face, but somehow she still looked beautiful. "Why are we playing this game? Why aren't you trying to escape?"

All good questions, all ones he wouldn't let himself answer. "Because it stops with me." Where it had started.

Her eyes flashed with the lightning. "What? What stops with you?"

Everything. The past and the present, the danger and the truth, the insidious wanting. The whisper of inevitability. But he didn't say the words, just watched her from eyes he knew to be cool and impassive.

"You can't do it, can you?" she asked, and the disappointment, the disillusionment, in her voice almost sent him to his knees. "I bared my heart in there to you, but you can't answer a simple question in return." Her mouth twisted. "You can't trust."

He took the accusation like a blow. Then, because she was right, because his hands ached to do something stupid like touch her, he balled them into tight fists. He could no longer trust himself to move, not without falling deeper into a hole he was no longer sure he could pull himself out of.

"Trust me, angel," he drawled with the insolence that never failed him during interrogations. "There are some things you're better off not knowing."

"Me?" she returned. "Are you sure about that?" Her eyes flared. "Or maybe the real truth is," she added, sounding more like a prosecutor by the minute, "it's yourself you're trying to protect. Yourself who's better off without me knowing."

The wince was automatic. "Maybe we both are."

A hard sound broke from low in her throat, not raw passion like before, but sheer disgust. "If you really believe that," she said, but didn't finish, just brushed by him and walked inside, leaving him standing in the rain.

Through the golden glow of a single lamp, he saw the pictures the second he turned toward the bed. Brenna had gone into the bathroom and closed the door, leaving only a shaft of light spilling from beneath. She'd not said a word since she'd left him on the balcony. He wasn't sure how long he'd stood there in the drizzle, five minutes, ten, maybe twenty, but when the rain stopped and the thunder faded into the distance, he had turned and walked into the ballroom, found her standing rigidly at the wall of windows overlooking the dark, angry ocean.

"It's time for bed," he'd said, putting a hand at the small of her back, but she'd moved away from him, his touch, toward the door, where the guard had stood ready to escort them to their room.

He'd hurt her. She'd dredged up her past for him, but when she'd asked him a simple question in return, he'd denied her. And in doing so, he'd succeeded in doing what he'd set out to do—push her away.

Never had success tasted so bitter.

Now he strode toward the big bed, where a stack of computer-generated pictures awaited atop the floral comforter of orange and yellow hibiscus. Disgust gripped him. He knew Jorak had been watching them, but seeing the evidence of that stacked neatly on the bed sickened in a way he hadn't expected.

Brenna. Christ, there she was, as she'd been that first night, dressed in black and standing beneath a sycamore tree. The two of them standing close, Ethan gripping her shoulders. Touching her.

The look of dread on her face twisted through him. How had he not seen it that night? How had he not noticed?

Because he'd been blind, he knew now. The need to destroy Jorak Zhukov had distorted his ability to see clearly, to interpret clearly, leading him to find motive and deceit where none existed.

The urge to rip the picture to shreds was strong, but Ethan resisted, unable to destroy the image of Brenna as she'd been that first night, when she'd selflessly walked into his life to warn him, without giving her own safety a second thought.

And then there they were, here in this very room, by the bed, kissing. The memory flared through him, not of the demanding kiss he'd intended to deliver, the one that would prove she was affiliated with Jorak, but a press of mouth to mouth that had caught him completely off guard.

Ethan let the picture fall to the floor, only to come face-to-face with another image, this of their bodies intimately tangled. In bed. He'd told himself he was only playing for the cameras, comforting a woman after a bad dream, but now he stared at the raw emotion on his face, the way his hand lay protectively against her back, and something inside him started to tear.

At the beach, just that afternoon, standing in each other's arms in the surf. No wonder Jorak thought them lovers. To all the world that's how they looked.

Frowning against a truth he didn't want to see, Ethan flipped to the last picture, and felt himself go very still. Only Brenna graced the photo, Brenna standing by the bed and holding the picture of Allison.

Crying.

Tough, gutsy, invincible Brenna, who'd seen her mother die and held herself responsible for her grandmother's death, who'd been ridiculed and scorned and shut out her entire life, who'd been used and discarded, who'd picked up the phone anyway and called a man who was no more than a stranger, simply because she didn't want anything bad to happen to him, was crying.

Because of him.

Deep inside, that little fissure turned violent, ripping away pretenses and plans, leaving a surging darkness that could no longer be denied. And he couldn't do it. Couldn't keep living the game, the charade, not when doing so put Brenna in the line of fire. There was really no choice.

The bathroom door opened, and he looked up to see Brenna standing there in the ivory nightgown, silhouetted by the light behind her. And he didn't stop to think. Didn't stop to analyze. He crossed to her and took her into his arms before she could push him away, put his mouth to hers before she could tell him to go to hell.

Long moments later he pulled back and tore open his white dress shirt, ripped off the fabric then flung it over the camera nearest the bed. "No more cheap thrills," he said very clearly, very deliberately. Then he methodically and relentlessly obstructed the view of every other camera in the room.

Tonight would be a night neither of them would forget, and he would allow no witnesses to what went down in this room. No prying eyes. No vile photographs.

Chapter 11

"Is anyone out there?" Brenna banged on the hard wood of the door to the main hallway. Heart pounding, she glanced toward the unmoving form on the floor, then resumed her pleading. "Someone please, dear God. You have to help me."

Footsteps then, nearing the door. The click of the intricate series of locks. She sucked in a sharp breath and braced herself, commanded herself not to be afraid.

"What is it?" the guard asked, pushing open the door.

She stared at him blindly, then gestured to the heap at the foot of the bed. "It…it's Ethan," she said. Adrenaline rushed hot and hard. "He got rough and I hit him, and now he's not moving."

A slow smile curled the guard's mouth. He was the same young man with dark hair and thick arms who'd escorted them from the ballroom. The same man whose touch ignited a wave of dark slimy revulsion. Now a gleam moved into his eyes as he studied her torn gown and tangled hair, her swollen mouth. Muttering under his breath, he pushed past her for a closer look.

Mistake. Ethan attacked the second the man cleared the door, charging him with the lamp that had once sat on the bedside table. He slammed it against the back of the guard's head, sending him to his knees. Ethan closed in on him, and for a minute Brenna thought he was going to kick the guard in his gut, much as Jorak's man had done Ethan that night by the James. But he didn't do that. He merely squatted beside the groaning man and put a hand to the side of his neck, then squeezed.

The man went lax.

"That should keep him out awhile." Ethan stood and dragged the inert form to the bed. He helped himself to the man's semiautomatic and walkie-talkie, the knife he wore in a harness around his hips, his wallet, then he bound his wrists and his ankles, secured a dirty T-shirt over his mouth, and tucked him in neat and tidy.

"Don't let the bed bugs bite," he drawled, then turned to her and grinned. "Not bad for a city boy, huh?"

Brenna just stared. From start to finish, Ethan's plan had taken less than sixty seconds to execute. From those first tenuous moment along the James, she'd known Federal Prosecutor Ethan Carrington's expensive designer suits concealed a lot more than a body of hard muscle and hot flesh, a clever mind and will of steel. He was a man of intense patience and relentless dedication, a ruthless precision for getting what he wanted.

God, she could only imagine what it would be like to have all that energy focused on her. To have him want her as much as he wanted revenge.

"Not bad," she said turning from him. It hurt to look at him, hurt to see the coldness in his eyes, after the way he'd looked at her earlier. Hurt to know that she'd given him a little piece of herself but he would give her nothing in return.

"Come on." He grabbed the bundle he'd hidden on the other side of the bed. "We need to get out of here."

She nodded, followed him to the door. He looked down the

darkened hallway, then took her hand into the warmth of his and slipped into the shadows.

"What about the cameras? Won't the guards come looking when they see you've covered the lenses?"

Ethan hugged the cool stone wall. "Nah," he drawled. "They think we're making love."

Her breath caught, but somehow she kept moving. Making love. Just the phrase, the immediate, ensuing image, heated her blood. "Why would they think that?"

The corridor dead-ended, prompting Ethan to pause. "You're a beautiful woman," he said, and his voice was so quiet she barely heard it above the strumming of her heart. "We've barely kept our hands off each other all day."

True, dear God. Very true.

He looked right then left, hesitated, then pulled her down the shorter of the two halls. "What man wouldn't get you in bed the second he was alone with you?"

The words, the matter-of-fact argument of the prosecutor, did cruel, cruel things to her heart. It slammed against her ribs, kept slamming. Earlier she'd realized she had to put a stop to the longing, the wanting, but when she'd come out of the bathroom and seen him standing in the glow of a single lamp, with his shirt off and the yellow light emphasizing the hard lines of his chest, something inside her had died a little death.

He'd crossed to her before she could so much as breathe, taken her into his arms and kissed her, hard, thoroughly, and for a few dizzying minutes, she'd forgotten everything, the truth of who and what they were, their circumstances, the fact that she knew to survive this man, the intensity that hummed between them, she had to close herself off to him. There'd been only the shock waves, not the dark, punishing kind she experienced when Jorak or his men touched her, but a thrilling, drugging electricity that made her want more.

Then he'd skimmed his mouth to her ear and whispered his plan, and everything had come crashing back. They were actors on a stage. Puppets at the end of Jorak's rope.

"That won't buy us all night," she pointed out.

He reached the door at the end of the hall and laid a hand against the hard wood. "Don't sell yourself short." He let out a rough breath. "But you're right, at least for tonight."

She watched him finger the security panel. He lifted his other hand and flashed the guard's badge across a small screen, and within seconds the red light blinked green.

In some foggy part of her mind disbelief registered, but she fought it, knowing for now she was better off not thinking too much. Ethan knew what he was doing. Jorak thought he'd abducted Ethan, but Brenna knew that wasn't true. Ethan had been hungering for this opportunity, access to his longtime enemy. He'd been planning. He'd been prepared. And again, she thought, this man was no ordinary lawyer.

"We don't have much time," he whispered, pulling her into the night. Muggy air enveloped them like a lover's embrace the second they stepped outside, the tangy smell of salt and rain and decay. Ethan slipped along the exterior of the compound, keeping his back to the stucco wall, until they reached the muddy path that led to the beach. "Can you run?"

She looked at her feet, covered only by sandals Jorak had supplied. Grabbing the bottom of her nightgown, she yanked it above her knees. "I can run."

"Good girl." The kiss surprised her. It was hard, it was fast and then it was over. He had her hand again and was tugging her down the muddy trail. Her feet slipped and she felt the slimy dampness of dirt and sand slinging up along her legs, but she didn't care, just kept running.

The beach almost stopped her cold. The beach. Dear God. As long as they'd been inside the compound, she'd felt safe, because she knew, she knew the final showdown happened on the beach.

But then she remembered the hot glare of the sun, and knew that as long as the moon dominated the sky, the beach would not be washed in red.

An eerie calm stood like a groggy soldier in the wake of the storm. The surf crashed gently against the beach. Stars again glimmered against the dark night sky. Ethan led her to the far side of the cove, where the pier jutted out over the water. Several boats bobbed in the tide.

Alarm gripped her. It was dark and they had no idea where they were. In a boat, they could drift for days....

"There's got to be another way—"

Ethan dropped her hand and turned to her. "There is." He jogged to the end of the pier and released one of the boats, jimmied with the motor until a low purr flirted with the roar of the ocean, then launched it into the night.

Realization dawned. If Jorak's men thought Ethan and Brenna had escaped on one of the boats, they would follow. They might still search the island, but not as intensely.

"Come on." Again, he took her hand. "We don't have much time."

They were running then, through the wet, clingy sand to the dense vegetation at the back of the beach, slipping through a grove of dripping palms and vanishing into a tangle of vines and other overgrown plants.

Pain stitched into her side, but she ignored it, focused on putting one foot in front of the other. Vines slapped at her, tangled, pulled. She would have sworn she felt the warm trickle of blood on the side of her face, but she didn't say anything, didn't slow, just followed Ethan deep into the darkness.

She had to be exhausted. They'd been running over an hour, sloshing through mud puddles and cutting through vegetation that probably hadn't been disturbed in decades, fighting with vines, but she'd not complained, not tried to pull back, just kept pace with him.

Ethan slowed, let himself pull oxygen deeper into his lungs. He was a trained athlete. He ran nightly. He'd been schooled to survive. But Brenna...he'd dragged her into a mess.

On the beach they'd had the resurgent light of the moon and stars to guide them, but here in the tangle of undisturbed jungle there was only an oppressive blanket of damp darkness, and he refused to dwell on the fact they might not be alone.

He'd snapped. It was as simple as that. He'd seen the pictures, all the emotion on Brenna's face, on his face, emotion he'd been denying, damning, and he'd known he had to get her out of there. He was prepared for whatever went down between him and Jorak. He was prepared to go down, if that was what was necessary. But not Brenna. Christ, not Brenna. No matter what it took, he was determined to make sure she made it off this godforsaken island alive. Because more than he wanted revenge, justice, he wanted her to be okay. To live. To have the normal life she no longer thought herself capable of.

Her courage awed him. This wasn't her fight, wasn't her battle, but she'd walked into his life anyway, because not trying to help, she'd told him, would be unconscionable. In return he'd given her nothing, not even the answers she deserved.

"I met Jorak Zhukov at Harvard," he told her, surprised by the harsh rasp of his own voice. The admission fell flat against the quiet of the night. "We were both law students." The meeting had seemed innocent enough, at the library, studying at the same table. "He told me his name was Dimetri Pasquel."

For the first time since they'd left the compound, Brenna stopped running. She sucked in sharp breaths, and when Ethan turned to look at her, his heart twisted at the sight of blood smeared on her face, all the stains and tears on the ivory nightgown. "Christ," he muttered. "Why didn't you tell me?"

She shoved the hair back from her face. "Tell you what?"

"You're hurt." He moved without thinking, lifting his hand to wipe the smear of blood from her cheek to find a tiny cut.

"It's nothing," she said, but didn't remove his hand from her body. "You don't have to do that."

Ethan kept rubbing. "I never meant for you to get hurt." He'd never meant for a lot of things.

"Not that," she said, breathing hard. "About you and Jorak. You don't have to tell me."

He just stared at her. Very little light squeezed through the canopy of vegetation, the first tentative strains of dawn, barely enough to make out the lines of her face. "I think I do."

She frowned. "Ethan—"

"It's okay," he said, and though he wanted to keep touching her, running his fingers along her face, along her entire body to make sure she wasn't hurt elsewhere, he knew they had to keep moving. Soon their absence would be discovered—if it hadn't already been. "Just come on," he said, and again they were running.

"He was a skinny kid," he told her, letting the past wash back over him. "Awkward." He could still see him that evening in the library, wearing a Red Sox baseball cap and a threadbare rugby shirt. "We got to talking, first about law school, then about other things."

Brenna kept pace with him. "You felt sorry for him."

"I did," he admitted. "I'd grown up living a life of privilege, but my parents instilled social responsibility. I saw this kid, putting himself through school in a country that didn't automatically welcome him, and I didn't know how to turn my back on him."

She squeezed his hand. "You can't blame yourself."

Ethan tripped on a root and staggered forward, steered her so she didn't make the same mistake. "He told me he was from Croatia. That he'd lost his family to the persecution there, and had come to America to live with his grandmother."

"To seek refuge," Brenna murmured, and there was a hard edge to her voice. "He played you like a song."

The bitter taste of being played a fool pooled at the back of Ethan's mouth. It seemed like so long ago, another lifetime since he'd let himself be so gullible to something so intangible as friendship. He swallowed against the truth, ran harder.

"He said he wanted the life his parents had dreamed of but never had the chance to live." And like a total sap, Ethan had fallen for the sterling piece of sucker fiction.

Brenna swiped at a low-hanging vine. "You became friends."

Ethan let the vine fall back to slap the side of his face. "We did." It had seemed so easy, innocent and uncomplicated. Late-night study sessions had given way to chess and campus parties. "I invited him home with me that Thanksgiving. Mom

always made a big deal about holidays, and Dimetri's grandmother had died, and the family decided he shouldn't be
alone.''

His sisters had been charmed by his dark eastern European
looks and accent. ''That's when he met Allison.''

They were running, but he felt Brenna tense. ''The girl in
the picture.''

The memories twisted harder, surging forward after years of
exile. Guilt sliced deep, jagged. Sweet, sweet Allison. He'd
known her forever. His mother had made it annoyingly clear
she'd welcome Ally as her daughter-in-law. Tall and blond,
she'd exuded a radiant innocence that was more seductive than
a centerfold in a string bikini. He'd always felt protective of
her, hadn't thought twice about introducing her to his friend.
To Dimetri.

The man who would ruin her life.

''They hit it off immediately. Ally had a heart of gold, and
the second she heard his story, about the cruel slaughter of his
family, he had her.'' Wholly and completely, without reservation. ''He pretended to love her, too.''

Brenna said nothing, just kept running alongside him.

''They married a few weeks later.'' And sometimes when
Ethan lay alone in the cloying darkness of his bed, it was Ally's
face he would see, on her wedding day, when he'd stood by
Dimetri's side and watched his friend walk down the aisle, the
bright smile to her face, the beaming light to her eyes, the off-
the-shoulder silk dress of white. She'd been a virgin until she
met Dimetri. She'd been untouched. She'd been saving herself.

A fresh surge of disgust churned through Ethan, but again
he forced it aside, as he'd trained himself to do. Feelings got
him nowhere. Feelings only blurred his focus, distorted his
ability to see black for white, truth for lie.

Feelings destroyed.

''What happened?'' Her breathing was hard, but her question
was soft, laced with an empathy he did not deserve.

''A few months went by. Everything seemed normal. I had
no idea—'' A loud shrill sound aborted his words.

He stopped dead in his tracks, listening to the noise pitch lower, wobble, drone like a warped storm warning. "Took longer than I thought," he muttered, tugging her forward. He had to find somewhere to hide her, damn it. Somewhere Jorak would never find her, never touch her, never destroy her the way he'd destroyed Allison.

"It was March," he forced himself to continue, focusing on the past rather than the growing cesspool within. "I got a phone call." Much like the ones Brenna had placed. Vague. Allegedly urgent. Requesting a meeting by the James. "I'll never forget how damn cold it was." He'd always tested himself, dressing in shorts and T-shirt to run, even during the dead of winter. He'd shown up that night clad in his normal attire, not at all prepared for the bone-chilling cold cutting through the shivering trees. The river had continued to trickle over the slabs of rock, but crusts of ice caked many of them. "And that's when everything changed."

"You learned the truth?"

"The informant met me there." A hooded figure had stepped from behind a sycamore and, with a few whispered words, yanked the world from under Ethan's feet. "I learned the truth about Dimetri, that he was living in the States under an assumed name. That he wasn't a war orphan, wasn't trying to build a better life for himself."

The siren continued to wail, droning, relentless.

"He was really the son of a deposed eastern European military leader, who was wanted in conjunction with heinous war crimes." A man who'd single-handedly and cold-bloodedly ordered the execution of entire villages, including the rape of innocent women, the slaughter of children. The man who'd seven years later gone after Ethan's sister Miranda.

"He'd planted his son in America to learn everything about our culture, our value system, that he could—how we think, how we play, how we fight." And as his primary instructor, he'd chosen none other than the son of a United States senator.

A low sound broke from Brenna's throat. "Ethan, I'm sorry."

For years he'd kept the truth bottled up inside him. His father knew, but no others. Not even Elizabeth. He'd never been able to force himself to spit out the words, the truth. The shame was a black stain that could never be erased, only learned from.

"That Thanksgiving, when I invited him into my home, he hacked into my father's computer and gained access to crucial military information." Ethan bit back another surge of disgust. "Information he used to order the execution of an entire team of Navy SEALs."

Around him, through the thick tangle of vegetation overhead, the sky was lightening into a grayish peach, but Ethan saw only black. Dark, punishing. It pushed from all directions, spilled through him, pooled in his lungs.

"Oh, God," Brenna said, and her voice was low, sad. "Ethan." She stopped abruptly, holding on tight to his hand and forcing him to stop, as well. There in the darkness, with the alarm blaring over the sounds of the night and the sun trying to lighten scars that would never go away, she looked up at him with those incredible fairy eyes of hers, eyes that made him long to slip back in time to his childhood, to the boy who'd been enchanted with the lore of Ireland.

Her movements registered in slow motion, the step toward him, the press of her body to his, the lifting of her arm, the hand against his face. Her voice then, soft, strong. "It wasn't your fault."

But it was. Totally and completely. Because of him, because of his inability to see Dimetri Pasquel for the monster he was, men had died. Families had been destroyed. And Allison—

Jesus.

He could still see her, lying so horribly still. He'd never seen so much blood....

He moved without thinking, crushed Brenna in his arms without realizing his intent. He just needed to hold her, hold on, feel that she was warm and alive and vital, that he'd gotten her away from Jorak in time, but then she was holding him, too, and some forgotten place inside him thrummed hard and deep.

"It's okay," she murmured, running her hands along his back and pressing her face to his neck. "It's okay."

But it wasn't okay, and he knew it. There was only one way to make it okay.

He pushed from her—when he wanted only to drag her to the muddy ground and take more—ran harder, not holding her hand, but freely against the night that wouldn't stop slipping away.

"Ethan!"

But he kept running, pumping his arms and lengthening his strides, breathing hard, no longer from Jorak's men, not from Brenna, but from a darker vigilante, one that had eroded the core of who he was for seven long years.

"Ethan, wait!" she called again, this time from not as far behind him, and in a blinding flash, sanity returned, and he knew it was time to quit running. He slammed to a stop and bent forward, braced his hands against the hot damp skin of his thighs and tried like hell to breathe.

Couldn't.

And then Brenna was touching him again, running her hands over his sweaty arms and back in a compassionate gesture he didn't come close to deserving. But God, how he wanted.

"I went to the FBI." The need for justice, to punish, had nearly blinded him. Hell, that was a lie. It *had* blinded him, totally and completely, just like the illusion of friendship had. "We arranged a sting."

Brenna kept touching him, kept murmuring softly, but he didn't look at her, couldn't, not when the soft light of dawn would let him see what was reflected in those whitewashed sapphire eyes.

"It was at night." The dead of night. And Ethan had sat outside in his car, oblivious to the bite of the cold, knowing only that in minutes Dimetri's lies would come to an end, and he'd never hurt anyone ever, ever again. "A SWAT team moved in just after midnight. They kicked in the door, and even down on the street I could hear the gunfire. The shouting."

The scream.

"They told me to stay in the car and wait." Somewhere in the distance, the alarm went quiet, as though the entire island was braced for what came next. But for as long as Ethan lived, he would never be braced, never be prepared. "But I couldn't. I got out of the car and ran." It was the longest hundred yards of his life. "And then there she was."

Brenna sucked in a breath. Her hands stopped moving. "No..."

He stared down at the mud sloshed up over his shoes, the streaks of slime on his legs, and no matter how badly he wanted to twist around and see Brenna, tell her to keep her hands moving, touching, he couldn't. Wouldn't let himself.

"The son of a bitch got away," he rasped, and the hot surge sluiced back through him. "Allison was the one left lying in a pool of blood." Allison who'd been fourteen weeks pregnant.

For a moment everything stood still. Brenna, Ethan, the island. But then she was there again, not just touching, but draping her entire body over him, as though she could somehow change the truth. "God, Ethan, I'm sorry."

All at once he pushed upright and stared blindly ahead, noticing for the first time what appeared to be a road cutting through the jungle. "So am I," he said, taking her hand and pulling her forward. "So am I."

Finally it all made sense. A horrible, twisted sense. From the moment she'd met Ethan Carrington, from the moment he'd looked at her through those piercing eyes, searching for a link between her and Jorak Zhukov, she'd seen his scars, and she'd wondered. Something had twisted this man, she remembered thinking. Something had shaped him. Something, someone, had destroyed his ability to trust.

She'd thought it a woman, and now, watching the tall man with the raven hair walk ahead of her, a man who exuded strength and confidence even as guilt gnawed away at him, she realized she'd only been partially right. Yes, the loss of Allison had hurt him deeply. But she hadn't been the only one to die that night. Far from it. Part of Ethan had died, as well, the youthful confidence she'd seen in the picture of him and Allison, when he'd looked ready to take on, to conquer, the world.

And it was Jorak Zhukov who had killed him. Jorak Zhukov who had betrayed him. Jorak Zhukov who had taught him not to trust, not only others, but worse, far worse, himself.

The truth staggered her. And finally she knew why Ethan Carrington demanded fact and evidence, why he had to feel and see and taste before he could believe. She knew, and she understood, and deep inside, on a level she'd tried to destroy, to wall off from the world, she hurt.

"Here's an opening," he said, and his voice, low, urgent, yanked her back to the muddy path circling what looked to be an abandoned resort. Morning shimmied around them, the soft hazy light of dawn, the cry of an island full of birds. She looked through the mist and focused on the chain link fence, where Ethan stooped near a tear.

"You go first," he said.

She did as he instructed, moving on autopilot to crawl through the hole in the fence. There was nothing all that discernable about the other side, more overgrown vegetation and puddles of mud, but excitement whispered through her.

"My God," she said under her breath, and stared at the massive structure in the distance, Mayan in design, steadily being reclaimed by nature. "Do you think it's safe?"

Ethan joined her. "Safer than the compound." He took her hand, and instinctively she curled her fingers around his. The ease with which she did so shocked her. For so long she'd avoided human contact, but now she couldn't get enough. Not with this man. The need to touch, to run her hands along his body and take away the pain, smooth the hard lines, took her breath away.

"What do you think happened?" she asked.

He started forward. "Who knows. They could have gone bankrupt, I suppose." They passed under a stunning concrete archway, next to which sat a crumbling sign which read Palacea de Maya. "Maybe a hurricane."

Brenna breathed in deeply, despite the strong smell of decay surrounding them. The main hotel building loomed about a hundred yards down the path, a weathered stucco structure that looked like an ancient palace. There were columns and arches, small windows, and as they grew closer, she noted intricate carvings in stone.

"This was a happy place," she said, and deep inside she felt it.

Against hers, Ethan's hand tightened. "How do you know?"

She stopped walking and glanced to the right, where a structure that looked eerily like a temple rose up through the dense vegetation. "Places carry memories," she said. "Every bit as real and vital as humans." The sensations would hit her, wash over her, just as they did with people. "When I was in high school, a group of kids I wanted desperately to be friends with invited me for a night of joyriding." All it took was the memory, and her throat went tight. "I went, never questioning their motives. We drove and drove, until finally they stopped the car in front of an old house and all started to get out."

But Brenna had just sat there, gasping for breath. The sensation, the cold, the darkness, had pushed down on her like a wet wool blanket. "I couldn't get out of the car."

Ethan turned to look at her, lifted his free hand to brush the sweat-dampened hair from her face. "Why?"

"The house," she said, and even to her own ears her voice sounded distant. Mechanical. "It was the scene of a murder. A man took out his own family, killing one child at a time in their beds where they slept." She paused, forced herself to swallow, felt herself sway.

But then Ethan was more than holding her hand, he was supporting, holding her up.

"Killed his wife," she whispered. Degraded her first. "Then himself." A cry broke from her throat. "And the kids thought it was funny. They wanted to go inside. They wanted to spend the night."

Against the bright light of early morning, Ethan's eyes went dark. "And you?" he asked, his voice unbearably gentle.

She blinked up at him, pulled herself back from the memory. "I wouldn't get out of the car." She'd been lucky to simply breathe.

Against her face, Ethan's hand stilled. "Did you convince them to leave?"

She looked away from him, toward the pyramid-looking structure in the distance. The Mayans had been architecturally advanced, she remembered reading. They'd built their structures in accordance with the solar calendar, creating fascinating displays of shadow and light, mysteries that remained to this time. "No."

Ethan swore under his breath.

For some foolish reason, his anger on her behalf soothed. She wanted to turn her face into his hand, to press her lips against his palm, but instead she turned to see his eyes. "They took the keys with them and it was the middle of January, and sleeting, and so c-cold." She paused, refused to let her teeth chatter in memory. "But I would not get out of that car. I...couldn't." Couldn't walk knowingly into a place where evil lingered. "Because I knew."

His hand fell away. "And that's how you know this was a happy place."

She felt the smile curve her lips, and for a dangerous moment, let herself believe that Ethan Carrington, man of concrete fact and cold, hard evidence, believed her. "There's a little sadness in the air," she said, glancing to the other side of the main building, where what looked to be tennis courts stood abandoned, weeds jutting up between cracks in the weathered red concrete. "But it's not dark and it's not evil. It's more sorrowful for something beautiful lost."

She paused, drew in another breath, found not the putrid stench of mud, but the tangy scent of fruit. Mango, maybe. "I think you were right," she said. "I think it was a hurricane."

He stared at her a long moment, then started moving again, pulling her toward what looked to be the reception area. "We need to get out of the open."

They heard it at the same time, the low rumble of what

sounded like an engine. And then they were running again. She broke toward the building, but Ethan tugged her toward the crumbling ruins of what looked to be a small-scale replica of a Mayan city.

''They'll look in there first,'' he said, and she knew that he was right.

Behind them the rumble stopped, replaced by the echoes of doors opening, then closing. Then shouting.

Jorak's men had caught up with them.

Chapter 12

Ethan pulled her behind an overgrown banana tree, then led her deeper among the small buildings made of weathered but uniform stone. She recognized the elaborate structure with viewing areas on three sides as a ball court, where Mayan warriors would play a game similar to soccer, different only in that the winning captain lost his head. There was a statue to one of the gods, Chacmool, she thought, the god of fertility on whom the Mayans relied to bring crop-quenching rains.

"This way." Ethan ran toward a massive army of decomposing columns. The ivy-covered structures flanked another templelike building, but he didn't run toward the dark opening, veering instead toward the entrance to a cave.

Darkness obliterated every trace of the storm-washed morning. A chill pervaded the walls, dampness, but not severe, and Ethan led her deeper inside, toward the trickle of water.

"A *cenote*," she realized loud. An underground river. Mexico had few bodies of water flowing above ground, but within the bodies of its caves lay an intricate network of sunken rivers flowing toward the ocean.

Ethan stopped, kept holding her hand. "Want a bath?"

She couldn't help it. Maybe it was the complete absurdity of his question, or maybe the way he tossed it out, lazy, casual, as though there wasn't a squadron of men combing the grounds looking for them. But, God help her, she did. She wanted a bath. They'd been running for hours, through the thick, muggy jungle, tromping in puddles and hacking their way through vines, and her body practically screamed with filth and exhaustion. "Is it safe?"

Too late, a little voice inside asked, from what? The men outside, or the man with her?

Drips of light squeezed from a fissure in the rock overhead, enough that she could see Ethan staring toward the mouth of the cave, little more than a speck in the distance. "Lizzie and I went to Cancun for our senior trip," he said. "There are these eco parks nearby, and they let you snorkel in the underground rivers."

She toed off her sandals and dipped her foot into the water. Cool. That was her first thought. Refreshing.

"They won't look in here," he was saying, and on an instinctive level, Brenna believed him. And if by some chance they did, the river offered an escape route.

She didn't stop to think. She didn't stop to consider. She stripped off the torn nightgown and slipped into the cool fresh water. It swallowed her like a bowl of fresh gelatin, and relief sang happily to every nerve ending.

And then Ethan was doing the same. She heard the rip of his zipper and told herself not to look, but could no more have stared in the other direction than she could have ignored his dominating presence in her dreams only a few weeks before.

Pinpricks of light flirted with his bare chest, farther down to his hips, where he was unceremoniously shucking off his cargo shorts. She watched them fall, felt the breath jam in her throat when she saw the dark-gray boxers hugging his buttocks and thighs, the unmistakable bulge she'd felt through her clothing but longed to feel more intimately.

The rush of heat prompted her to slip beneath the surface of the water. When she came up with cool water dripping down her face, Ethan was paddling toward her. "Feels great," he said, and then his calve, bare, hairy, brushed hers.

She braced herself, looked beyond him to the ledge, searching for his boxer shorts. Seeing them.

"Head downstream for now," he instructed, and through the wavering light, she saw that he had one hand out of the water, and in it, he held the sleek black semiautomatic he'd lifted from the fallen guard. He'd stashed their clothes high on a ledge. "On the outside chance they shine a light in here, I don't want them to see us."

She did as he instructed, turned and stroked her way through the water, not freestyle as she loved, but the quiet, easy movements of breaststroke. The cool water sluiced around her body, taking with it the fatigue and exertion of the long night.

"As soon as they're gone I want you to rest," Ethan said from beside her.

"You, too," she said, but from the low sound he made in his throat, she knew he had no intention of lowering his guard until—

Until what? That was the variable she'd yet to figure out. He had a plan, that much she knew. He was too clever not to.

"Ethan, about what you told me earlier. It wasn't your fault."

"Shh." With one arm he drew her to him, and she realized the *cenote* was shallow enough here for him to stand. He leaned against the rocky side of the cave and pulled her into his body, flesh to flesh, tucking her head under his chin. "Don't talk."

Once, not so long ago, she would have resisted the way he anchored her to him, would have resisted the command. But the hard heat of his body soaked into hers, and with his arm securely around her, she could almost believe they were both going to get out of this alive.

"Relax," he said, threading his fingers up into her damp hair. "Just let go."

Her body hummed in response to the roughly whispered words. Lethargy stole through her, heat, a tickle from her exposed breasts down between her legs. She felt his body grow increasing stiff, but the age-old panic didn't claw its way through her, didn't stab into her throat.

"Ethan," she murmured, lifting her face to his, and then his mouth was there, on hers, and he was kissing her, not hard and urgent like the last time, but soft, tender. She opened for him, let him sweep his tongue into her mouth, and there in the darkness of the cave, with the cold water lapping around them, she would have sworn she'd found heaven.

But then he turned away, scraping his whiskers along her jaw, staring the direction from which they'd come. "Rest."

And that's when she realized it. There were no cameras here. No one watching. No pretense to maintain. There was just the two of them, and the truth of who and what they were.

Ethan had subjected himself to a lot of tests in his life. His grandfather had taught him how to live off the land, and as a fifteen-year-old, he'd done just that for ten days, living alone in the woods, with nothing but the clothes on his back. He'd hunted and fished for his food. He'd found berries and leaves. He'd made a fire. He'd willed himself not to be cold, even when the temperature dipped into the forties and an annoyingly cold drizzle fell from the sky.

At VMI, he'd survived the equivalent of basic training. He'd learned what sleep deprivation did to a man. He'd learned how to disconnect his mind from physical discomfort. He'd learned to disconnect his body from mental anguish.

Later, when his sister Kristina died, he'd made himself be strong, the rock for his shattered family, when all he'd really wanted was fall to his knees and cry. She'd been his sister, a bright, beautiful light, and he'd loved her, but in the end he hadn't been able to protect her from someone he'd mistakenly called friend.

Twice, damn it. Twice he'd mistakenly called a man friend. Twice that man had crushed something precious and vital.

All those tests had hardened him, prepared him for the years to come. But Lord have mercy, none of them prepared him for standing chest deep in the cool water of the shadowy *cenote,* with Brenna's naked body draped around his, her head resting against his chest, while she slept.

He hadn't expected her to drop off. He hadn't expected her to let go like that, to…trust. Even now, the memory of her naked body sliding against his, her surprisingly full breasts against his chest, her legs wrapped around one of his, her soft, broken breathing, made him go so hard it hurt.

He'd braced himself for the dreams, the images that had ripped her from sleep the first night they'd slept together. But they hadn't come. She'd shifted occasionally, her flesh sliding against his, soft, inviting, and he'd remembered the sweetness of her kiss, almost like a sacrificial offering.

Now he watched her standing on an upstairs balcony of what had once been a luxurious guestroom. She faced the ocean, barely visible through the fading light and dense vegetation, but its roar left no doubt as to proximity.

She'd changed into the sundress he'd grabbed for her while gathering supplies before leaving the compound, and the soft white fabric whipped about her legs. Her hair, finger combed and air dried, fell in soft waves against her shoulders.

She'd barely spoken since she'd awoken, since her eyes had opened, wide, dark, and stared into his with an intensity that still had the power to rattle him.

"You need to eat."

He didn't expect her to turn toward him, but she did. "So do you."

He gestured toward the soft yellow blanket spread out where a bed had once been, where bread and cheese and water now awaited. "From last night," he explained. "I pocketed them during dinner."

She glanced toward the ocean, then a cracked outdoor bathtub in the corner of the balcony, then moved into the empty room. "Thanks."

"I don't think Jorak's men will be back," he said. At least not tonight. In all likelihood, they'd fallen for the ploy of the boat set out to sea. And by morning what they thought wouldn't matter. "We should be safe for the night."

She sat and crossed her legs, reached for a bottle of water. "Then why won't you put that down?"

He stared at the semiautomatic in his hand, the way his fingers curled around the sleek curves like a lover's caress and forced himself to set it on the floor beside her.

"You have to quit blaming yourself," she said, pushing a dinner roll toward him. "None of this is your fault."

He took the bread and tore it in two, watched her sitting there, with her hair falling softly against her face. "It wasn't supposed to go down like this, damn it," he practically growled. It was his penance and he was prepared to pay. Craved to pay. But not hers, damn it. Not hers. "You weren't part of the plan."

She looked up, met his gaze. "It's going down exactly the way it's supposed to."

Something hot and violent flashed through him. "Bull. You shouldn't be here right now." Shouldn't be in the line of fire.

"You don't know that," she said with a calm acceptance that ripped at him, and again he realized just how deep her scars penetrated.

"The hell I don't," he said, and forgot all about that control he'd be holding in a death grip, the test he'd been administering to himself, the test he had to win.

The one he was about to fail.

He pushed aside the bread and stretched toward her. If his eyes were a little too hot, his voice a little too rough, too bad. It was about time Brenna Scott realized that whatever the hell was going to go down between Ethan and Jorak was not predetermined. "I am not," he said very slowly, very succinctly, through tightly clenched teeth, "repeat, *not* going to let that bastard hurt you."

He'd die before he let Jorak hurt another woman Ethan lo—

The thought, the word about to grate from his throat, staggered him. Intensity, he remembered thinking. Adrenaline. That was all.

Brenna's eyes, those whitewashed pools of sapphire, remained eerily calm. "You might not have a choice."

The urge to grab her shoulders and shake her, shook *him*. "The hell I won't."

"Ethan—"

"What did you see, damn it?" And this time he couldn't hold back. He reached for her, took her arms in his hands but didn't shake, just pulled her closer to him, held her tight. "Tell me what you saw, on the beach."

Finally she reacted. Finally that calm facade she wore like a tight-fitting glove unraveled, and her eyes went dark. Her face, kissed by the sun, went pale. "I've already told you."

"No, you haven't," he said, and knew. She'd been holding back. He held her gaze with his, a timeless prosecutor technique that never failed to produce results. "Not everything."

The sound she made was so raw he barely heard it. She twisted against him, but he wasn't about to let her run, not now, not when the truth stood between them like one of the ancient, inexplicable Mayan relics that dotted the Mexican landscape.

"Tell me."

The words were deliberately quiet, purposefully forceful, and he literally saw them rip away the last vestiges of her denial.

"You," she said, not in anger or resignation, but with a sadness that swamped him. "I saw you," she said. "I felt *you*."

And the way she said it, with dread drenching her words, made it obscenely clear that whatever she'd seen, felt, had rocked her badly. "What, damn it? What did I feel?"

"Her," she ground out, "You saw her. You felt her."

Ethan released her abruptly and sat back on his heels, tried to breathe. Couldn't. *Her?* No way. No possible way Brenna could know that. Not yet. "Who, damn it? Who did I see, feel?"

Brenna's eyes dimmed and her eyelids fluttered, and for a fractured moment, he thought he was going to lose her, but then she inhaled roughly and met his gaze. "She's not supposed to be there,'' she said, and the words were rote, almost mechanical, like she was reciting a scene from a movie, ''but you look up and though the sun nearly blinds you, you see her, standing at the end of the beach beneath a banana tree, and suddenly everything you planned, everything you waited for, doesn't matter, because there's only fear, a terrible, shredding fear that you didn't do enough, and now something's going to go wrong and *she's* going to be the one taken down, and you can't let that happen.'' She exhaled raggedly, pressed on. ''So you run. You know you shouldn't, you know you might die in the process, but you don't care. All you care about is her. So you run.''

Dark spots clouded Ethan's vision. Shock thickened his throat. Christ have mercy, there was no way in the world she could know. ''And what happens?''

Brenna's eyes went wild. She shoved the hair back from her face and shook her head, but nothing chased away the devastation in her gaze. He'd seen that look before, too many times to count, at too many funerals. Too many trials. It was the look of someone who'd just lost a loved one to a heinous act of violence, that bottomless, stunned, confused look. Dazed. The kind that reached inside and twisted his guts into tight knots.

It was the look he'd denied himself after Kristina, and after Allison.

''You go down,'' she said on a rush, then blew his mind. She reached for him, touched him of her own will, put her hands to his chest and stared up into his eyes. ''Everything turns red, and you go down.''

The pain in her voice, the anguish in her eyes, gutted him. He fought it, fought her, fought a truth that couldn't come to pass.

''No.'' Damn it, no. ''That's not how it's going to happen,'' he said, and then he couldn't help it, couldn't just sit there and watch her fall apart, watch her look at him through those dark, raw eyes, certain that tomorrow death would come calling, and there wasn't a damn thing they could do about it.

He moved without thinking, hauling her against him and

taking her mouth with his. He couldn't say why, just knew he couldn't sit there and pretend one freaking second longer, couldn't deny the irrational insanity that had gripped him the first moment he'd heard her voice.

Her lips were soft and moist, trembling, but they moved against him with a hunger he'd never expected from her. There was a sound low in her throat, one he didn't recognize but that fed his own hunger, fed his need, and instinctively he lowered her to the blanket and deepened the kiss.

Need fired through him, the need to touch, to taste, to take Brenna to a place where no one could ever, ever hurt her again. Including himself. He forced himself to go slow, be gentle, when his hands wanted only to explore every inch of her.

"I'm not going to let that man touch you," he promised against her open mouth. And he wouldn't. No matter what it cost him in the end, he would not let this incredibly brave, foolishly selfless woman pay the price of his stupidity.

The words were intended to ease the horror he'd seen in her eyes, but instead she went very still. He could feel her breathing, labored, choppy, but her hands no longer curled against his flesh.

He pushed up on his arms to look down at her. "Brenna?"

She lay there with her hair fanned out beneath her, cheeks flushed, mouth wide and bruised, swollen and damp from his kisses. "No," she whispered. "This isn't about me. I'm not your problem."

The denial, soft, laced with a sickening smear of resolve, pushed him close to an edge he'd trained himself to avoid. "Problem?" The word came out harder than he'd intended, but damn it, for a woman who claimed to see what others couldn't, she wasn't very good at seeing what was right before her eyes. "Is that what you think you are?"

It was dark outside, the moon casting little light into the abandoned room, but still, a shadow washed across her face. "I wasn't part of the plan," she said, and this time it was sorrow that tinged her voice. "You said that yourself."

The hell with that. Even the boldest of defense attorneys had learned never to throw Ethan Carrington's words back in his face. Because even though she was correct in recounting what he'd said, she didn't have a damn clue what he meant. That was the problem with words. They could be shaped and twisted, forced, patched together to create any lie known to mankind. Evidence, however, didn't lie.

Holding her gaze, he took her hand and drew it to the bulge at the front of his shorts. "Does that feel like a problem to you?"

Her eyes went dark. "Yes," she whispered, but her tongue moistened her lips. "A very big problem."

Her smile, slow, tentative, stunned him. "Tell me you don't want me," he forced himself to say, because damn it, that was the right thing to do. No matter how badly he wanted her, needed her, he didn't want it to be one-sided, and even though he knew with a few more deep kisses and carefully placed touches he could make her see that this problem was a good problem, a very damn good problem, the choice had to be hers. "Tell me to stop, and I will."

She didn't want him to stop. She didn't want him to roll from her, to lose the weight of his body, so hot and hard, pressed against hers. She didn't want to go one second longer without feeling his mouth taking hers in that gentle, demanding way that was all Ethan Carrington. Only Ethan Carrington.

Without feeling what came next.

The realization robbed her of breath. She wasn't sure how they'd gotten from sitting down to dinner to lying sprawled on the blanket with Ethan propped above her, staring down at her through those penetrating eyes, desire blazing hotter and brighter than the dizzying array of stars decorating the night sky. She only knew her heart pounded and her body yearned, and the darkness she'd been waiting to press down on her, the darkness that always, always came, the darkness that had twisted Adam's passion into rage, had not come.

Brenna grasped at the frayed edges of everything she'd ever believed about herself—that she wasn't capable of this kind of intimacy, that she wanted nothing to do with the jumble of emotions swirling through her. But no matter how hard she tried to deny, to understand, to cling to what she'd once believed as gospel, denial slipped through her shaking fingers, leaving her with only the truth.

She didn't want him to stop.

The fact that he was willing to, despite the unmistakable ridge pressed into her thigh, despite the heat in his eyes, made her all the more certain.

The last time a man had stopped, it hadn't been because he'd asked her what she wanted.

It had been at the point of a gun.

"There aren't any cameras here," she whispered, glancing around the sprawling room that had once been a luxurious hotel suite. A broken marble fireplace gaped dark against the cracked plaster, like a toothless old lady.

"Cameras?" Confusion narrowed Ethan's eyes.

She swallowed hard, tried to breathe. "Cameras," she said again. "Jorak. He's not watching. We don't have to pretend."

"Pretend?" The word sounded torn out of him, ripped from somewhere dark and disbelieving, much like the word *problem* had sounded only minutes before. "Is that what you think this is about?"

She wanted to say yes. She wanted to believe yes. But the word would not form.

"I'll tell you when I was pretending," he growled, lowering himself over her. His mouth brushed hers, not in a lingering kiss but whisper soft. "Whenever I stopped," he said, placing little kisses along her jawbone, then nibbling over to her ear. "Whenever I lay awake all night holding you, rather than running my hands along your body."

Her heart kicked hard. No one had ever spoken to her like this. No one had ever touched her like this, not on the outside, certainly not on the inside. "Ethan—"

"I pretended when I made myself stop kissing you," he went on, "last night at dinner, earlier today in the *cenote*." He shifted, his big body settling between thighs she instinctively spread for him. Lifting a hand to her neck, he splayed his fingers wide. "And worst of all, I pretended last night when I found you standing in the rain but wouldn't let myself touch."

The tiny cry escaped before she realized it had formed. She'd wanted him to touch her last night. She'd stood there in the fine mist, aching, wishing the dreams that had yanked her from her sleep, the ones that had left her gasping for air, with the embers of a dying scream burning in her throat, wishing those dreams had been different dreams, dreams of the way she felt when he so much as looked at her, touched her. That he would walk up behind her and pull her into his arms, tell her—

Tell her this wasn't pretend.

"This," he said, returning his mouth to hers, "is not pretend."

And Brenna was lost. All those walls she'd tacked up between herself and the world, herself and Ethan, crumbled, and she reached for him, held him to her, let her hands run along the hard planes of his back. His flesh was hot to the touch, sending a different kind of shock wave singing through her.

"Yes," she whispered, loving the way his mouth played hers, the feel of his lips slanting against hers, their tongues rubbing. Heat arced through her, stripping away the fear she'd once felt.

"I don't want to hurt you," he said, sliding a hand to her chest, where his fingers toyed with her nipple.

"You're not," she managed, arching into his touch. She wanted to thrash, to glory in the sensation of his hands playing with her breasts, the stunning dance of color that dimmed her vision. She closed her eyes to it, let the pleasure wash through her.

Desire made her bold, whereas always before, fear had made her recoil. Now, with Ethan, she let her hands travel, as well, sliding over his buttocks, loving the firm feel of the muscles there. She wanted to feel the heat of his skin beneath his shorts, but knew that would come soon enough.

"So soft," he murmured, kissing his way along her jaw and down her neck. Longing flooded her, and again she twisted, wanting his touch in a way she'd never imagined possible. His fingers were talented, playing with her nipple, tracing small circles that made her breasts ache for so much more. The sensation streamed through her like an arrow, pooling between her legs.

"The buttons," she whispered, and he needed no more encouragement than that, just slid his hand to the column of small discs and immediately fumbled them free, allowing the cotton sundress to fall open.

She wasn't wearing a bra. She'd had one on under the nightgown she'd worn when fleeing the compound, but she'd shed the restrictive garment in the seductively dark confines of the *cenote,* and she'd not put it back on.

Cool air whispered across her exposed breasts, and lying there with her eyes closed, she waited for the return of Ethan's fingers or his mouth. But one second turned into two, two to three, and she restlessly looked up at him, found him hovering above her, staring down at her through those hot, dark eyes of his. The lines of his face had gone soft, drawing her attention to the whiskers shadowing his jaw. His lips were slightly swollen, moist.

A flash of modesty swept through her, but she forced it aside. No man had ever looked at her like this. Only one had ever seen her breasts, and he'd been all over her like a starved mongrel.

"Hey, now," Ethan said, lifting a hand to her face. "What's wrong?"

She blinked up at him, couldn't stop herself from turning her cheek into his palm. "Wrong?" Everything felt amazingly right to her.

The heat was still in his eyes, but tempered by hesitancy. Concern. "You just checked out on me."

Breathe, she told herself. Just breathe. The past was just that. That night had nothing to do with this one. Nothing to do with Ethan. "Touch me," she whispered, swallowing against the tightness in her throat. "Please."

A hard sound broke from his throat. "You're going to kill

me yet,'' he muttered, but then dipped his head toward her
chest, and his mouth opened against her nipple, his lips sucking
gently, and Brenna knew he wasn't going down alone. Pleasure
licked through her, hot, swirling, an urgent sensation that had
her wrapping her legs around his and holding on tight.

"Yes,'' she whispered, digging her fingers into his back. His
other hand was sliding down her stomach, between her legs,
and then his fingers were there, discovering just what his kisses
did to her, the heat. The wetness. He pushed inside, one finger
probing gently, sending a wave of delirium to every pulse point
in her body.

Desire and need crashed through her, blinding her to everything else. She grabbed for the fabric of his T-shirt and yanked
it up his back, toward his shoulders, working with him as he
helped her rip away the unwanted cotton. Then she slid her
hands between their bodies and fumbled with the clasp of his
shorts. Using two fingers now, he lifted his hips for hers, giving
her the access she needed to pull down the zipper.

"Easy,'' he said, but was wrong. There was nothing easy
about the frenetic rhythm of her heart, the urgency clawing at
her.

"Don't make me beg,'' she rasped, and suddenly the tongue
sliding around her nipple stopped, the fingers inside of her
stilled, and he pulled back and stared down at her, swore softy.
Almost reverently.

"You're sure?''

His voice was rough, and it did cruel, cruel things to her
heart. "I've never been more sure in my life.''

He trailed his other hand along her collarbone, then up her
neck, to her jaw, and she would have sworn she saw sorrow
flicker through his eyes. "I don't have any protection.''

She blinked, but then the haze cleared, and she realized what
he was saying. Reality slammed home, the magnitude of what
they were doing, the fact that she could create a child with this
man. *A child.* Something she'd always yearned for but quit
dreaming of years ago.

"I'm safe,'' she said after a rapid calculation of her cycle.

She felt the twist down low, the moment of protest, but didn't know whether it stemmed from fear of the unknown or acceptance of the possibilities.

From outside, a warm tropical breeze whispered over their bodies, bringing with it a soft musky scent and drawing her attention to the pounding of the surf beyond the tangle of vegetation. Ethan said nothing, though, just kept looking at her through those profoundly sad eyes.

Then he spoke. And when he did, when his hoarse voice scraped over her, the only sound she heard was that of her heart breaking. "I can't offer you tomorrow, angel. You need to know that."

Emotion scratched her throat, unearthing a truth she'd lived with for countless days and weeks, months. Years. "I stopped believing in tomorrow a long time ago." She heard the emotion drenching her voice, but didn't try to strip it away. Facts were facts, and facts were the commodity this man prized above all others. "Tonight, Ethan. That's all I want." Slowly, she lifted a hand to his face and let her fingertips trail along the stubble of his whiskers. "Can you give me that?"

He grabbed her hand, drew it to his mouth. "You deserve more."

Then give it to me!

But she'd seen the dream, seen the beach turn to red, and knew that tonight was all they had.

"Life isn't about deserving," she said. "Life is about making the most of each moment." She shifted beneath him, cradling him between her thighs. In some place deep inside her, some place buried, repressed, regret bled through, but she pushed it aside. "They're all we really have."

His eyes were dark. "Sweet Mercy," he rasped, "you deserve so much more."

Never in her wildest dreams could she have imagined that it would come to this, that she would find herself lying half naked on the floor of an abandoned luxury resort, begging the man she'd seen running down a beach drenched in red to make love to her. The first morning she'd picked up the phone and jabbed out his number with shaking fingers, she'd been driven only by the knowledge that she had to contact him. Warn him. After years of holding herself apart from the world, with nothing more than a simple touch, a gentle brush of shoulders between strangers, she'd connected with Ethan Carrington and couldn't let him walk unknowingly into the line of fire.

Now *she* stood in the line of fire, and for the first time in her life she couldn't find one single part of her body to care. To protest. Instead she smiled up at this man who'd come to her in her dreams, at the thick raven hair and gleaming green eyes, the hard jaw covered by several days' worth of whiskers, and on pure instinct, she lifted a hand to the back of his head and urged it toward hers. "Then don't say no."

Chapter 13

Ethan was a strong man. It wouldn't be hard, he told himself. Just push up from her arms and untangle their legs, roll away. Walk away. It wouldn't be hard. But as he looked at her lying beneath him, watched the moonlight play with the soft lines of her face, watched it shimmy in her eyes, not whitewashed sapphire like usual, but dark, glimmering, full of promise, he saw something else, something that completely demolished his capacity for rational thinking.

Salvation.

"Like I could." For the first time in his life, he'd flat-out lost a test. A challenge. He'd commanded himself not to touch this woman, not to complicate an already impossible situation, but as his mouth took hers, he knew he was about to go down hard.

Honor, sanity, rational thought, they crumbled like the shards of white granite beneath the weathered columns flanking the hotel. There was only need and hunger, a driving, relentless passion that blinded him to everything but the beautiful woman sprawled beneath him, a woman who had every reason, every right, to hate him, fear him, resent him. But didn't.

He moved his mouth restlessly against hers, reminding himself to go slow, when there was nothing slow about the rapid slamming of his heart. Or the thrumming of his pulse. He wanted to touch every inch of—

Touch. It hit him on a rush, the devastating impact of touch she'd told him about. "Angel," he rasped against her open mouth. Dark thoughts clouded in on him, of what this could be doing to her. "What," he managed, forcing his hand to quit caressing her breast, "about the shock waves?"

Beneath him, she again curled her legs around the backs of his thighs, again dug her nails into his back. "They're wonderful," she staggered him by saying, then stunned him even more by sliding a single hand between their bodies and finding him jutting against her thigh. She curled her fingers around his width, and slowly started to torture him.

Ethan almost lost it right then and there. In a rush he relieved her of the rest of her dress and slipped down her panties, almost groaned when he felt the moist heat of flesh pressed against his. She was the most amazing woman he'd ever known, and in a moment she would be his.

Tonight, Ethan. That's all I want.

He could give her tonight. He could give her every second of every minute of every hour. He could make them powerful, make them memorable, make them last until the sun brought the day neither of them wanted to arrive.

Emotion scratched his throat and burned the backs of his eyes. He ignored it, determined not to let tomorrow ruin the moment, the feel of Brenna twisting in his arms, squeezing him with her fingers and driving him mad with need. He sprinkled kisses along her jaw and down her neck, until he found her breasts, those beautiful full breasts with the softest pink nipples he'd ever seen. He had to taste more of them, more of her.

The moan rumbling in her throat almost pushed him over the edge. He slid his hand between her legs once again, and like the last time, found her hot and wet and ready. She un-

urled her fingers from around his thickness and stopped the
orture, shifted restlessly until he pushed against the heat.

"Your hand," he managed, fumbling through the darkness
or her fingers, threading them with his and extending their
arms over her head. "Hold on tight."

Her lips curved in a lazy smile, and he felt his heart twist,
hard. He'd never seen her like this. She'd always been so se-
ious. So grave and somber. But now she gazed up at him
through heavy-lidded, slumberous eyes, with her cheeks
flushed and her lips swollen, that gorgeous blond hair tangled
from his hands, and he damn near forgot to breathe.

"Tonight," she whispered, and he couldn't deny them any
onger, couldn't wait. He gave. He rocked his hips and pushed
inside, found her warm, tight, and pulled out a little, pushed
again. He loved the dazed look that came into her eyes, the
dark, doused look that came only from passion, and he pushed
harder, breaking through the tightness and thrusting deep inside.

Her cry, low, shocked, stopped him cold. Or maybe that was
the stark realization that he hadn't just pushed through tightness, but something else, something no other man had touched.
And for a shattering moment he couldn't think. Couldn't move.
Couldn't so much as breathe.

Brenna was a virgin. Or at least she had been, until she'd
risked her life by walking into his, only to wind up here, now,
like this, naked on the dirty floor of an abandoned hotel room,
with her dress in a heap beside her and a man on top of her,
taking a gift to which he had no right.

Shame flooded him. He pulled back from her, pulled himself
from deep within her. Or at least he tried to. Her legs, curled
around the backs of his, clamped down hard, and her hand,
fingers entwined with his, squeezed. "Ethan—"

"You should have told me." His voice broke on the words.
Something else came dangerously close to breaking on the
truth.

The light in her eyes, hazy with passion only a few minutes
before, dimmed. "Told you what?"

There was a fierce clawing inside of him, a push-pull between burying himself as deeply as possible and never letting her go, and pulling out and walking away, pretending this moment had never happened. "You've never been with a man before."

The dim light of the stars showed moisture glisten in her gaze. "Until you."

The simple honesty rocked him. "Brenna—"

"It was my choice," she whispered, lifting her free hand to his face. A finger swiped beneath his eye, and in some shell-shocked place, he felt the slide of moisture. "I wanted it to be you. Tonight."

He was still buried inside of her, and when she arched up against him, he pushed deeper. And when a soft sound of satisfaction rumbled low in her throat, he pulled out a little, thrust back in. Gently, at first, stronger as he saw the light in her eyes return, the elusive smile curve her lips.

With the moon shining in on them, they moved together. He returned his mouth to hers, kissed her deep while their bodies found a rhythm of their own. Her fingers curled into his back, and he felt her tense, felt her brace, and knew he could hold back no longer, not when he'd finally found a place where the past didn't burn, and the future didn't taunt.

He buried himself deep, and she accepted him, all of him, without question or challenge or reservation, without judgment, but with an earthy sensuality that whispered through every pore of his body. He collapsed on top of her, and when he started to roll away, her grip tightened, and she held him that way, her legs wrapped around his, her arms curled around his middle, their slick bodies joined intimately, the light of the moon spilling in on them, reminding him that soon, tomorrow would come.

But not now.

Contentment drifted through her like the foggy mists that often claimed the land surrounding her grandmother's house. On those dewy spring mornings she would steep a cup of green tea and take Gryphon out into the deeply wooded area, savor the solitude.

She didn't feel solitude now. The contentment was the same, but her body hummed with a soul-shattering vibrancy. She could literally feel the rhythm of her heart as it pounded against Ethan's, his against hers.

Outside, through the warped and peeling French doors hanging crookedly against their frame, the night had grown darker, warning that soon morning, with its palette of pinks and oranges, would break. It always happened that way. Dark always preceded light. Normally that thought brought comfort.

Now she refused to let herself imagine those first peachy hues of dawn when the birds would again start to sing.

"How?"

The question, spoken in that thick, sleepy voice of his that made her blood sing all over again, startled her. She glanced up at him, and through the darkness saw the glow of his green, green eyes. "How what?"

His hand, still against her back, slid up to tangle in her hair. "How can there have been no one?"

Her throat tightened. Even as he'd thrust deeply into her body, carrying her to a mystical place she'd only imagined existed, she'd known this moment was coming, known a man like Ethan Carrington would never be content knowing only the outcome. He would never be satisfied with a destination, not without knowing how he'd gotten there.

But while his question was from the prosecutor's bag of tricks, his voice was not the hard, take-no-prisoners tone that made him so successful in the courtroom. It was the man's voice, surprisingly hoarse, heart-stoppingly tender.

The smile started in her heart, streamed to her mouth. She'd never imagined something so complex, so impossible, could be so devastatingly easy. "It was never right before."

Confusion clouded his gaze. "I find that hard to—" He broke off abruptly, his jaw going tight. "But it has been wrong."

It took effort, but Brenna kept herself from wincing. She

wanted to roll from his arms and grab her sundress, cover herself, even though darkness concealed her nakedness. Yes, it had been wrong before. Horribly, grossly, disgustingly wrong.

"Angel," Ethan whispered, and though she didn't want to look at him, didn't want to see the truth he'd just stumbled across, when his finger tucked under her chin and he tilted her face to his, she swallowed hard and looked up into his eyes.

His voice was disturbingly quiet. "Did someone hurt you?"

Images slaked back over her, and this time she did try to pull away, but Ethan didn't let her, just held her steady and kept his eyes on hers, so intent, so…caring. "Yes." She closed her eyes to the truth, but the memories were there, as well—stark, suffocating. "I…I—" God, she'd never told anyone, not even her grandmother. "I told you about my mother."

She heard him let out a rough breath, heard the stream of hot, violent curse words under his breath.

"She wasn't just murdered. She was—"

Ethan crushed her against his chest before she could force the ugly word past her throat. His whole body engulfed her, enveloped her. He drew her between his legs and held her with his arms, but there was more, he was holding her closer than that, deeper. "Ah, God," he was murmuring. There was a sickened edge to his voice she'd never heard before, as if his heart was breaking and he didn't know how to stop it. "Ah, God, no."

For one of the few times in her life, the urge to fight, to deny, to run, did not consume her. There was only Ethan and the feel of his body against hers, the comforting words he murmured into her hair, words she'd waited a lifetime to hear. "I didn't know what it was at the time," she admitted. Just that it was ugly and wrong and…that it hurt. That she never wanted a man to touch her like that. Never wanted to feel like that. Hurt like that. Be violated like that.

"Of course you didn't," he muttered and kept stroking her, stroking, stroking, running his hands through her tangled hair. "You were seven years old."

The tears started then, a lifetime of them, rushing from her chest and scraping against her throat, spilling from her eyes. "And then Adam—"

Ethan stopped rocking her. Stopped stroking. Stopped murmuring. He eased back and took her face in his hands, killed her breath with the fierce look that streaked into his eyes. "Adam?"

She nodded, bit down on a lip that wanted to tremble. "Dave Brinker's partner."

Ethan's eyes flashed. "So help me God, if he laid one hand—"

"No." She cut him off before he could continue. "It wasn't like that." Not exactly.

He didn't move, other than the brutal tightening of his jaw. "Tell me."

Her heart kicked hard. She looked up into his eyes, then out toward the night, where the stars grew dimmer and the roar of the ocean grew softer, the breeze more gentle. Soon. Soon morning would break.

"He asked me out." She turned to look at Ethan, knew that no matter how hard it was to admit the truth, this man would settle for nothing less. She saw it in the glint to his eyes, every rigid line of the body that had loved her so thoroughly through much of the night. "I thought he was interested in me."

That was the galling part. Her own naiveté.

"And?"

"He wasn't." After all this time, shame still flooded her. "He was jealous. Jealous of the time Dave spent with me. Jealous of the partnership we'd formed."

Ethan swore softly.

"We went out several times." Dinner, movies, all the normal things she'd never done. "I never realized he'd wedged himself between me and Dave until it was too late. I thought the three of us were working together, that the information I was giving Adam, he was also feeding to Dave."

Ethan closed his eyes, opened them a moment later. "But he wasn't?"

"I should have seen it," she said, and this time she did pull away, push to her feet. She stood and walked to the French doors, stood there naked against the waning tone of the night. "I should have realized he was only using me."

Ethan came up behind her and put his hands, so big and capable yet heartbreakingly gentle, to her shoulders, drew her against his chest. "Don't blame yourself."

"One night we went back to his place." She forced the words out. "He put on some music and we were dancing, and then he was kissing me." Against her shoulders, she felt Ethan's hold on her tighten. "I…I tried," she said, then turned in his arms to look into his eyes. "For once in my life I wanted to be normal."

His mouth curved into a sad smile. "You're perfect just the way you are."

The words, rough, quiet, seeped through her skin and shimmied around her heart, brought an ache that made it hard to breathe. "I let him undress me."

She wasn't sure what she expected from Ethan, but he just looked at her, looked steady, like he was bracing himself for what came next. The prosecutor, she knew. Waiting for the rest of the story.

She forced herself to swallow. "I let him touch me."

The muscle in the hollow of Ethan's jaw started to twitch, but still he said nothing, just stood there, naked and waiting.

The old Brenna would have looked away from him then. The old Brenna would have aborted her story and retreated into that place where no one could hurt her, ever, ever again. But standing there in a whispery pool of fading moonlight, she realized she didn't want to retreat. Not from this man.

"It hit me so hard," she blurted out. Her voice broke but she didn't care. "All at once, it was like a sledgehammer coming down on me, and everything I hadn't let myself see before flared to life in vibrant, horrible color." She'd gone still at first as the images flashed through her mind at dizzying speed, blurred at first, the edges sharpening with each sickened thud of her heart. Then she'd started to back away. "There was so much ugliness in that man, I don't know how I didn't see it to begin with."

Finally the hard lines of Ethan's face softened. "He seduced you."

"That's no excuse," she bit out, appalled because he was right. She'd been so gullible. "It happened fast, like a dam breaking. As soon as I saw him for the man he was, I saw other things, other images, and I knew, God I—" She gagged on the words, the memory, but Ethan never faltered, just held her steady. "I realized all the information I'd been giving him about the suburban slayer had stayed with him."

Ethan's jaw tightened. "What information?"

Her lungs shut down on her. "That he knew. That the slayer knew we were on to him."

Ethan swore softly.

"Adam had told me he'd sent my grandmother into protective custody that afternoon, but standing there naked in his bedroom, with him all hard and leering at me, I knew he'd lied to me, and that my grandmother wasn't safe. That Dave's wife—"

Ethan pulled her into his arms and buried his face against her tangled hair. "Christ have mercy," he swore under his breath. "That's when it happened."

She wrapped her arms around the thickness of his waist and held on. "That night." She paused, tried to put distance between herself and the memory, couldn't. "I tried to leave, to get to them in time, to warn them, but Adam wouldn't let me. He told me I was crazy, a freak, imagining things." She paused, pulled back to meet Ethan's eyes. "That's when I pulled his gun."

Ethan looked down at her a long time before a smile slowly curved his lips. "That's my girl."

"He didn't think I'd use it," she told him, "but I knew how to shoot, and when I missed his groin by half an inch, he changed his tune."

A low rumble broke from Ethan's throat.

"I forced him into the bathroom, secured a chair against the doorjamb, then got out of there as fast as I could."

The smile, the pride, that had been lighting Ethan's face dimmed. "But it was too late."

She looked down, saw their two bodies pressed intimately together, hers soft and pale, his hard and tanned. "Yes."

His hands returned to her hair. "I'm so damn sorry."

"I was an idiot to trust him, to let myself get involved." She fought back the ancient grief. "To think for one second that I could have a normal relationship."

He stabbed a hand into her hair, then tilted her face so she had no choice but to see the light burning in his eyes. "Then what's this?" he asked hoarsely.

Tears blurred her vision, but not the truth. "This is tonight," she said, pushing up on her toes and pressing her mouth to his. In some distant corner of her mind she heard the low growl in his throat, but rather than discouraging her, it sent even more urgency spearing through her. She opened her mouth and ran her tongue along his, her knees almost buckling when he opened to her, let her in.

"Angel," he murmured, backing her against the door, where the warm breeze spilled in and the moon rained down, beyond which the ocean roared like the blood through her veins. Feverishly she ran her hands along the hard planes of his body, and when his knee nudged her thighs apart, she didn't protest, instead she opened to him as he'd opened to her, let him in.

"Tonight," she whispered, shutting her eyes to the first pinkish strains of dawn pushing up from the tangle of dense vegetation. "Tonight."

Against a carpet of sand so white, so sugary it defied logic and possibility, the turquoise surf crashed with increasing urgency. Wave after wave, breaking hard, foaming, washing up over the sand, then abruptly pulling back, leaving a fleeting glimmer before the next onslaught.

The flash of red hit without warning. A churning wave of it, surging up from the horizon and sloshing over the beach, washing away the serenity. Seagulls, mildly dipping for fish moments before, squawked and hurried away. Gunfire exploded.

He was running then, shouting, swearing through the sudden crush of darkness. "Stand down!" he roared. "It's over."

The flash of sunlight blinded with the force of an explosion, but still she saw him, a tall man in torn cargo shorts and no shirt, running against an impossibly blue horizon. He wasn't looking back. Wasn't paying attention to the MP-5Ns suddenly raised in his direction. He just kept running, shouting, the surf sucking at his legs.

From behind him, a small Latino man tackled him, and he staggered, went down hard. Refusing to stop, he pushed to his hands and knees and lunged forward.

He never saw the gun. The explosion of white blinded her, blanketed her, snuffed out her voice and her breath...

"No!"

On the blanket thrown haphazardly against a concrete floor, Brenna jerked herself awake. Her heart crashed in her chest with painful precision, hard, urgent, violent like the surf breaking beyond the tangle of forgotten vegetation. Sweat and the damp dew of morning bathed her naked, slightly sore body. Struggling to breathe, she lifted a hand to her burning throat, fully expecting to find a rope constricting her breath.

"Ethan."

The sense of abandonment sliced in first. She surged to her feet and spun around the forgotten hotel suite, saw the morning sun spilling against weathered plaster and bare floors, the gaping, empty fireplace, the truth.

Sex was one thing, and sex was good, but Ethan was not a man to allow anything more. She knew this. With him revenge, justice, evidence, always came first. He didn't believe in things that couldn't be touched or seen, and the unchained urgency swirling through her definitely fell into that category. She couldn't blame him. She didn't trust feelings, either.

The horrible chain of events she'd seen in her dreams, the violent confrontation she'd been trying to prevent, was coming to pass. Ethan had left her, returned to Jorak.

And the woman on the beach.

Pain stabbed into her throat, churned in her stomach. She grabbed the blanket and wrapped it around her body, wondered what foolish notion had led her to believe, for one fraction of one second, that this time would be different.

Tomorrow always, always came.

"Tell me, my friend. Did you not find my accommodations satisfactory?"

"You know me," Ethan said with an indifferent shrug. "I get edgy if I'm cooped up too long."

Standing along the edge of the beach, wearing another of his ridiculous white suits, this one with a blood-red rose tucked in the breast pocket, Jorak Zhukov smiled. "You always did like running in the dead of night," he mused, but then his eyes hardened. "We will find her, you know."

The urge to struggle against the two men holding his arms behind his back was strong, but now was not the time to fight. Brenna was safe. He'd seen to that. She'd been sleeping soundly when he left. The sight of her curled on the blanket, with just a whisper of sunlight surrounding her, had all but shredded him, but he'd forced himself to fold the blanket over her and turn away, walk away. It was the right thing to do. The only thing to do.

By the time she awoke and realized what was going down, everything would be over. "This doesn't concern her."

Jorak swiped sand from the linen of his suit. "You made it concern her," he said, then cocked his head skyward.

Ethan heard it, too, the low hum of an engine. The helicopter, he knew. The one that would land soon and kick the rest of his plan into motion.

"It is time, yes?" Jorak asked, returning his attention to Ethan. He squinted against the bright morning sun. "I hope you said your prayers last night."

The laugh came all by itself, low, guttural. "Something like that." He'd lain there in the darkness, with Brenna's body draped around his, the thoughts in his mind blurring into a chant. *Let her be okay. Let her make it out of this alive. Let her find the happiness she deserves.*

"How do you live with yourself?" Jorak asked, his voice pitched low. The helicopter came into view then, a state-of-the-art piece of military refinement. "How do you look at yourself every morning and know that you killed your best friend?"

Ethan felt his jaw go tight. "I didn't kill her."

Jorak's face, once marked by the strong, handsome lines of his Eastern European heritage, now gaunt and ravaged by his time on the run, twisted. "I still hear her scream. At night. When I'm lying in my bed, I still feel her in my arms. See the confusion in her eyes when the door burst open." He paused as the helo hovered over the beach, sending a hard spray of sand against them. "Hear her scream when she went down."

Remorse clogged Ethan's throat. "Maybe you should have thought of that before you lied to all of us."

Jorak watched the chopped set down. "And maybe you should have thought of that before you sicced the FBI on us."

"Trust me." Adrenaline kicked hard. "I did."

Jorak said nothing, just kept watching. The sun glared down on them, insanely hot for the early hour, the burning rays not even diluted by the steady breeze. The sea, impossibly turquoise, crashed against the beach. A trio of seagulls dipped for their breakfast, completely oblivious to what was about to go happen.

"Well, well, well," Jorak mused, and something about his voice, the abject pleasure, almost a lover's purr, sliced into the steady thrumming of Ethan's heart. He turned toward the man he'd once called friend, saw him smiling, not at the helicopter, but toward the edge of the beach. "Two guesses what she spent the night doing."

Time stopped. Or maybe that was just Ethan's heart. He followed Jorak's gaze, saw the two armed guards, saw her. The sun glinted down on her tangled blond hair, illuminated the flush on her complexion. Her sundress, a pretty white cotton he'd grabbed for her the night before, hung on her body, dirty and torn.

The wave of red staggered him. It clouded his line of vision, obliterated all the plans, all the deliberate pieces he'd so carefully aligned. There was only Brenna and the truth.

"No!" On a violent twist, he broke from the guards holding him and ran, shouted, swore, fought his way through the cloying blanket of darkness. He had to reach her, reach her fast. Before the man with whom he'd once broken bread broke something else that could never be replaced.

"Stand down!" he roared, peripherally aware of the door to the helicopter opening. "It's over."

The flash of sunlight blinded him, but still he saw her, a slim silhouette against the impossibly blue horizon. She wasn't moving. Wasn't running, wasn't taking cover. She just stood there, her flimsy dress flapping wildly, the surf crashing against her calves.

Pain exploded against the base of his skull. He staggered, went down hard, refused to stop. He pushed to his hands and knees and lunged forward.

He saw the gun too late. The explosion of white blinded him, blanketed him, snuffed out his voice and his breath...

"No!"

Her voice carried to him on the hot breeze. Sand stung his eyes and burned his body, but he pushed up anyway. Somewhere close by was another hum, louder, louder, and when Ethan went to push himself up, Jorak's foot came down on his back and pressed him hard to the sand.

"I warned you," he said, and his voice no longer sounded mild, cultured, but hard and deadly. "I warned you what would happen if you betrayed me."

Ethan bit back the coppery taste of blood. "I know the consequences of betrayal."

At the other end of the beach, the second helicopter, this one a military-issue Black Hawk, touched down, sending another wall of hot sand against them.

"Bring her here," Jorak barked, and Ethan twisted to see the guards pushing Brenna toward them. She walked with her head high and her shoulders straight, looking achingly beautiful despite the ugliness unfolding around her. Ethan saw no fear in her eyes, only a calm acceptance that ripped at his gut.

Jorak held out his hand, and immediately one of the guards placed a black semiautomatic into his palm. "Now she pays."

Dark spots clouded Ethan's vision. He struggled to see, to breathe. To think. This wasn't how it was supposed to go down. "Wait," he gritted out, twisting beneath Jorak's foot. "The person you've been searching for, the reason you brought me here, is on that helicopter." He tried to suck in air, got hot sand instead. "Kill her and you'll never have the answers you want."

Jorak narrowed his eyes. "Do I strike you as a fool?"

"No," Ethan said, fighting for control. His whole life, damn it. Practically his whole life he'd masked his emotions, stretched tape over the gaping cracks through which volatility wanted to seep. Now everything he'd learned betrayed him. "You strike me as a man who's waited a long time for answers."

Jorak's mouth flattened to a hard line. He stared down at Ethan a long moment, then lifted his foot, but kept the gun trained on his chest.

Ethan got to his knees first, then pushed up to his feet. Brenna was so close now, so close he swore he could almost smell the musky scent that had intoxicated him during the long hours of the night. So close the semiautomatic would blow her away. There were no emotions on her face, only a trickle of scratches, mud, and a red spot on her neck, from where he'd loved her a little too intensely.

They urge—*the need*—to touch staggered him. Somehow he squelched the hot surge of emotion and focused on the Black Hawk, where two heavily armed men in fatigues emerged through an open door. Two men he'd been plotting with for months. Two men he trusted with his life.

And with the life of the woman he loved.

Hawk Monroe stepped into the sand first. His strong, Viking face was a stony mask, betraying none of the driving emotion he normally wore for the world. Behind him, Sandro Vellenti reached back into the helicopter, then urged a third figure into view. Slight. Dressed in all black. Hooded.

Anticipation drummed through Ethan, hot and hard and ridiculously sweet. This. God, this was the moment he'd been waiting for, hungering for, craving for over five long years. He'd planned it so meticulously....

His two future brothers-in-law, men trained for combat but driven by honor and loyalty, escorted the hooded figure across the glowing sand, the naked morning sun burning down on all of them. The seagulls had returned, dipped gracefully behind the trio. The wind whipped sand into a frenzy.

Twenty-five feet away, Hawk and Sandro stopped.

From out of nowhere, more of Jorak's men swarmed the trio, all heavily armed, ready to shoot.

Ethan squinted against the sun and met Sandro's eyes, gave a silent nod of his head, and the other man, a former special forces operative, pulled the black hood from the figure's head.

Long, silky blond hair whipped in the breeze. Her skin was soft, like peaches, he'd always thought, but her eyes, eyes that had once shone with friendship and hope and love, burned hot.

And Jorak...the man she'd pledged to honor and love for all the days of her life, dropped to his knees.

Chapter 14

Ethan wanted to feel satisfaction. He wanted to feel the sweet kiss of triumph. But standing beneath the glare of the hot Yucatan sun, watching the complete lack of emotion on Allison's face, he felt only the bitter tug of regret.

Once this woman had been like a sparkler on the Fourth of July. Bright. Vibrant. Full of life. But Jorak Zhukov had changed that. Snuffed it out forever.

He looked at the man now, looked at him kneeling in the sand, staring at Allison through stricken eyes as if she were a cruel apparition, and knew it was time.

"A trade," he said coldly. He hadn't wanted it to come to this. He hadn't wanted to involve Ally. But she'd insisted, said it was the only way. "A woman for a woman."

Brenna forced herself not to move. Not to make a sound. Not to reveal a single sliver of the shock screaming through her. This, dear God. This. This was what she'd been seeing for weeks now. Ethan on the beach, the woman in the distance.

The dress was wrong, but everything else was excruciatingly right.

Allison was alive. She'd survived.

She was the woman for whom Ethan would give his life.

The wind whipped hot sand against Brenna's face, but still she stood, and still she watched. It *was* like viewing a movie, a hated, disgusting movie. A movie to which she knew the ending, despite how many times, how many ways, she'd tried to rewrite the final scene. Her heart ached as she watched Ethan standing there, the raw emotion on his face as he looked toward Allison.

The burning hatred as he focused on the man who'd betrayed them all.

She wanted to touch him. The need burned like a physical pain. It was the ultimate irony. She who had spent a lifetime avoiding human contact, now craved it with a single-mindedness that stunned her.

Because she knew. She'd felt Ethan's pain. She'd experienced this moment with him in her dreams over and over and over. She knew how hard his heart pounded. She knew the violent kick of adrenaline. She'd felt the unbendable will, the determination to do whatever it took, even give his own life, to keep the woman he loved safe.

She also knew what came next. And that's why she'd run from the decaying hotel. That's why she'd made enough noise for Jorak's men to find her. That's why she stood there now, still as a statue, waiting.

The future isn't etched in stone. It's fluid, ever changing. Something to be cherished, not feared.

Chest tight, throat burning, eyes stinging from the hot spray of sand, Brenna watched Jorak hiss out a low breath and stagger to his feet, walk toward his wife as though pulled by an invisible rope. The slim woman, once blue-blood beautiful, now ravaged by a ferocity that came only through betrayal, watched him approach, her expression never revealing a hint of any of the emotion Brenna sensed churning beneath the placid surface. Not the contempt. Not the rage. Not the love that had long since twisted into fragments of hatred.

"Allison," Jorak muttered, and reached for her. She stepped from between the two stone-faced men and let her husband put a hand to her face, let him push the hair from her cheek.

And Brenna shivered. She knew what that man's touch brought. She knew what it revealed. What he'd done.

"I thought—" he began in a thick voice, but Allison cut him off.

"I know," she said, and finally, Brenna caught the first betrayal of emotion in her steely eyes. "But it was all a lie."

Jorak's hand slid to cradle her cheek. "The child?"

"A boy," she whispered. "I buried him next to Mama."

From her vantage point twenty-five feet away, Brenna saw the revelation hit Jorak like a powerful physical blow. He swayed, but Allison reached out to steady him.

Brenna slid her gaze to Ethan, saw him make eye contact with the man with the dark blond hair pulled into a ponytail, then the fierce looking man with the olive skin and midnight eyes. It was all fleeting, fast, and within a heartbeat she noticed four heavily armed agents slipping from behind the big black helicopter to fan across the beach.

"They put me into witness protection," Allison told her husband in a voice that no longer shimmied with enthusiasm, but rasped from what sounded like damaged vocal cords.

Jorak swore hotly. "I never knew—"

"There's no way you could have." The wind slapped against her outfit of all black, smearing the cotton fabric against the outline of her body.

Brenna braced herself, but nothing prepared her for Ethan to turn to her, the hot, edgy look in his normally penetrating eyes. He seemed to be telling her something, something urgent, but though she sensed the importance, she didn't understand.

"Dimetri," Allison said, breaking the moment, "I've dreamed of this moment for years." Confusion doused Brenna, confusion at the purr of the other woman's voice, a stark contrast to the glitter to her eyes. "Hungered." Then she pulled the gun.

And Brenna knew.

But Jorak didn't seem to understand. He didn't move, didn't flinch. He just kept staring into the eyes of the woman he'd betrayed in the most heinous ways imaginable, to whom he'd lied, almost gotten killed.

Two of Jorak's men saw, though, and they surged closer, shouted in warning. But still Jorak didn't move.

Allison lifted the semiautomatic, pointed it at his chest. "Dreamed of justice," she amended. "Dreamed of making you pay."

One of the guards charged, but Jorak waved him away. "No!"

"It was me," Allison said, and the last hideous piece clicked into place. All the emotion, the pain, the contempt Brenna sensed had festered for seven long years, bubbled over. "I was the informant. I was the one who discovered your double life, your deception." Her lips lifted into what could only be called a snarl. "I was the one who went to Ethan."

Brenna's heart staggered at the revelation. The irony. This woman, this woman he loved, whose death he sought to avenge, was in fact the one he'd been hunting, had wanted to kill, since the night his lies had caught up with him.

The one he blamed for her death, rather than blaming himself.

"It's time," she said, and pulled back the trigger.

Jorak staggered back, but her shot was never fired. One of the guards tackled her from behind, and all hell broke loose. Jorak roared to his feet and turned toward Ethan, lifted his MP-5N and fired.

Brenna didn't stop to think.

The future isn't etched in stone.

She didn't stop to decide.

It's fluid, ever changing.

There really was no choice to make. Not anymore. Not when every thought she'd had for the past two weeks, every hot, aching breath she'd drawn, every beat of her heart, every shock wave, had all propelled her toward this moment. This man.

Something to be cherished, not feared.

She lunged.

One second stretched, snapped, broke into a fractured lifetime. A lifetime that had begun with a phone call in the dead of night, a lifetime that had taken on new meaning when she stepped from behind the sycamore tree. A lifetime that had forced him to look into mirrors, see truths, experience feelings, for the first damn time.

Peripherally, Ethan saw Sandro running, heard Sandro shouting, but the impact never came. Not of the bullet. Only of the woman, the weight of her soft body against his. He staggered back and fell. She collapsed on top of him.

He instinctively rolled, shielded her from the spray of bullets. He would give his life, he knew, his life, to keep her safe. Sandro tossed him a weapon, and then Ethan was firing, his future brother-in-law hunched down beside him. The rapid-fire of gunshots drowned out the squawk of seagulls, the crash of the surf. Smoke swirled on the hot breeze. And still Ethan fired. So did Sandro. So did Hawk. Until there was only quiet.

Ethan coughed against the oppressive smell of gunpowder and blinked hard, cleared his vision, saw Jorak sprawled on the sand, red pooling around him. Allison was on her knees by his side, the gun loose in her limp hand. All across the beach, federal agents rounded up Jorak's men.

Finally, at last, it was over.

"It's okay, now," Ethan said, turning toward Brenna. Hot words burned his mouth, the sickening reality of what could have happened to her when she'd foolishly thrown her body in front of his. "You can get up—"

But she couldn't. Not when she lay behind him sprawled in the shimmering white sand, with a sickening smear of red spreading across the white cotton of her sundress.

His heart, pounding rapidly moments before, stopped. Just

stopped. He crawled toward her, shouted at Sandro. "We need help!"

"Angel," he murmured, reaching her and running his hands over her hot, gritty body. The truth staggered him. She'd knowingly thrown her body in front of a bullet. For him. "Why—"

"Had to," she murmured. Pain glazed her eyes. "T-told you. C-couldn't let you d-die."

The broken words slayed him. Quietly. Brutally. She *had* told him. She'd told him that from the very beginning. *I'm here because I couldn't let you walk into danger without warning you.*

God.

The frenzy around him faded to nothingness. He pulled her in his lap and cradled her against his chest and rocked, just rocked, murmuring nonsensical words as hot sand stung his face and hot moisture burned his eyes.

He was alive. She could feel him holding her, the warmth and vitality of his body, hear the low pitch of his voice, that thick, rough Virginia drawl that made her blood sing.

Her throat burned with words that wanted to be said, but the effort required too much energy. She'd been holding on long enough as it was. Holding on forever, it seemed, trying to atone, trying to prove her grandmother hadn't lied to her.

You were right, she thought as a flash of white blinded her, and then there she was, her granny, not lying in the pool of blood like she'd seen her so many times when she sought only the solace of sleep, but standing on the front porch in a pink flowered apron with a pitcher of lemonade in her hands. And the smile on her face, bright, welcoming, ethereal, resounded through Brenna like a blast of eternity.

She'd been right, her granny had. The future wasn't etched in stone. Brenna hadn't been able to save her mother or the head cheerleader, she hadn't saved the little boy a monster ripped from his mother's arms, she hadn't seen Adam for who he was, and she hadn't saved her grandmother, Dave's wife,

God, Dave himself, but finally, at last, she'd come through in the end.

Ethan was safe.

She saw them all then, on her grandmother's porch in a semicircle of white so bright, so pure it made her heart ache. Her mother and grandmother. The children. Dave and his wife, arm in arm, smiling, as deeply in love as they'd always been.

And finally, quietly, to the low murmur of Ethan's voice and the broken thrumming of his heart, the steady rocking, the gentle stroking of his hand, she let go.

"She should be awake by now, damn it."

"She lost a lot of blood. She'll wake up when it's time."

"It's been four days."

"I know." Miranda Carrington looked from the ominously still woman on the bed, the tubes running to and from her slim body, back to her brother, who sat in a chair dragged as close as physical space would allow. "They say she's going to be okay, though, Eth. You have to remember that."

He scrubbed a hand over his face. "She won't even move. It's as though she doesn't want to."

His sister sighed, reached for his hand. "You won't do her any good wearing yourself down to nothing."

"She's right, you know," came a soft voice from behind him. "Sooner or later you have to go home and get some rest."

He twisted to see Elizabeth, who'd entered the room without him even hearing, and love squeezed his heart. His family didn't even know Brenna, but they'd been standing by his side every minute of every hour since he'd stepped from the military airplane. "Am I being ganged up on?"

Elizabeth's smile was soft, sympathetic. "Maybe."

"Definitely," Miranda corrected. It was dreary outside, a drab fall day, but she lit up the room like a psychedelic light. "Not to be cruel, but frankly you look like hell and we—"

"I don't give a damn how I look."

The second the words were out of his mouth, the second he

saw her wince, the light in her sparkling eyes dim, he regretted his words. "Ah, hell, Mira, I'm sorry."

Elizabeth breezed to his side and squatted so that she looked him in the eye. "A shower and a shave, a nap in your own bed, clean clothes. That's all we ask."

"I'll stay with her," Miranda volunteered. "In case she wakes up while you're gone." She lifted her mobile phone. "I'll call you before a second can pass."

The weary breath escaped all by itself. A shower. A shower sounded like heaven. And maybe he could use some sleep. God knew he'd had very little since they'd returned to Richmond. The doctors had operated well into the night to remove the bullet that had slammed into her gut but missed all vital organs. They'd expected her to open her eyes within hours.

Instead it had been days.

"It should be me in this bed," he growled, and hot remorse burned the back of his throat. For years he'd hungered for justice, to see Jorak Zhukov brought down, to see Allison freed from the prison of the past. Both goals had been achieved, but the emptiness inside didn't go away. It festered.

Elizabeth's hand squeezed his knee. "But it's not you, Eth." Her touch was as soft as her smile. "And as much as you wish you could change things, you have to realize you're not doing her any good punishing yourself like this."

"She knew." Ethan looked from Elizabeth to Miranda. Still, even after replaying the scene on the beach hundreds of times, the truth staggered him. "She knew what was going to happen that day, but she came to me anyway."

Miranda smiled. "She sounds pretty special."

His sisters didn't know the half of it. He hadn't, either. Not at first.

"Come on," Elizabeth said, taking his hand and dragging him to his feet. "Just for a few hours."

She was right and he knew it, but that didn't make walking away easier. He leaned over the bed and took Brenna's pale, lifeless hand, squeezed gently, then brushed a kiss over lips dry and cracked, despite the balm he'd been applying every few hours.

"Come back to me," he murmured. "Come back."

She didn't want to wake up. She didn't want to see Ethan standing like a soldier over her bed, staring down at her through those penetrating eyes of his. She didn't want to feel his hand on her body, the intensity of his touch.

She didn't want to feel the ache in her heart, the stinging reality that it was time to say goodbye.

But she had no choice. She had no idea how long she'd drifted, aware of her family on one side, Ethan on the other. Every time she'd gravitated toward her grandmother, her mother, she'd feel Ethan's hand squeeze hers, hear his low sexy drawl, and as though he possessed an invisible rope, he pulled her back.

Pain hurt less, her grandmother had told her, when it was fast, like a bandage ripped from her skin rather than eased away one millimeter at a time. Brenna knew that.

But the sight of him hurt. Her eyes were dry, gritty, the room washed in what had to be early-morning sun, but still she saw him, not standing, but sprawled in a chair dragged close to the bed. She knew he'd gone home to shave at some point, but dark whiskers again shadowed his jaw. His mouth was slightly open. His hair badly needed a cut. His eyes were closed.

She swallowed against a dry throat and wanted to just drink him in, savor the moment. Even in his sleep he looked alive and vital, strong.

Even in his sleep guilt glowed like an unwanted badge of honor.

He wore a wrinkled gray button-down, untucked. His jeans were well-worn, threadbare, torn in a few spots. She wouldn't have thought the man even owned such ratty clothes.

And in his hand he held her grandmother's necklace, the Celtic cross dangling from his fingertips.

Deep inside, she sighed. Emotion bled from her heart and tightened in her chest, burned her throat. She hadn't known.

She hadn't known it possible to love like this, so deeply and intently, so purely. So wholly.

"Brenna."

The sound of his voice washed over her like a gentle caress. Before her heart could so much as beat, he was out of the chair and propped on the side of the narrow bed, reaching for her hand, despite the IV needle jutting from one of her veins. "God, angel, you're awake."

She didn't want to smile. She didn't want to feel. But she might as well have tried to block the sun from streaming through the window. "You look like hell."

He laughed. It was a wonderful sound, one she'd never heard from this driven man, who worked so hard to keep his deepest desires from the world, rich and lyrical, with a hint of lazy Virginia good ol' boy, and it streamed through every cell of her body. "You look beautiful."

The words did cruel, cruel things to her heart. "W-water?"

He automatically reached for a pitcher by the bed, poured water into a cup, grabbed a straw and brought it to her dry, cottony mouth. "Drink."

She did. The liquid felt wonderful sliding down her throat and moistening her vocal chords. "Allison?" she asked.

His gaze darkened. "Let's not talk about that."

The scene on the beach played through her mind, like it had so many times as she'd hovered in that foggy place where she was aware of all that happened around her but somehow seemed disconnected from it. "Is she okay?"

"She's fine," he clipped out. "It's you—"

"You should be with her."

Ethan squeezed her hand. "I'm where I need to be."

Need. The word was sweet, but not what she wanted to hear. *I can't give you tomorrow.* Her heart clenched. She knew that. She'd always known that. And she didn't want to be a duty to this man, a cross to bear. She wanted—

God, she wanted.

"S-sleepy," she murmured, and heard the thickness to her own voice.

Ethan's expression lightened, a smile replacing gravity. "Rest, then." He leaned over and brushed his mouth over hers. "There's plenty of time for talking later."

Groggily she gazed up at him, felt her eyelids grow heavy, saw his image blur. "You…rest…too."

"What do you mean 'she's gone'?"

The nurse, a tall, dark-haired woman with sympathetic eyes, glanced at the orderly, then back at Ethan. "Just that," she said. "I came on duty this morning, but she wasn't in her room."

Ethan bit back the first thing that came to his tongue, then glared from the vacant hospital bed to the bright batch of sunflowers in his hand. "For the past two days she's barely been able to talk for ten minutes without falling asleep." His fingers tightened around the innocent stems of the flowers. "Now you're telling me she just got up and walked away?"

The nurse winced. "It's highly unusual."

Deep inside, something started to tear. "I want to talk to whoever's in charge."

"Maybe this will help," the nurse volunteered, handing him a piece of folded paper. "We found it on her pillow."

He took the scrap of white and opened it, stared down at the shaky handwriting. Two words. Two little words, but they told Ethan everything.

Tomorrow came.

Swearing softly, he dropped the flowers and walked from the room.

Chapter 15

Beneath a bloodred sky, Ethan slowed his car as he approached the wood-frame house deep in the outskirts of Richmond. It would have been easy to miss, if he hadn't been looking so intently. Oaks surrounded the structure like an army. Even the wraparound, screened front porch seemed protective, designed to shield occupants from the world at large.

"I'm sorry," Doc Magiver had said an hour earlier. "We haven't seen Bree since she got back to Richmond."

The older man had been reluctant to disclose her address, but in the end Ethan had prevailed. Now he turned off his ignition and stepped from the car, let the soft bite of fall wind surround him.

This was where she lived.

He surveyed the land, only a short drive from downtown proper, but seemingly a world away. There was a stillness to the homestead, a blanket of quiet wrinkled only by the occasional rustle of the wind, call of a bird.

It stunned him how hard his heart was beating. He couldn't remember the last time he'd been nervous. It was an emotion, a vulnerability he'd taught himself not to feel. But sleepless nights had a way of erasing longstanding lessons. So did reality.

He started toward the porch, acutely conscious of the crunching of his shoes against the gravel. He heard the dog bark first, fast and high, only moments before he saw the blur of black and white.

The Dalmatian rushed around the corner and skidded to a stop in front of Ethan, immediately stood up to slap two front paws against his sweatshirt. "Hey, boy," he greeted, taking hold of the paws. Then he stared. This dog, with its bright eyes and soft moist nose, with a full belly and a strong, whipping tail, this was the half-starved, beaten pup he'd found along the James. The one he'd taken to Doc Magiver that hot steamy night, when he'd first seen Brenna standing behind a counter, when her whitewashed sapphire eyes had seared into him, when he'd forcibly brushed against her while walking to an exam room.

"Look at you," he murmured, taking in the dog's obvious health. He slid a hand to his neck, where blood no longer seeped from a nasty wound. Only scar tissue now, a bright red collar.

The hope caught him by surprise. If the dog was here—

The screen door pushed open with an obvious groan, and a striking young woman emerged to stand on the top concrete step. "Sailer, down," she clipped in firm tones.

The Dalmatian dropped to all four paws, but kept gazing up at Ethan through wide, expectant eyes. His tail swished with unmistakable strength.

"Sorry about him," the woman with the long, glossy black hair said. She took another step toward Ethan. "Can I help you with something?"

Familiarity niggled at him as he stared at her. Tall, willowy, dark hair and dark skin…but the eyes. Whitewashed sapphire. And his heart staggered hard. "I'm Ethan Carrington."

She put her hands to her hips. "I wondered how long it would take."

The blunt response made him smile. "I'm here for Brenna."

The sparkle in her eyes, a sparkle he'd rarely seen from Brenna, abruptly faded. "Well, she's not here for you."

More blunt words, but these didn't make him smile. He felt his body go tight. "I'll wait."

"Won't do you any good," she said, taking another step. The cool breeze whipped dark hair around her face. "Bree's gone, and I don't expect she'll be back anytime soon."

Ethan just stood there, the dog at his feet and the wind at his face, but saw only the truth. The note. "Tomorrow came," she'd written, but he could no longer deny what she'd meant. Goodbye.

He shoved a hand in his pocket where he found her silver chain, and his fingers curled around the weathered Celtic cross. The only tangible proof she'd ever walked into, then out of, his life. He didn't need the cross, though. He didn't need that piece of evidence, not when she'd left her mark on every corner of his life. Every corner of himself. He felt her with him with every breath he drew, every beat of his heart.

At night, when he stood at his window and stared into the darkness of Monument Park across the street, he saw only her, as she'd been the last night they'd been together, when she'd given him a gift he hadn't come close to deserving. Then sometimes he'd see her there on the beach, with the warm breeze whipping the dress around her ankles, that cruel, punishing moment when the plan he'd pieced together had shattered and nothing mattered but getting to her before Jorak had the chance to hurt her.

His throat burned. He stared at the woman who looked so like her, but wasn't her, and felt the bleed start deep, spread fast.

I stopped believing in tomorrow a long time ago.

He ran hard. He ran fast. He ran with the single-minded intensity of a man with nowhere to go but an urgent need to get there. He ran with no regard for the exhaustion screaming through his body. No acknowledgment of the cold bite of the wind or the fine mist falling softly against his hot, exposed skin.

Snow, the weatherman had promised. The first snow of the season. Damn early, but Ethan didn't care. He pushed himself harder, farther, his feet pounding on a decaying carpet of leaves, no longer red and orange from their fiery fall show, but brown and decaying. To his left the James ran unusually fast over the network of flat rocks, and in some hazy place of his mind, he wondered whether the water would bite or sting, or whether he would feel it at all.

Six weeks. It was November. Thanksgiving lurked just around the corner. Then Christmas. Then Miranda's wedding. His parents were back from Ravakia. His sisters were a blur of constant activity as they prepared for the festivities. They fussed over him, as well, refusing to take a hint and back off.

And still Ethan ran. Jorak was dead. It was hard to believe that the man who had defined Ethan's life for seven long years had gone down in a gunfight on a beach off the coast of Mexico. Hard to believe that the moment Ethan had craved for so long had passed with barely more than a ripple on Ethan's life. Hard to believe that too late he'd discovered he'd let Jorak control him all these years. He'd brought the man down, but as Ethan kicked in the last quarter mile of his daily five-mile run, he felt as though Jorak had gotten the last laugh after all.

Night came early this time of year, and the daylight of thirty minutes before had faded into shadow. The trees stretched up against the dark-crimson sky like shadowy specters, naked now, exposed, much as Ethan's heart had been since walking into the brightly lit hospital room to find the bed empty. An increasingly cold breeze rattled through their branches. Glaring at them, Ethan pushed himself through an invisible finish line.

And went very still.

Very, horribly still.

He could still see her standing there, beneath the branches of the ancient sycamore. She looked small, dwarfed by a mammoth dark-brown trunk that made her look more like a doll than a woman. Dressed all in black she blended with the night, but for the fall of silky blond hair. The dog sat at her feet—

Ethan blinked hard. There'd been no dog that muggy fall evening when his world had tilted on its axis. There'd been only the woman, standing in just that spot, staring at him in just that manner.

The adrenaline that had fueled his run surged anew. He sucked in a choppy breath but didn't move, just kept staring at the apparition, waiting for it to slip into shadows the way she did almost every night, when he imagined her standing at the base of the monument to General Robert E. Lee across from his town house.

The dog moved. It was a big dog, huge and sleek, with black smudges against a coat of soft gray, almost like a small horse, and it lumbered to stand between Ethan and the woman.

"Gryphon," she said softly. "Easy, boy. It's okay."

Her voice might as well have been a gunshot. Once, the low, throaty sound had burned through him like the moonshine his grandfather had shared with him a lifetime ago, but now the voice slammed into his gut like the shot that had felled her that deceptively beautiful day on the beach.

"Brenna?" He felt himself start to move, felt legs that had effortlessly pounded mile after mile start to buckle. The wind whipped harder, sharper, but no chill penetrated his hot damp skin.

A tentative smile touched her mouth, the mouth he'd dreamed of for six long weeks. "You came."

His hands burned to touch, but he kept them at his sides. "I've been here every night since I found your hospital bed empty." If possible, she looked even more striking than he remembered. She'd been pale in the hospital, unnaturally so, but now color softened her cheeks.

"Where have you been?" The question practically ripped out of him. "Why did you go?"

She lifted her chin, let the increasingly cool breeze play with her hair. "Shh." The soft sound shimmied between them. "I didn't come here to see the prosecutor." She met his eyes, revealing calm confidence glowing in hers. "I came for the man."

The words staggered him. He stopped close enough to touch, but didn't, forced his hands to stay at his sides, even though his fingers itched to tangle in her loose hair. The big dog eyed him suspiciously.

"I couldn't let you die," she said, and her voice was softer now, almost a whisper. "Tomorrow came," she added thickly, "but I couldn't stay there on the other side of the island, not knowing what I did."

Everything came roaring back, the intensity of their night in the abandoned hotel suite, the beauty of the gift she'd given him, the agony of leaving her sleeping on the soft pallet. The horror of seeing her at the edge of the beach.

"I left you there for a reason," he said, working hard to keep the rough edge from his voice. That wasn't what she needed.

Her smile was soft, quietly knowing. "It wasn't your choice to make." The wind whispered harder, sending blond hair spilling against the side of her face. "It was mine," she added, brushing it back, all but a strand that clung to her lips. "And when I woke up in the hospital and you were there…" Night was falling, but even through the darkness he saw the shadow cross her face. The pain. "I knew you'd been there all along—and I knew I had to leave. I couldn't drag tomorrow out any longer." She hesitated. "I thought it was best if I made a clean break."

He felt everything inside of him go hard, but banked the reaction. Instead he echoed her words of only a moment before. "It wasn't your choice to make."

She winced. "I did it for you," she said, and God help him, her voice broke on the words. "And for Allison."

Somewhere nearby, a lone bird wailed against the night. "Allison?"

Her eyes misted over. "The woman you love," she clarified.

"The woman I—" He broke off the words abruptly and stared down into her upturned face. And knew. That first night fired through him, the prophecy she'd shared, the claim of the woman on the beach. The woman he'd give his life for.

His heart kicked hard. "Angel," he said thickly, "you've got it wrong."

She shook her head, almost fiercely. "She was the woman I saw on the beach. The one you'd give your life for."

She'd been right. He'd scoffed at her, accused her of being affiliated with Jorak Zhukov, but all along she'd been right. She'd known, long before there was the sliver of possibility. "If that's the case," he asked, needing her to see the truth, *feel* the truth. "Then why are you here now?"

That got her. She blinked at him, narrowed her eyes as though he'd just asked her to explain the inexplicable. For a moment she looked away from him, toward her right, where the James rushed over the granite slabs. "The dreams," she said, looking back at him. "They haven't gone away." Her eyes took on an ethereal glow that fed some place deep inside. "They're…more intense."

For six weeks he'd looked for this woman, refusing to give up hope even when every sign pointed to the futility of his search. She'd left him. She didn't want to be found. She'd made that clear. He'd screwed up. He hadn't seen the truth. He hadn't told her. But now here she stood, and his body burned at her words. "The same dreams?" he asked, even though he already knew.

She glanced down at her Great Dane, who sat patiently and loyally at her feet, then back at Ethan, revealing even more color to her face, a flush much like the night when he'd run his mouth over every inch of her body. "No."

He did it then, what he'd wanted to do from the moment he'd seen her standing in the shadow of the sycamore, even those fleeting moments when he'd thought her an apparition. He stepped forward and touched her, very gently, a finger to the underside of her jaw. "Tell me."

She quickly looked away from the heat he knew burned in his gaze. "It doesn't matter."

"It does to me."

"That's not why I came here," she said, and her nervousness, uncharacteristic and strangely charming, almost undid him. "I came here for closure." She looked up abruptly, pierced him with whitewashed sapphire. "I came to say goodbye, to make the dreams go away."

He felt himself smile, knew the curve of his lips would be dark and lazy. "You're so wrong," he said, and couldn't believe that everything inside him that had been cold had suddenly turned warm. "Allison is a friend and I love her, yes, but not in the way a man loves the woman he wants to spend his future with."

Through the deepening shadows, Brenna stared up at him. There was confusion in her eyes. "I...I don't understand."

"Neither did I. Not at first." He'd been in some serious denial. "I'd quit believing in things I couldn't see or touch." Evidence, he'd believed. Tangible facts and clues. He'd staked his whole life on them, never realizing they, too, could be distorted or misread. "I refused to let myself trust the kind of emotion that could twist me up inside and strip away my ability to think." He slid his hand to cup the side of her face. "Until you."

Her eyes went dark. "Me?"

He looked down at her and let himself see the truth he'd been trying so hard to deny. "I was drawn to you immediately." From the moment he'd first heard her voice, her intriguing invitation. "Compelled to seek you out."

"Because you thought I worked for Jorak."

"That's what I told myself," he admitted. "At first." But no more. He lifted his other hand to her waist and pulled her against his body. "You're not the only one who's been having dreams, angel." His words were slow, purposefully thick, as he let the heated images wash through him. Sleep had not come easily, despite the fact he'd come to crave what he found there. Brenna, always Brenna. Bathed in moonlight and nothing else. Smiling. Extending an arm toward him. "I've had a few of my own."

* * *

That was her cue. It was time to go. She'd heard enough. She'd seen what she needed to see. Him, she'd told herself. She just needed to see him one more time. The dreams would go away, she'd convinced herself. She'd quit waking in the middle of the night, her body hot and damp and burning from the lingering feel of his touch. His mouth.

His love.

The woman she'd trained herself to be, the woman who walked on the outskirts of the world, who didn't believe in tomorrow, told her to walk away. Now. Fast.

The woman she'd become that night in the abandoned hotel, when she'd given herself to Ethan and the promise of his touch, refused to let her move.

It was hard to look at him, hard to meet his penetrating green eyes and see the heat burning there. But it was impossible not to. In the weeks that separated him, she'd tried not to let herself see him, tried not to remember, but here, now, seeing him in an old T-shirt damp with his perspiration and the same shorts he'd worn that first night, despite the frigid temperatures, the tousle of his hair, and whiskers darkening his jaw, the raw glint to his eyes, it was impossible not to remember.

Not to want.

"What kind of dreams?" she asked with a mild curiosity that pleased her—but how her heart pounded against her chest.

A slow smile curved his mouth, inviting her to stare at his lips, lips she would swear she could still feel against her skin. "Dreams about you," he said, and his voice was pitched low. "Dreams that pick up where we left off in Mexico."

The wind whipped like icy needles against her skin, but she felt only a surge of heat.

"Except we're not in an abandoned room this time," he said, and if possible, his eyes went even more smoky. His hand was still on her face, not moving, just sending his imprint deeper into her. "There's a bed," he said. "Silk sheets." His smile turned wicked. "Sometimes we use them."

Her mouth went dry. "And other times?"

''There's the shower,'' he said softly. ''A hot tub.'' A naughty light glinted in his eyes. ''The floor.''

Brenna wasn't sure how she stayed standing. If his hand hadn't been on her, she might not have. His words stirred some place deep inside, and too easily she saw, she felt, everything he described, because, heaven help her, she'd had those dreams, too.

''You,'' he said, and suddenly the gleam was gone from his eyes, replaced by a seriousness that wrapped around her heart in a tight squeeze. ''You, angel. You're the woman you saw. The one on the beach. The woman I'd give my life for.'' His eyes burned hotter than the stars fighting with the high thin clouds. ''That's why I risked everything to get you out of the line of fire—because I couldn't let my thirst for revenge touch you. Hurt you.''

Never in a million years. Never in a million dreams. She'd seen Ethan and she'd seen the scene on the beach, but she'd never seen herself. ''That's not possible.''

He laughed then, a low, rich sound that seared into her bloodstream. ''Don't you see?'' He pulled her closer, sharing with her the hot, hard planes of his body. ''In trying to prevent what you saw in your dream, you only made sure it came true. If you hadn't walked into my life, if you hadn't tried to warn me, there would have been no woman on the beach.''

No. Denial vaulted through her, but the truth of his words glowed brighter with every beat of her heart.

''And I might have died,'' he added quietly.

And for a moment all she could do was stare. And remember. ''Gran…'' she whispered, staring up into his eyes. ''She always said the future isn't etched in stone. That it's fluid, ever changing.'' Tears thickened her voice, burned her eyes. ''Something to be cherished, not feared.''

Ethan answered by drawing her close and leaning down to put his lips to hers. ''I cherish a lot, angel,'' he murmured. ''It took losing you for me to realize what you'd been trying to tell me, that if I couldn't trust myself, I had nothing.''

She lifted a hand to his face, welcomed the tickle of his whiskers.

"I love you, Brenna," he said, and her heart lost a beat on the words. "I love you more than I knew possible."

"Ethan, you don't know—"

"Yes, I do," he said quietly, cutting her off with his words and another soft kiss. "And so do you. That's why you're here tonight, whether you admit that to yourself or not. That's why you walked into my life." He put his mouth to the corner of hers. "You told me you don't believe in tomorrow, but everything you've done proves that you do. It's not etched in stone, Brenna. It's a blank canvas waiting to be painted."

For years she'd taught herself to live in a cocoon, to pretend she could watch the world go by and not want to join it. To believe she was better off not getting involved, that loving only led to heartache. But as she opened to Ethan, invited him in, the truth streamed through her. It wasn't loving that hurt, but losing that love. Tomorrow didn't have to be a dark place.

"Tomorrow, angel," he murmured, pulling back to meet her eyes. She smiled at him through the moisture in her own, stunned to see the same moisture in his. "That's what I want to give you. Tomorrow, and every day afterward."

And when he put it like that, it all seemed so unbelievably simple. "Starting with tonight," she whispered, returning her mouth to his.

He kissed her back, long, slow, gentle kisses that heated her blood and sent an entirely new kind of shock wave trembling through her. "Tell me about these new dreams of yours," he murmured as he nibbled her lower lip. "I want to know what I have to look forward to."

She pulled back and smiled, reached for the bottom of his T-shirt and slipped her hands inside, flattening them against the warmth of his stomach. "I'd rather show you instead."

Epilogue

"Dance with me."

Miranda Carrington Vellenti looked up from an elaborate spray of heavily scented lilies and magnolias to find her husband of one hour and twenty-two minutes watching her with mischief glimmering in his dark, dark eyes.

Over eight months had passed since the storm-washed morning in Portugal when he'd walked into her life wearing black and carrying a briefcase that was really a machine gun, but still, the sight of him gave her heart an immediate lurch. At the time, when she'd looked at the stranger wearing the dark sunglasses, she'd never in a million years imagined that come the following January, she'd walk down a red-carpeted aisle dotted by white rose petals, to the altar where he stood in a breathtaking black tuxedo, watching her, waiting for her.

The reality still had the power to jam the breath in her throat.

"It's not time yet," she said, glancing around the restored plantation home they'd chosen for their wedding reception. "The music hasn't started yet."

A slow smile curved his lips, revealing startling white teeth against olive, Mediterranean skin. *"Bella, bella, bella,"* he said in that low, raspy voice of his, one of the few reminders of the violence of his former life. "How many times do I have to tell you not all music comes from radios or compact discs?" He glanced toward the far corner of the parlor, where a jazz band had just begun to set up, then put his hand to the small of her waist and drew her against his body. "Don't you hear it?"

The memory washed over her and through her, of the first time they danced, that long-ago night in a musty wine cellar. There'd been no official music that night, only the purr of the wind and the whisper of candles, and—

She lifted a hand and opened her palm against the black lapel of his tuxedo, felt the heat, the intensity, the rhythm, clear down to her bones. "Drums?"

Against hers, his body started to sway. "The next best thing."

Staccato, she remembered saying that night. Just like the rhythm of her own heart. Impossibly content, she melted against him and let the music of their hearts carry her away.

Her wedding day. She'd dreamed, but never had she imagined a love could be so perfect, so pure and blinding and right. With her cheek resting against his chest, she glanced around the parlor, noted that many of the guests had stopped mingling and now only stared. She saw her parents, icons of propriety and dignity, but they were smiling as they watched their youngest daughter dance with her husband, to music no one else heard. And then there were Sandro's parents, estranged from him for so many years, standing at the edge of the makeshift dance floor, arm in arm, watching their son with love and pride glowing in their eyes. Through love and time, all those broken fences had been steadily repaired, and now there was only the future, stretching endlessly before them.

Time to live again, she remembered Sandro telling her the morning he'd walked back into her life, and she knew that truly it was.

"Dance with me."

Elizabeth Carrington turned from the sight of her sister and new brother-in-law dancing to music no one else heard, to find her fiancé watching her through butterscotch eyes that had the power to stop her heart. For a moment she said nothing, did nothing, just drank in the sight of him in his outrageously sexy black tuxedo, with his dark blond hair queued behind his head and emphasizing his wide, flat cheekbones. It was impossible to see him like this and not remember another night, another request for a dance. Not in a parlor filled with wedding guests or even on a dance floor, but in an elaborate ladies' room of white marble.

"It's not our turn," she forced herself to say, even though her body burned to be pressed against his, to feel his arms holding her close.

He lifted a hand to finger the strand of black pearls at her neck. "I thought you weren't afraid of taking chances," he reminded.

Once the words would have ignited her temper, prompted her defenses to snap into place. Now she only smiled. "I'm not afraid," she said. "I just don't want to take Miranda's moment."

"Ah." The word was deep, smooth, a sound uttered from low within his throat. Then he lifted a hand to her face, not to touch her cheek as she expected, but to snag a bobby pin from her hair.

"Wesley!" She swatted his hand away, but not before the damage was done and a wisp of hair fluttered free.

"You know I prefer your hair down," he drawled.

And she smiled. She did know that. "Can't always get what you want, though, can you?"

His eyes went dark. "Oh, I don't know about that," he drawled, taking her hand and dragging her toward the back of the room.

Laughing, she went with him. "What are you doing?"

He tugged her into the big hall and then to the sprawling staircase, didn't break stride when he swooped her into his arms and took the steps two at a time. "You said you weren't afraid."

A wicked thrill twirled through her. Dear God, he wasn't really—

But this was Wesley "Hawk" Monroe, who tore through life with no regard for rules or propriety. And of course he was. That was only one of the reasons she loved him.

"We can't," she said, but already her body hummed.

He pulled open a door and strode inside, then kicked it closed and turned the lock. "I warned you what would happen when you wore that dress," he reminded her.

Grinning, she glanced down at the sapphire sheath her sister had chosen for her bridesmaids, and automatically remembered the first night she'd tried it on for Wesley, the low light that had come into his eyes. He'd tucked a finger under one of two thin straps, much as he did now. Slowly he began to slide. "I told you what this dress makes me want," he drawled.

In another lifetime, the lifetime before Wesley had blazed into her life and taught her what it mean to live, truly live, the words would have terrified her. Now they thrilled. She wasn't afraid anymore. She knew how to let go and savor each moment. How to love.

Eager, she lifted her hands to his chest and slid the tuxedo jacket from his shoulders. "To take it off."

"Dance with me."

Brenna turned from watching Miranda and Sandro dancing to music no one heard, to where Ethan stood behind her, watching her with an awe he no longer fought. "Soon," she said, smiling up at him. "Soon."

He plucked two flutes of champagne from the tray of a passing waiter and handed one to her, kept the other for himself. "Then to moments yet to come," he said, lifting his glass to hers.

A slow smile curved her lips and touched his heart. "To times yet to come," she echoed, clinking her glass to his.

This was his baby sister's day, and she looked radiant in her silk dress of shimmering white, but to Ethan, Brenna outshone even the bride. She wore black much as she had the night she'd stepped from behind a sycamore and walked into Ethan's life, but rather than helping her to blend with the shadows, the sleek dress she'd chosen emphasized her curves and accentuated the fair coloring of her face and hair. Her eyes, those whitewashed pools of sapphire ringed by cobalt, glowed with a joy, a peace he'd never imagined he'd see from her.

Never imagined he'd feel.

But he did feel them, intensely, hammering through every inch of his body. Because of her and the love she'd brought to his life. For so many years he'd been driven by the need for evidence and fact, things he could see and touch, but she'd taught him the greatest gifts in life were those that which could not be seen with the eye or felt with the hand, but rather those that emanated from deep inside, like the love that had led him to purchase the ring waiting deep in the pocket of his tuxedo.

"Look," she said, taking his hand and tugging him toward the verandah.

He let her lead him outside into the crisp air of a January evening. The day had dawned cloudless and blue for Miranda's wedding, but now with the approach of dusk, the sky had dimmed, and clouds pushed close.

"Do you see them?" she asked.

He followed the direction of her gaze, expecting to find her staring at the army of stately old live oaks guarding the plantation or the elaborate gardens adorning the grounds, but her face was tilted upward, and yes, he saw. "Shape-shifters," he murmured.

"What do you see?" she asked.

Once the question would have struck him as simple, maybe even foolish. Naive. Once he would have barked out the obvious. He saw a violet sky and cumulous clouds.

But then, once he'd been a fool.

Now he looked up at the twilight sky and slid a hand into his pocket, fingered the ring. He saw so much—a future with her by his side, children, birthday parties and picnics, summer vacations and anniversaries. But for the first time since he was a little boy, he also saw…

"Sailboats," he whispered, trusting the thrum of his heart more than he'd ever trusted any piece of cold hard evidence or concrete fact. "I see sailboats."

*   *   *   *   *

*The Carringtons' story may
have ended…but new secrets are just
beginning to be uncovered!*

*Don't miss the newest in-line continuity from
Silhouette Intimate Moments,*
FAMILY SECRETS: THE NEXT
GENERATION
Launching in June 2004 with
A CRY IN THE DARK
by Jenna Mills.
*Available only from
Silhouette Intimate Moments.*

*And now, for a sneak peek
at this exciting new continuity,
turn the page….*

Prologue

The cry ripped through the late-afternoon silence.

Gretchen Miller stopped folding her daughter's pink-and-white play outfit and looked up abruptly. She held herself very still, listening intently, as only a mother could.

Violet.

Her heart kicked hard. She sprang to her feet and ran across the hardwood floor of her suburban Boston home, toward the staircase leading upstairs, where her daughter napped.

"Sweetheart?"

She heard her husband's voice, but didn't slow. Couldn't. Not when her daughter needed her. After years of longing for a child but believing the miracle would never come her way, she'd dedicated herself to motherhood with a ferocity that even she had never imagined. Gone was the woman whose life had once consisted solely of ancient writings and academic pursuits. In her place lived a mother who thrived on art projects and play dates.

"Violet?" she called, reaching the top of the stairs. She tried to strip the concern from her voice, but adrenaline drowned out her effort. The cry had been sudden and intense, drenched in distress and fear. If her little girl was hurt—

Wide blue eyes greeted Gretchen the second she raced into the pink room with the white canopy bed. Sandy blond hair framed her daughter's pixie face. She sat in a small chair in front of the art table. In front of her crayons lay scattered across a sheet of drawing paper.

Gretchen drank in the scene—the beautifully, perfectly normal scene—and tried to regain her equilibrium.

"Whatcha drawing?" she asked, moving to squat beside her little girl. With a hand she fought to steady, she gently brushed the hair back from Violet's slightly pale face.

Her little girl gazed up at her, her eyes darker than usual, her pupils dilated, almost trancelike. It took a moment for Gretchen to realize her little girl was still mostly asleep.

"Come now," she cooed, lifting her daughter into her arms and carrying her back to bed. She deposited her among the messy sheets and stretched out beside her. "How about we nap together?"

"Everything okay?"

The soft Texas drawl had her glancing toward the doorway. She and Kurt had been married for three years now, but his rugged handsomeness still stole her breath. "I thought I heard something," she said. "A cry."

With a gentle smile he strolled to the bed and leaned down, kissed her softly on the lips. "Looks like everything's okay now."

Emotion swarmed the back of her throat. Fighting tears she didn't understand, she looked at her little girl, sleeping now, her breathing deep and rhythmic, as though five minutes before she'd not sat with crayon in hand. "I hope so," she whispered.

But deep inside, an innate sense warned otherwise.

The cry drowned out the gentle strains of the lullaby.

Lieutenant Marcus Evans, celebrated U.S. Navy SEAL, man of steel, staggered against the chipped Formica counter. For a brutal, heart-stopping moment he was back on the navy frigate that had failed miserably trying to tiptoe through a minefield. The impact rocked him hard, jump-started his heart.

Samantha.

On a violent rush of adrenaline he ran from the kitchen of the rented Naples, Florida, beach house, to the sprawling, sun-dappled room beyond, where his wife sat in a rocking chair, their five-month-old daughter, Honor, at her breast, their two-year-old tinkering with a building set at her feet.

The serenity of the scene stopped him cold. Through a curtain of flaming red hair Samantha, esteemed ambassador to the small country of Delmonico by day and gloriously creative wife by night, looked up and smiled. "Something wrong?"

His mouth went dry. "That's what I was going to ask you."

"Is it time yet?" Little Henry, an astonishing combination of his mother's refined, classic beauty and his father's rough edges, bounded to his feet and raced across the room. "You promised we could go in the ocean and you'd teach me how to be a seal, like you."

Marcus hoisted his son into his arms, all the while his heart threatening to burst out of his chest. His son. His and Samantha's. Sometimes he still couldn't believe it. "Give me five, champ," he said, ruffling the boy's dark hair. "Why don't you go put your trunks on."

The second Henry's feet hit the sandy tile floor he was off, racing toward his room in a flurry of energy that stunned even Marcus.

Samantha shifted Honor from one breast to another. "You've got that look," she observed.

"What look?"

Her mouth twisted into a wry smile. "The Superman look," she said. "Like you think there's someone you need to be saving."

He wanted to laugh. He tried to laugh. He knew that was the right response. But God help him, he could find no laughter, not when his pulse still pounded. A Navy SEAL, he'd learned to trust his sixth sense. Not only trust it, worship it. The tingling at the back of his neck, the churn to his gut—without the warnings Samantha would have died one horrible day three years before, and he would not be standing here staring at her in the rocking chair, with the sun streaming down on her face and his daughter suckling greedily.

"Just a feeling," he muttered, trying to scrape away the nasty sense of unease. His family was fine. He could see that for himself. There was no more danger stalking them. No more shadows. No more deception. That had all ended years ago, in what seemed like another lifetime.

But God, the cry had been so real. So panicked and incessant. A small cry. A child's cry.

"Weady?" Henry said in his two-year-old voice, skidding into the room. He'd stripped off his tattered "Property of the United States Navy" T-shirt and pulled on a pair of khaki swim trunks. No water wings for his boy. His son had inherited his love of and comfort with water.

"You bet." Already bare chested and in trunks himself, Marcus indulged in one last, lingering look at his wife and daughter. Then he grinned at his son. "Last one to the water is a rotten egg," he taunted.

"Hoo-wah!" Grinning, the little boy took off toward the door, threw it open, raced outside. Laughing, Marcus charged after him, into the warm breeze of a lazy, sunny Florida afternoon.

But deep inside, the chill, the uncertainty, lingered.

Something was wrong. Very wrong.

The cry stopped him cold.

Outside, the temperature soared near one hundred degrees, but the chill went through Jake Ingram like a frozen knife. He held himself very still for all of one punishing heartbeat, then he ran. Through the sunny foyer of his Dallas, Texas, home, up the stairs, toward the master bedroom.

"Mariah!" Fear gripped him. Just yesterday the doctor had pronounced his wife in perfect health. Their unborn baby was thriving. He'd seen the image on the sonogram screen, the heart beating strongly, the little legs and arms wiggling. It was as though his son or daughter had been waving hello, dancing madly.

But now Mariah was home three hours early.

And he'd heard the cry.

"Honey—" He stopped abruptly, stared.

She emerged from the bathroom with her dark hair streaming down her back and a smile curving her lips. "What do you think? Do I look fat?"

The breath left his body on a painful rush. He told himself to move, to speak, to do something, anything, but all he could do was stare at his wife, standing beneath the skylight in a skimpy red bikini, with the most beautiful baby in the world straining against her abdomen.

She frowned. "That bad?"

"No." The word almost shot out of him. And then he was across the room tugging her into his arms, loving the feel of their child nudging against his abdomen. "You look perfect," he murmured, burying his face in her hair and drawing in the fresh clean scent that was all Mariah. After all this time, the intensity of his love for her still staggered him. "I just—" how to explain? "—thought I heard you cry out."

She pulled back and gazed up at him, amusement dancing in her sharp, intelligent eyes. "I think maybe you're taking this visualizing a little too far."

He forced a smile. "Maybe." From the moment they'd learned they were finally pregnant, Mariah had teased him incessantly, telling him it was time to start preparing for the sleep deprivation sure to come. She'd suggested he begin visualizing himself with a crying baby in his arms, pacing the dark confines of the house late at night.

"How about a swim?"

Again he let his gaze dip over his wife's body, more lush now in her fourth month of pregnancy, more feminine. He loved being in the pool with her, slippery flesh sliding, legs twining, especially late at night, when she had a fondness for skinny-dipping. "Sounds great."

She pushed up on her toes and brushed a kiss over his lips.

"Hurry down," she said, then swept out of the room, leaving him staring after her.

She was fine. He'd seen that for himself. Happy. Radiant. Glowing. Nothing was wrong. There was no one or nothing sinister lurking in the shadows. Not anymore. Their lives had returned to normal. The threat to him and his brother and sisters had long since been neutralized. He'd talked to Gretchen just that morning, and Marcus had called only the night before.

Jake walked to the window, looked down through the thick canopies of a cluster of post oaks and saw his wife stepping into the black-bottom, lagoon-shaped pool. She dipped beneath the water, came up seconds later with her hair wet and slicked back from her face, water cascading down her body. Normally the sight fed his soul.

But standing there in his sunny bedroom, next to the big king-size bed his tough, gutsy, FBI-agent wife insisted upon cluttering with an array of girlie throw pillows, he couldn't push back the slippery edge of darkness. He'd heard the cry, damn it. He'd heard it. Loud. Panicked. Urgent. Like a summons, a plea. And deep in his gut he knew the truth.

Something was very wrong.

Chapter 1

The remnants of the cry echoed, low, soft, deceptively benign, like the distant rumble of thunder from a passing summer storm.

Standing behind the reception desk of one of Chicago's elite hotels, The Stirling Manor, Danielle Caldwell ignored the unsettling sensation, concentrating instead on the collection of sun-dappled roses and fragrant lilies. Once, she would have been urgently seeking out the source of the disturbance, crafting a way to help. Once, she would have risked everything.

Once, she had.

Now she hummed softly as she slid a yellow-and-pink-splashed rose into the snow-white lilies. Her brother would have accused her of trying to drown out her destiny, but Danielle no longer believed in such nonsense. Destiny, chance, did not rule her world. There were no such things as lucky or unlucky stars. You created your own fate, made your own choices.

Never again would she chase shadows. Never again would she splurge on instinct.

But the disturbance lingered at the back of her mind, dark and unsettling, choppy like the waters of Lake Michigan on a storm-shrouded day.

She knew better than to look. She knew better than to indulge. But she glanced around the richly paneled lobby anyway, toward the collection of formal sofas and wing chairs situated next to a stone fireplace. A large Aubusson rug stretched in a leisurely way across the hardwood floor. A huge mahogany bookcase held leather-bound books.

The scene was perfectly normal—a few lingering guests, a woman curled up with a book—almost a carbon copy of a hundred other afternoons since she'd joined the hotel's staff. And yet, something was off. Something was different. It was like a move playing at the wrong speed, motion slowed just a fraction, elongated, jerky. Not quite real.

Because of the man.

He sat in a wing back chair near the fireplace, tall, impeccably dressed. His button-down was a dark gray, open at the throat. His trousers were black. In his hands he held a newspaper—the same section he'd been holding for close to an hour.

She'd never seen someone sit so very, very still for so very, very long.

The disturbing current pulsed deeper. She knew she should look away, quit staring, but the whisper of fascination was too strong. He was tall. Very tall. Too tall, too broad in the shoulder, to fade into anonymity. She'd noticed him, *felt the ripple of his presence,* the second he'd walked into the lobby. He carried an aura of authority like so many of the powerful patrons of the hotel, but the shadows were different. They were thick and they were dark, and they swirled around him like flashing warning signs.

Just like they did her brother Anthony.

Look away, she told herself again, but then his eyes were on hers, and for a fractured second it was all she could do to breathe. They were a deep brown like his hair, yet the darkness eddying in their depths defied color.

His expression never changed. There was no amusement at

catching her staring, no quick swell of masculine triumph, no discomfort, no irritation, just the cool, impassive gaze of a man who saw everything, but felt nothing.

It was a look she'd never seen before, and it scorched clear to the bone.

Frowning, humming more loudly, refusing to let the man affect her one second longer, she grabbed another rose, this one a pure deep yellow with a long, dark green stem, and debated where to place it for maximum impact. Until she'd come to work at the hotel styled after an English manor house, she'd never imagined something as simple as a vase could cost more than she earned in a month. Granted, it was lead crystal and made in Ireland, but still. She'd always found old mason jars and chipped drinking glasses worked just fine.

"The lights are on, but apparently nobody is home."

Danielle looked up to find Ruth Sun, one of the hotel's long-time assistant managers, smiling at her. "Pardon?"

The woman's dark eyes twinkled. "You haven't heard a word I've said, have you?"

Danielle's heart beat a little faster. Everyone in the hotel knew Ruth had the boss's ear. She'd been around forever. One bad word from her, and all Danielle's hard work could be for nothing.

"You know how I get when the flowers arrive," she said lightly. "Everything else—"

"Fades to the background," Ruth finished for her. "I noticed." Her smile faded abruptly, and she reached out to grab Danielle's wrist. "Dear, you're bleeding."

Danielle blinked, stared down at the trail of dark red blood running against the pale skin of her arm. "I..." Focused on the man, she hadn't felt a thing. "It's just a prick."

Ruth made a maternal clucking noise, one that should have comforted, but instead unleashed a sharp curl of longing. "You need to get that cleaned up."

Danielle nodded, but didn't move. "Did you need something?" she asked. "Before?" When she'd been oblivious to everything but the echo of the cry that had ripped the fabric of the quiet June afternoon, and the man with the disturbing eyes.

"Not really." Ruth reached into a cabinet behind the long reception desk and came up with antiseptic and cotton. "Just thought you'd want to know someone was asking about you."

"About me?"

Ruth poured antiseptic onto the cotton. "What your name was, how long you'd worked here, that kind of thing."

Danielle went very still. She worked hard to keep her face clean of all emotion, but when Ruth pressed the cotton to her skin, the sharp sting made her wince. God, she'd been so careful, covered her tracks so cleanly. "Who?"

Ruth kept dabbing. "A man."

The dread circled closer, tighter. No wonder she'd been edgy all afternoon. He'd finally come looking for her, the brother she'd not spoken with in two long years. Her heart leaped at the prospect, abruptly slowed. "What did he look like?"

The assistant manager looked up from her handiwork. "I'm surprised you didn't notice him. He's been sitting in the big leather wing chair most of the afternoon. Dark hair. Tall." Ruth let out a dreamy sigh. "Very, very tall."

With eyes like pools of midnight on a cloudless night. "The guy in the gray button-down?" Danielle asked, and her heart beat a little faster. A lot harder.

"That's him," Ruth said. "Real good-looking guy."

Intense, Danielle silently corrected. Striking.

Gone.

"All better," Ruth pronounced, but the words barely registered. Danielle stared across the lobby, toward the elegant wing chair that now stood empty, the newspaper abandoned to the floor.

The quick slice of unease made no sense. "Where did he go?"

"He's right—" Ruth's words broke off. "That's strange. He was there just a second ago."

Her heart kicked up a notch. Frowning, she glanced around the lobby, toward the elevator, the sweeping staircase, the elegant front doors. Found nothing. Not the man anyway. There were other patrons—the businessmen, the elderly couple from Wichita, the honeymooners from Madison—but the tall man with the flat eyes was just…gone.

Except she still felt him. Deeply. Disturbingly.

"You going to get that?" Ruth asked.

She blinked and brought herself back, heard the low melody of her mobile phone. Through a haze of distraction she reached for the small black device, for which only three people had the number—her manager, her sister and her son's day-care center. "Hello, this is Danielle."

"Turn around."

She stiffened. "Come again?"

"Paste a smile on that pretty face of yours and turn around, away from the old woman."

Everything flashed. The motion of the lobby dimmed, slowed, seemed to drag. "I don't understand—"

"Just do it."

Her heart started to pound. Hard. Instinct warned her to obey, even as an age-old rebellious streak dared her to lift her chin and defy. She'd done that before. Many times. And the cost had been high.

Slowly she turned from the comforting din of the hotel lobby and took a few steps away from Ruth. "Okay."

"Good girl." The voice was distorted, genderless.

"Who is this? What do you—"

"I have your son."

The world stopped. Hard. Fast. Violently. She no longer faced the hotel guests, but knew if she turned around she would see nothing. No movement. No life.

But then the words penetrated even deeper, beyond the fog of shock and the blanket of horror, to the logical part of her, the part Jeremy had honed and fine-tuned, sharpened to a gleaming point, and another truth registered.

She was being watched. Someone, someone close, knew her every move.

The man. God, the man who'd been watching her, asking

questions. The one who had vanished, but whose presence lingered.

"You what?" she asked, slowly indulging the need to look. To see.

"Don't move," the voice intoned, and abruptly she froze. "If you want to see him again, you'll do exactly what we say."

The world started moving again, from dead cold to fast forward in one horrible dizzying heartbeat. Everything swirled, blurred. Blindly she reached a hand for the counter. Her son. God, her precious little boy. Her life.

"No cops," the man continued. It had to be him, she knew. The man from the lobby. The one who'd been watching her. Asking about her. Who'd vanished mere seconds ago. "Call them and negotiations end."

She wasn't sure how she stayed standing, not when every cell in her body cried out, louder and harder than the distorted cry she'd picked up an hour earlier. And she knew. God help her, she knew why she'd been on edge. Why she'd been disturbed. Her son. Someone had gotten to her son, and on some intuitive level she'd known.

But just like with his father, she hadn't been able to prevent.

"What do you want?" she asked with a calm that did not come easily to her Gypsy blood. She'd been in situations like this before, after all, dangerous, confusing, never with her own son, but she'd gone where law enforcement could not go.

"Call the day-care center. Tell them Alex walked home on his own."

She swallowed, hard. That was feasible. The day-care center was only a few blocks from her small Rogers Park home. Alex knew the way. He was an adventurous kid, always in constant motion. Clever. Daring. It would be just like him to wander off when no one was looking.

"Then what?"

"Wait for instructions."

Deep inside, she started to shake. A sick, cruel joke, she wanted to think. A prank. Payback for the sins of her past. But she'd·met relatively few people since moving to Chicago, could think of none who would be so cruel.

A mistake, she thought next, but even as hope tried to bloom, reality sucked the oxygen from her lungs. She wanted to spin around and run, to shout at the top of her lungs as she searched for the tall man with the dark eyes, but with great effort she kept herself very still.

"I'm calling them now," she said with the same forced calm.

"Good girl." A garbled sound then, something between laughter and scorn. "Do not betray us, darling. One word about this call to anyone, and your son will pay the price."

The line went dead. And for a long, drowning moment Danielle just stood there, breathing hard, praying she wouldn't throw up.

Then she ran.

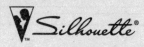
Silhouette®

COMING NEXT MONTH

SIMCNM0404